whisper in the wind

Venita Coelho is a screenwriter, novelist and artist with ten published books to her credit. She has won The Hindu Goodreads Award for Best Fiction for children twice, in 2016 for *Dead as a Dodo* and in 2019 for *Boy No. 32*. Her collection of feminist ghost stories, *The Washer of the Dead*, was longlisted for the Frank O'Connor award.

She lives in Goa where she runs an alternative school called The Path Shaala. She is working towards her second exhibition of paintings.

VENITA COELHO

whisper in the wind

First published by Tranquebar, an imprint of Westland Publications Private Limited, in 2019

1st Floor, A Block, East Wing, Plot No. 40, SP Infocity, Dr MGR Salai, Perungudi, Kandanchavadi, Chennai 600096

Westland, the Westland logo, Tranquebar and the Tranquebar logo are the trademarks of Westland Publications Private Limited, or its affiliates.

ISBN: 9789388754606

10 9 8 7 6 5 4 3 2 1

This is a work of fiction. Names, characters, organisations, places, events and incidents are either products of the author's imagination or used fictitiously.

Typeset by SÜRYA, New Delhi

Printed at Manipal Technologies Limited, Manipal

Portuguese Goa

1947

The Words of a Madman

I met a madman today, who told me that all the stories in the world are whispered in the wind. Listen, he said—and the wind will blow a story into your head.

There are many stories in this house. Tales of all shapes and sizes. Sad tales, happy tales, unguessed-at mysteries. Tightly knotted enigmas. I can hear the wind stirring them. Which one is my story—the one that I alone can tell?

Listen.

What is that sound? A wind-up musical box playing on insanely in this empty house? Music? No. Too scattered. Music a child might play, on made-up instruments.

Another shimmer of odd mismatched notes. I can feel the hair on my arms rising. What could those sounds be? The house has been uninhabited for five years.

It is an old Portuguese house, with tiles on the roof and unnumbered rooms burrowing into each other. Corridors lead out into tiny courtyards that lead to yet more rooms. A wide porch wraps around the front of the house. The windows are paned in circles of mother-of-pearl. But it is all sadly neglected. I was promised a grand Portuguese manor. Instead, I find myself living in a near ruin with neither running water, nor electricity. But I will be resolute. It was difficult enough getting permission to come here.

I held a knife to my wrist to get Mother to agree. I had to go to the kitchen to find a knife and I scared the cook into hysterics. There were potatoes rolling all over the floor from an upset basket, and the cook was shrieking, 'No! Baba, don't do it. Baba, no!'

My mother never took her eyes off me as she said, 'His name is Mr Irani. And he will now put down the knife so we can discuss terms.' I put down the knife and we discussed terms. It was clear that the terms were a concession that would never be made again.

I was to be indulged in this one folly and after that return to be a dutiful son. To take over the family business and be wed to a suitable girl. Parsees do not marry non-Parsees. And besides, we are *the* Iranis. I do not mean to boast, but we are among the richest families in Bombay. No ordinary daughter-in-law will do for my mother. Besides, with our family history, it is quite unthinkable. There could never be, for me, a match unsuitable to my class.

Personally, I think it is only the unrest across India that reconciled her to my spending a month in Goa. There have been rallies across the country. Three of our factories have had to be shut down. There are demonstrations in the street every day. The trains are running behind schedule for the first time since the British built them. My mother was spat upon—spat upon!—in the street for the imported silks that she wears. At least, in Goa, no one is demanding freedom from the Portuguese. Or at least, not yet.

So, here I am. With one month and a whole book to write and my entire future dependent upon it. I will be resolute and not complain. The life of an artist is not an easy one. I must get used to struggle and reversals of fortune.

I turned my attention to the more prosaic business of getting the house fit to live in. The caretaker promises he will have the electricity turned on soon, and that his wife will come and cook and clean for me. But, until she does, it is up to me to manage.

I first thought I would clear several rooms, having grand plans for a study, library, etc. But, within half an hour of wallowing in dust, I gave up and cleaned only two rooms—what would be my bedroom, and another nice cheerful room to work in. It is the first time I have ever been required to clean anything. My respect for those of the working class has increased tremendously. Dusting and wiping are far more arduous than I could have imagined.

My working room is perfectly circular and has eight windows. They give a full view of the hills below me and the little lane that runs below this house. The effect is of floating on a sea of tree-tops. I spent a pleasant hour pretending I was marooned alone in this little part of the world and that the village did not exist. My pleasant fiction was broken by sounds that carried up on the breeze, and I deduced the existence of a school and a church nearby. The church bells resound from time to time, and all day long I have heard children at their lessons. Down below me, rising through the trees, is a single stone tower—gapped and broken, the arched belfry empty. The broken finger beckoned imperiously. I went.

I followed a small path that, unexpectedly, came out on to a sight that stopped me dead. It wasn't just a tower. A whole church lay in ruins below me. Flying buttresses had crumbled mid-leap. The roof was gone, and wind and rain had for long washed the floor. The walls were breached by banyan and tamarind. Gulmohar had showered red petals on the ruined altar. Crumbling stairs led up the side of a wall and ended in mid-step. The choir stall stood remote and unreachable above the heads of the faithful.

There were still a few saints in the niches, their faces ground down to nubs. A scatter of candles, burnt down to the sockets, showed that the faithful still recognised them.

I looked down. The stones I was walking on had names and dates incised on them. Gravestones of the faithful. I was walking upon someone's grave.

I heard the hoot of monkeys, and a troop of them crashed into the trees overhead and then traversed the hall, leaping from arch to arch, some scampering across the floor, others pausing on the altar to stare at me. They chattered in the branches of the tamarind, their voices ricocheting around the ruin. As their whoops faded into the distance, I could hear something else. A child's voice. Tired with shouting. Edged with panic. Calling—'Sara! *Saaaa* … rah!'

The sound was haunting in that place, echoing among the broken walls. I walked out to where the sound was, climbing over heaps of toppled stone.

'*Stop*! *Statue*!'

We used to play the game when we were young. At the call of 'Statue!', you had to freeze into stillness immediately. The command surfaced out of my childhood and arrested me.

'You'll fall in!'

I looked down. My feet were one step away from a gaping maw in the stone flags. It was an old well, overgrown with plants, bearded with grass and almost invisible. I backed away carefully. A few stones went tumbling into the well and the sound of them hitting water came from a long way down.

A small girl stood regarding me solemnly across the well. 'It's very deep,' she said. 'If you fall in, you won't come out again. We're not allowed to play here.' She must have been about nine years old and the miasma of neglect hung about her. She wore a patched and ragged school uniform, her hair was uncombed and her nose was running. The girl wiped her nose on the back of her hand and said confidingly, 'I'm looking for Sara. Have you seen her?'

I told her I had seen no one but her that day. The girl sighed and turned away. I saw that one of her legs was quite withered away by polio. It was locked in an iron brace. The brace clicked and clacked against the stones as she limped away, leaving a fading spoor of sound. I could hear her raised voice diminishing in the distance—'Sara! Sa-*rah!*'

I was so shaken by my near-disaster, that I quite forgot to thank her. Mindful of snakes and more pitfalls for the unwary, I picked my way through the ruins. God knows what had brought them to this state. On my way to the village, every church I saw was well maintained and even the little roadside chapels were smart in their white wash.

A little further down, behind the church, there was a graveyard. And here I came upon my madman, sitting upon a grave.

He did not strike me as one at first sight, being most respectably dressed in a black suit and a tie that was covered in mouldy spots. He courteously raised a battered hat and asked me who I was and what I did.

'I am Jamshed Fali Irani. I'm a writer,' I said, a trifle stiffly. It was the first time I had actually described myself that way. 'I am here for some peace and quiet, to write my new novel.'

The old man leaned over and looked carefully into my eyes. 'Can you listen?' he asked.

'Listen?'

He nodded. 'To be a writer, first one must learn to listen. All the stories in the world are blown around in the wind—and you have to listen for the story that the wind will blow into your head.'

His eyes were intent on mine. Each pupil had a cobweb in it. So mesmeric was his aspect that I found myself listening. The churchyard was drowsy with the drone of insects and the rustling of the wind. Carrying on the wind was the voice of the little girl who had saved me. It piped wistfully through the afternoon. 'Saaa—ra!'

The old man nodded. 'I come here every day to listen. They all tell me their stories.' He waved a hand at the graves around him. 'This is a sleepy place and most of the time, they drowse. But sometimes they wake and whisper. I come to spend time with her. She likes to know I am near, and to talk to me sometimes.' He pointed to the grave he was sitting beside. The inscription read:

Helga Monteiro
Beloved wife of
Augustus Cajetan Monteiro
Born 1894
Died 1922
Dearly Beloved and Always Missed

I realised with a start that Augustus had been talking to his dead wife for twenty-five years. He was completely and utterly insane. No wonder the wind blows around inside his head. I hastily bid him goodbye and headed back to the house.

But the madman's words have stayed with me. And here I am. Listening.

Another soft shimmer of notes comes searching its way through the house. This uncanny music is the only company I have.

It strikes me that this is the first day in my life that I have been entirely alone. I am always surrounded and hemmed in by aunts, uncles, cousins, employees. And never a space without a helpful servant hovering in the background. Now, the only company I have are these sounds, dripping in broken bits through the house.

Tired of their distraction, I went in search of them.

Everywhere I went there were stories lying in heaps. I could hear them shifting and shuffling and waiting to be told.

In the dining room there was a grand tale of adventure spanning several generations and spilling over a series of black-and-white photos on the wall. A little bald-headed Indian posed among tall blacks in full tribal regalia in Africa. Indian women in flowered dresses smiled among household servants who proudly displayed their breasts. Two solemn Indians posed with their guns beside a dead lion.

A tale of desperate want and devotion was rubbed into the rosary laid on the sooty kitchen altar, the beads worn down over time with endless supplication.

And what's this in the kitchen? A household mystery in the cupboard, three tarnished silver spoons tied carefully together with red silk thread.

In the middle of the house is a forgotten courtyard. The stone mermaid combing dead wisteria from her hair hides a wistful story. Laid in her tail I found a scatter of seashells and two marbles.

But the most haunting story is carried in snatches on the wind. Standing in a corridor breached by a large banyan tree growing right through a wall with serried photographs, I listen carefully. The notes sound warped and distorted. I think it comes from the forbidden part of the house.

The caretaker who has rented me the house told me that the old lady who owned it died in her bed, and all her heirs are in Portugal. He said I could stay as long as I wanted, but there was one condition. Part of the house is forbidden. I was not to go past the locked door. Immediately, of course, the forbidden territory became irresistible. And inevitably, the sounds lay beyond it.

Led by the sounds, I found myself standing at the forbidden door. The odd sounds called through it, but there was nothing I could do. There are so many locks upon the door that it is impossible to even think of breaching it.

I found my way to my bed by candlelight through a corridor full of soft noises. Stopping at the door to my makeshift bedroom, I had a sudden sense of somebody nearby and wondered if it was the caretaker. 'Is anybody there?' I called.

Echoes. Small whispers. Nothing. Lost somewhere deep in the house, those haunting distant notes.

I lay in bed and listened to those odd, discordant voices calling through the darkness. Broken voices that came and went in snatches.

Right at the edge of sleep, my mind fumbled against the answer.

Wind chimes.

I awoke at that hour where night crosses a stretch of no man's land to dawn. What had awakened me? The chimes. The wind was rising and the fragments of sound were loud in the dark. I climbed out of bed.

This time the thread of sound led me surely through the labyrinthine house. In the dark I stumbled through crowded rooms, tripped over the debris of many years, and ripped through dense curtains of cobwebs, but never for a moment lost the thread that was leading me on.

Again, it led me straight to the locked door and the forbidden part of the house.

As I stood at the door, straining to hear, my hand touched a panel. To my surprise, the door swayed a bit. White ants had done their work on the wood. The locks were a hollow show of strength. I pushed—and a panel of the door fell through with a clatter. I squeezed myself through the gap.

I stepped into a vast hall lined with floor-to-ceiling windows. Each had a stained-glass inset; roses, lilies, a shattered lotus, an elegant fleur-de-lis. The windows had been left wide open. The dolour of dawn light was strengthening through them, scattering shards of colour on the floor. In each window, there hung wind chimes. Their twisted shapes cut through the darkness as the sun came up behind them. Their voices fell in echoing showers around me.

I stood facing one of the windows and regarded its particular chime. Somebody had made each of these chimes, I thought, knotting odds and ends together with bits of wire and string so that each sang in its own unique scale.

There were bits of bamboo clunking throatily. Glass, with its clear ringing soprano, chiming along with the lesser notes of little bits of metal threaded together in clusters. Strings of seashells sounded like rain falling on dry earth. Fragments of driftwood gave out a whole forest of strange sounds—clicks and shuffles and gurgles. A collection of rusty keys clinked against each other. Such were the mingled voices of wood and glass and metal. They were underlined by the sibilance of brushwood and palm sliding against each other.

In the middle of the room stood a grand piano, with 'Steinway & Sons' etched on a little silver plaque on the lid. It was covered with a thick felt of dust and droppings. The lid opened with a reluctant creak, and great clumps of grit fell to the ground. But the keys within were clear, shining in the half-light. I laid my fingers gently across them and was startled by the sudden sounds that they released. I hastily shut the lid.

There was nothing else at all in the hall. It was wholly empty. The wind dropped and the chimes diminished into silence. But it was a silence that was expectant. Waiting.

I still don't know why I did it. But, standing there, the sense of something nearby came over me strongly. Feeling foolish, my words jarring through the hall, I heard my own voice.

'I'm listening. Tell me your story.'

Screaming!

Screaming like a woman in agony. The hair stands on my arms even as I write this. I thought someone was being murdered in the house. I didn't know what I had let loose with my impulsive words.

The air fairly bubbled with the unknown banshee wailing. The sound scraped and wheeled about the house. It came from the direction of the kitchen.

I walked towards the sound, one hand trailing the wall, earthing me to reality, mind groping for an explanation.

When I stepped through the door, what I saw was strangely ordinary. A young girl stood across a well. She turned at the same moment and saw me. Both of us stared at each other, frozen in place. Another shriek wailed through the room. It came from the ancient pulley above the well as the abandoned bucket unreeled and plunged back into the water. The screech of protesting metal died into silence.

The girl's trembling lips moved and she whispered, 'Are you a ghost?'

My heart was jarring in my side. I could scarcely stand, my knees were so weak. And of all the questions! I couldn't help it—I burst out laughing.

The girl's terror turned to indignation. 'You scared me! Who are you?'

Well! I could be indignant as well. 'I thought *you* were the ghost,' I said. 'If you aren't a ghost, who are you?'

'I just came for a bucket of water. This well has the sweetest water in the village.' She turned to the well and cried out—'Oh!'

I joined her at the well and we both regarded her bucket floating free of the rope. 'Look what you made me do!' she said severely.

'Me?'

'Yes, you! I don't have another and I'm going to be late for work. It's all your fault!'

'My fault? Who was the one stealing water? Thief!' My own fright boiled over into fury. We both stood glaring at each other. Her feet were bare, her dress faded. She wore a single silver bead on a string around her neck. She must have been about sixteen years old. I concluded she was a servant—and a thief. Then, unexpectedly, she giggled, and the giggle transformed her completely.

'You should have seen your face,' she said.

I couldn't help smiling back. 'You should have seen yours,' I said.

The smile faded from her face and she regarded me with wariness. With a sudden movement, she climbed onto the ledge of the well. I had a wild impression that she was going to fling herself after her bucket and cried, 'Don't! Wait!'

The girl laughed openly at my panic and pointed across the well, 'I was only leaving.' As I watched, fascinated, her brown feet took three quick steps, balanced on the ledge of the well, and then she was on the far side.

I called across to her, 'Don't go! You haven't told me your name.' My voice echoed back from the water below me.

She looked at me with mischief in her eyes and said, 'But then you would know who the thief is.'

'Wait! Where are you going?' I called again.

She turned and pointed. A little square of white stood on the hills opposite, across the sea of green.

'Your bucket is still in my well,' I said, hoping to hold her back. 'When will you come back for it?'

'Tomorrow,' she said.

I looked down at the bobbing bucket. When I looked up, she was gone. I have absolutely no idea how to retrieve the pail.

God Promise

Beginnings
A Novel
By
J. Irani

I shouldn't have written this. Such a page smacks of vanity. But what a feeling it gives one to set it down in black and white! One day these words will be on a title page. Just typing them up gives me such a glow of satisfaction.

The glow has now faded. I have been in front of this page for hours. The church bells have rung twice, the children have had five separate lessons and have sung eleven hymns. Two men with fishing rods have gone down the lane and come staggering back, highly drunk. The problem is, I don't have a story. I went through my notebooks. I have been secretly developing several ideas across the last year. I thought I had enough material for three books, not just one. But now the conceits seem shallow and trifling. There is not enough there to go beyond a few chapters, let alone a whole novel. The words of the madman came back to me briefly and caused me some irritation.

Unable to settle down to work, I went wandering through the ruins of the house.

I open a door to the glassy stare of dozens of eyes. All manner of stuffed animal heads are arranged along the walls or in glass cases. There are spotted deer, some sort of antelope and a mangy lion that has a nest of termites spilling from its right eye. I wonder if it is the same lion the Indians shot, in the photograph I spotted the night before.

Africa runs like a deep theme through the house, turning up in small variations wherever you look. The curtain rods are actually African spears set up on brackets. The coat hooks are antlers from antelopes shot in the grasslands. Before I stepped into this house, I had no idea that Goans had gone all the way to Africa.

A tiny courtyard I stumble upon is black with soot from some forgotten conflagration. Two walls of the courtyard are almost rent asunder with giant fissures. Trapped in these I find charred fragments of paper. The writing is scarcely discernible, the words in elegant Portuguese. They seem to be some sort of record.

4 *Machos Humanas*	*Devidate*
2 *Femidade*	*Velho*
3 *Femidade*	*Enceinte*
3 *Machos Devidate*	*Bande*

I lose myself many times in the twisting corridors. In one such unmapped turn, I find myself in a music room which houses a gramophone and a collection of what look like ancient instruments. There, upon the walls, I recognise the piano that had stood, solitary and inexplicable, in the wind chime hall the night before. It appears and reappears, pristine and polished, in the photographs, holding the sequence together across the stretch of time they document.

Before me is a group of children stiff in lace and collars posed beside the piano with their tutor; here, a young girl sits on her mother's lap upon the piano stool; there, unmistakeably the same girl, although she is more of a woman now, her hands formal on the keys; then a sequence of photographs of her being felicitated and congratulated by a governor resplendent in his old-world uniform and medals; there are other men pompous in moustaches and formal dress. There are new locations, different pianos, what look like vast concert halls. Then, abruptly, when the woman appears to be about thirty, the sequence ends. There is one last photograph. It is difficult to recognise the sere old woman in it. She does not sit at the piano but stands beside it, one hand touching it as a child holds a parent's hand for comfort.

The story tantalises me with its black-and-white hints of a past. If only I knew it. Prodigious natural talent nurtured from childhood ... artistic triumph! And then, unexpectedly—tragedy. In the twilight of life, a retreat to this old house of her childhood. What could the reason be? A broken heart? A public snub?

I go to the kitchen in search of a cup of tea, though I am not quite sure how exactly one is made. I step into the kitchen and find myself facing a very large woman dressed in rusty black. She is holding a pistol.

It is really most annoying, the unexpected things that happen in this house! I am rather tired of dealing with the sudden shock. It is sheer luck that surprise holds me motionless, and that I do not fling my hands up in the air or any such foolish thing.

The large lady points the gun at me and lets loose a vast torrent of an unknown language. It is certainly not Portuguese so I take it for the local Konkani. It is threaded with the occasional English word. As my heartbeat slows down, I deduce that she is the caretaker's wife, come to clean and cook. But her stance is belligerent and accusatory. It seems that, while going about her chores, she has accidentally come upon the pistol and it has had as great an impact upon her peace of mind as it has on mine. She seems to think it is all my fault—leaving guns around. With a final burst of Konkani, she hands it to me and resumes her dusting.

It is a rather ancient gun, with a curlicued 'C' engraved on the butt in silver. Although I have never actually handled a weapon before, my vast reading has come to my rescue. I know that there should be a chamber in the gun, with bullets in it. With a little experimentation I open it and find a single bullet within. I close the chamber and experimentally aim the gun. The housekeeper turns around from her dusting at that moment and finds the gun pointed straight at her. She gives a shriek that makes me leap back and hastily lower it. Then she advances on me, shouting incomprehensible strings of angry words. She so alarms me, that I almost point the gun at her again. She points dramatically at the door and makes violent gestures. She is not having any gun in her kitchen. I hastily leave.

What am I supposed to do with a gun? For the time being I have kept it by my bed. But the sight of it has thoroughly distracted me and any chain of thought I begin goes immediately to guns and violence. I have no intention of writing a murder mystery. They have little literary merit and far too much blood. I am a serious writer and will not stoop to common titillating.

I give up and take myself down to the ruins with a notebook, hoping a change of scene will tempt the muse. I have only my title page and a whole book to write yet!

The ruins hummed with the sound of cicadas. The air was thick and clotted with afternoon heat. I found a stretch of unbroken wall and sat down in the shade of it. I looked at the blank page of my notebook.

The cicadas droned on. A little bird sang persistently, two notes up and two notes down. I sat, hypnotised by the heat and the singing and the blank piece of paper in front of me.

Dry leaves lazily drifted and settled at my feet. I found myself watching a little bit of paper that scuffled round and round with them in an eddy. Half asleep and dreaming, I picked it up and unfolded it. It was a page torn from an exercise book and a child had written on it in laborious letters: *'Sara come bak I miss you.'*

A second piece of paper fluttered down over my shoulder. I opened it. *'Please come bak Sara please. I am weting.'* I turned my head.

There were little bits of paper tucked into every single crevice of the wall. The wind touched them and set them shivering. A handful of them flew free like sudden butterflies.

I pulled out a wadded piece and opened it: *'Sara. Weting. I love you. Alice.'* I selected another at random. *'I have serched a lot. Come bak now. Alice.'* The cicadas sang. Bits of paper danced free in the wind, each one of them a prayer of desperation. *'Sara I am Alone. Weting and weting for you. Your sister Alice.'*

I didn't notice the little girl until she spoke: 'Have you seen Sara?' My heart gave a lurch at the sudden voice. It was my urchin of the day before, tucked into a niche in the wall. She held a grubby notebook and was occupied in carefully writing a fresh note in it. Her nose was still dripping.

'No,' I said. 'What happened to her?'

'She went away. She told me to wait for her. And I'm waiting.'

I sat down on a broken stone next to Alice, perfectly intrigued by this strange child. 'Why are you waiting here? Don't you have a home?'

She folded her note as she spoke. 'I'm from Mater Dolorosa.' My mystification must have shown on my face, so she expanded. 'The Mother of Sorrows. It's the orphanage the nuns run. I run away every afternoon and come here to wait. She was the only friend I had.'

Another story. 'Was she in the orphanage as well?'

Alice shook her head. 'Before. Now she's a big girl. She works. She used to work over there before she stopped coming to meet me. In her friend Nina's house.' She pointed to a patch of white on the hill. The very same house that my mysterious visitor of the morning had pointed to.

'Will you help me find her? Nobody helps me! Please.'

My blank notebook lay accusingly on the stones. 'I can't,' I said.

Alice said, 'Please! I have to find her. Please. I have to give her this.' She held out the carefully folded note to me. I hesitated. She regarded me consideringly for a moment and then said, 'It's all right. You can read it.' She unfolded it and held out the grimy scrap for me to read. *'No one loves me since you gone. I am alone. Please Sara come bak.'*

Well, really! I am here to write a novel. A serious work. I really have no time to run around looking for missing sisters. It was a request that I should immediately have said no to.

'Please,' said Alice, and there was a tremor in her voice.

I looked at the note again. The pencil marks were gouged deep into the paper, the words written with obvious effort. 'All right,' I said, 'I'll try.'

Alice's face lit up with delight. 'You will? Promise?'

I tried to retrieve myself from too large a commitment. 'I'll try, but I can't do very much, you see—'

'Say promise! Say *God* promise!'

Really! She expected me to perjure my soul without a thought. 'Promise,' I said.

A school bell clanged somewhere below us. Alice struggled to her feet, saying, 'I have to go. Thank you!' She limped away through the ruins, her brace ringing on the stones.

The papers in the wall fluttered and hummed like cicadas. I retrieved my unmarked notebook with a sigh. I was quite distracted and it was no use going back to the old house. Best that I got this over with immediately, so I could get back to the work I was here to do.

The white patch on the hill turned out to be a substantial house, tiled in the manner of the original Portuguese houses. The Portuguese came to Goa three hundred years ago, and the state has stayed under their rule ever since. The Portuguese were after trade and conversions and they got both. The population is now largely Catholic, and so every village has its tiny whitewashed chapels and its large church. The houses look like no houses anywhere else in India. They have fancy porches, windows that have mother-of-pearl in place of glass, and the roofs are covered with baked red earth tiles.

A huge wrought-iron gate guarded the house I approached and two stone lions sunned themselves on either side. One of them, rampant, stood over a flourish of letters that proclaimed 'Palais Casimir' and the other guarded a bell. Worked into the elaborate iron windings of the gate was an ornate 'C'. I had seen exactly the same curlicued initial earlier that morning on the butt of a gun.

The bell was a long time fetching anyone. Finally, a bent old woman shuffled to the gate and asked me what I wanted. I said I would like to speak to whoever lived in the house. The old woman said, 'Do you mean Dona Alcina?' I supposed I did. 'Who are you?'

I told her that Dona was unlikely to know me, but I'd like to meet her. I was a writer, I told her, conscious of a wince as I said it. It was the second time I had proclaimed myself one and that too on the strength of a single title page.

The old servant ushered me into a waiting room. As she turned to go, I gathered up my courage and quickly asked, 'Are there any others working here? Young girls?'

The servant stopped dead and gave me a long hard stare. One eye of hers was clouded with cataract, the other with suspicion. 'One,' she finally said, grudgingly.

I persisted in the face of her disapproval. 'What is her name?'

The servant pursed her lips in a manner that said volumes about unknown men who came asking about young servant girls, then she spat out, 'Constania.' Her one good eye dared me to ask another question, and I quailed. She shuffled off into the depths of the house.

It was a grand house. Overhead, the timbers of the ceiling were carved, and stippled glints showed that at one time they were gilded. A faint smell hung about the room. Not of age but rather of polish and spirits and hard work. It was the smell of Pride. Pride that had poured unending, ageless labour into preserving its glory. Of tiles hand-polished decade after decade; of silver buffed to shining; of a never-ending war against mould and wet and the chronic ills of age that old houses are prone to. Generations of servants on their knees had pursued Time round and round in this room, ceaselessly wiping his handprints from the heirlooms, dusting him out of the curtains, wiping him from the patina of silver. Here, Time had yielded to their labours and paused. It was the eighteenth century here in this house, and the Casimirs were still Portuguese aristocracy, bred to pride and wealth.

Their faces stared down at me from the photographs that lined the wall. Ladies dressed in lace and diamonds. Gentlemen in suits wearing satin sashes and rows of medals. Picnic parties posed on the grass. A military gentleman on his horse.

The fruits of their endeavour were scattered about the house. Hand-painted tiles from Venice, fine marble for the mantelpiece, pure mahogany for the pelmets. Everywhere there was the ornate 'C' of Casimir. It glinted from silver, was stamped on mounted china, hung carved and pendulant on the tongue of the old clock. It reminded me strongly of my own house, except that we are not so lavish with our initials. And our waiting room is certainly larger. It suddenly struck me that the ruin I now live in must have been something like this before Pride went out of it.

Laboured feet came shuffling down the corridor. 'Dona Alcina will see you now.'

Dona Alcina received me formally in her private
sitting room. She was in an upright chair and did not rise.
The room was a glory of polished mahogany and old
lace. Dona Alcina too was mahogany and old lace, except
where her hands and face shone out of the mourning
black like delicate translucent china, veined in hundreds
of cracks. Her hands were bent and twisted with arthritis.
She held a rosary and fumbled each bead through
gnarled fingers. She inclined a gracious head at me. I was
suddenly conscious that my shoes were dusty and my hair
uncombed.

'I'm here on behalf of a friend actually. She wanted me
to enquire … if this is not a convenient time … I mean, I'm
sorry to disturb you—'

A ripple of melodious Portuguese issued from Dona's
lips. The sour servant translated. 'Dona says to continue.
You do not disturb.'

I asked, 'You had a girl working here for you—can you
tell me what happened to Sara?'

The hands counting the beads suddenly convulsed. The
rosary clattered to the floor. A torrent of angry Portuguese
foamed from her lips.

The servant woodenly translated, her bland sentences
in contrast to the anger that was pouring forth from her
mistress. 'Who are you? Why do you speak that name
within these walls? What is your purpose in coming here?'

I was terribly taken aback. 'No one really … I don't
know Sara myself, I just—'

'That name is never mentioned within these walls. It is
forbidden. Have we not suffered enough?'

'If you could—'

'We know nothing of the girl.'

It was obvious the interview was over. I had never been so embarrassed in my life and every instinct told me to leave as quickly as I could. But the image of that painfully scrawled note came back to me. I persisted with one last question, recalling the name that Alice had taken. 'Perhaps Nina would be able to tell me something?'

This time the impassive old servant was startled into making the sign of the cross. Dona Alcina's face twisted. She grasped her cane and rose, struggling, to her feet. I needed no translator to understand the command that she spat out. Her cane thumped imperiously on the ground, then pointed to the door.

'If I could just speak to her for a minute—'

The servant snarled at me, 'Leave! Can you not see you're not wanted? Go!'

I backed away, muttering apologies. A crescendo of furious Portuguese drove me to the door. But before I plunged into the corridor, Dona Alcina's words halted me.

'Sara is dead!' she said. She spoke in accented English.

I turned back. 'How do you know?'

'I pray for her death every night,' she hissed. 'God is good. I know he hears me.'

She sat down in her chair. The servant gently replaced the rosary in those twisted fingers. I fled as far as the porch and stopped to take breath as the door slammed behind me. At that moment a little scatter of discordant sound was shaken loose and drifted around my ears. Hanging in the porch was a wind chime knotted out of bits of shell and driftwood.

A gun and a wind chime mark the connection between the two houses. What it is, I cannot for the life of me make out.

Sara the Angel

The village is a small cluster of houses around a central square, the whole dominated by the tall façade of the church that occupies one end of the square. The passage of the day is marked by the slow stretch of the shadow of the church across the square. The church bells mark the time for the entire village. Everyone takes their pace from the slow tolling of the bells and nothing ever moves in a hurry.

I stopped at the village shop on my way back for my purchases. The shopkeeper suggested burning cow dung cakes for the mosquitoes. I must have looked doubtful because he began extolling the many virtues of cow dung in lyrical words. I gave in and purchased a dozen cakes.

Next to the shop was a taverna. A motley clientele was seated there on wooden benches, looking as if they had grown there over the years. As I turned to leave, I realised that every eye in the taverna was avidly fastened on me.

As I juggled my many paper packages, a sudden thought came to me. 'Excuse me,' I said, addressing my question to the benches, 'I'm searching for a girl called Sara. Would you have any idea where I could ask for her?'

My question fell among them like a sensation.

'Sara!' cried a man whose paunch looked like he was hiding a pig under his vest. 'You want to know about Sara? We'll tell you.' He gestured for me to come over.

The men all squeezed together and made space on a bench. I hesitated. There was a peculiar penetrating smell in the air. It seemed to ooze from the eager occupants of the bench. I am really most sensitive to smell, and stayed on my feet.

The man grinned ingratiatingly. 'It's a little difficult to talk with a dry throat.'

I looked around and encountered a series of bloodshot and expectant gazes. Reluctantly, I ordered a drink that I had no intention of actually downing. The order was somehow transmuted into an order for drinks for everyone. When they arrived, I placed the reek. It came from the clear liquor in the glasses.

'Feni,' said another man, who was ferociously squint. 'The finest drink in the world. Made from cashew fruit.' He raised a glass in salute. He downed his drink and said, 'I don't know where Sara is, but the man she's with is in heaven!'

There was much raucous laughter at this sally. Another man chimed in with 'Know what a *byadgi* is? It's the chilli they put in the chorizo sausages. It's the little one that you remember the next morning. That's what Sara was, a byadgi.'

An old man with two remaining teeth joined in the reminiscing. 'Seemed all demure—like she'd learnt everything the nuns taught her by heart. But in the evenings, she'd be off to meet men. Running through the graveyard late at night.'

I asked, 'Why are you talking like she's gone away?'

A dozen voices clamoured to tell me, 'She has!'

'Ran away, she did.'

'Just vanished one night …'

The man with a pig belly gestured the chorus to silence and took over as official spokesman. 'She was off every night to meet someone. Then one morning she was gone. Left with him, I suppose.' He leaned over to whisper to me, 'Wish it was with me.' Laughter shook the taverna and I was inundated with voices.

'Started young, she did. She was a ripe piece.'

'Made my mouth water.'

'We have a word for women like her. *Chendi*.'

'I'd have liked to get her alone in the graveyard for a while! We'd have given the ghosts something to look at!'

The taverna echoed with the boisterous camaraderie of lust. It disgusted me. The sly innuendos, the wet lips, the leering eyes. I feared for Sara if she had ever found herself alone with one of these men.

A young man had been moving among the regulars, serving the drinks. He caught the word that was sliding so wetly from lip to lip and was moved to speak. But, when he opened his mouth, a tangled discord of sound fell out. Only one word among the clangour rang clear—'Sara!'

It was greeted with a chorus of catcalls. 'We forgot! Lorso was in love with her as well!'

Lorso ignored the raucous men. All his attention was focused on me. His lips contorted. He struggled to shape words. They fell, crippled and bent from his lips. Again, only one word slipped from his lips whole and distinguishable—'Sara! Sara? *Sara*?'

Pig Belly called out, 'She found herself a man with a tongue, Lorso. Women like men with tongues!'

Lorso's eyes never left my face. His mouth sawed and contorted and slurred the word again and again, 'Sara? … Saaa-rah … *Saaa—rah*?' Then he reached out and grabbed my arm.

'I don't know!' I said, wrenching myself free and flinging money on the table. The ribald shouts of the drunken men followed me as I walked away as fast as I could. My mother has repeatedly warned me about the evils of strong drink and I could now see for myself the ill effects clearly.

I must confess that the interlude in the taverna left me feeling sour and uncomfortable. I don't know what I expected Alice's sister to be, but it was certainly not the portrait that was painted for me at the taverna. Even at the Casimir house her name had provoked a reaction of hate. Who could have thought that asking after one servant girl could evoke such extreme reactions?

As I walked home, I was so deeply in thought that it was some time before I noticed the rustle of bushes behind me. Something or someone was following me, blundering through the undergrowth. I hastened my steps and hurried into the ruins. My pursuer came thundering behind me. I spun around, heart thudding loud enough to hear.

Facing me was the young boy from the taverna. His mouth was working and the word fell out differently wrought each time. It was a demand. It was a question. It was an entreaty. 'Sara? Saa-rah? Sara?'

'I don't know!' I said again, thoroughly exasperated. 'I don't know where she is. Just stop following me!' I set off down the path and Lorso followed, the name more and more strident in his mouth.

He reached out to grab my arm again, and I shrugged him off. With the gesture, my unwieldy armful of packages slid to the ground and several of them burst open. In high irritation, I bent to gather them up. Lorso stood expectantly over me. 'I don't know!' I shouted once more. 'Didn't you hear them? She's run away with a man. That's the kind of girl she was.'

Lorso grabbed my arm with another inarticulate explosion of words. All my misgivings came flooding back. His grip was surprisingly strong. He dragged me into the ruins while I struggled impotently. He stopped at a statue and let me go.

I stumbled back, putting distance between myself and him. But he was not looking at me at all. He was pointing. I followed the direction of his finger. A stone angel stood upon a plinth, wingless and blind, its eyes gazing vacantly at us. Lorso pointed at the statue and tried to say something. But words failed him. Instead, his hands moved and fluttered. I read the meaning that they began to weave. My paternal grandfather had been totally deaf, and the family had learnt how to sign to him.

'Sara was like—an angel? She was gentle ... kind ... good ... she sang—sang like an angel. She was a friend. The best friend you ever had. She went away ... without saying goodbye. Sara. Angel.'

The statue gazed down at us with its inscrutable blind smile. Lorso stared up at it, rapt in adoration.

Sara the angel. Sara the whore. I had no idea what to make of the double vision I had been handed. I chose instead to rescue my scattered groceries and hastily leave. What a most peculiar day!

The day wasn't over yet. As I climbed up the hill towards home, in the waning light I could see that someone was waiting on the porch.

It was a handsome man, dressed entirely in black. He was unadorned except for a gold signet ring that glinted on his right hand. He inclined his head in greeting as I came up the stairs.

'My name is Damon Casimir,' he said. 'You came to see my grandmother today.' He spoke English, but the soft cadence of Portuguese ran through the words. 'You wanted information on some servant girl.'

'Sara,' I said. 'Yes. Can you help me?'

'Neither I nor anyone in the village will be able to tell you anything about her whereabouts.'

He stood there on my porch, stiff in his pride. In the old woman the pride was old-worldly. Newly minted in the man, it was arrogance. I disliked him immediately. 'I made a promise to someone that I would find her.'

'Not all promises can be kept. It would be unwise to persist.'

I didn't immediately realise that I was being threatened. When I did, I was outraged. He had the arrogance to try and threaten me! I am an Irani. In the city of Bombay that means a lot. I have an old and respected name and enough reasons to be proud too.

I held back my fury and continued to be polite. 'I like to keep my promises. Perhaps Nina will be able to tell me something.'

Dusk had fallen as we spoke. Damon was no more than a dark shape against the twilight sky. 'Nina will not speak to you.'

'Why not?'

'It is not possible.'

He took a step forward. I was forced to take a step backward and ended up on the first porch stair, a whole head below him. It was a ridiculous position. My anger was compounded by my suspicion that he was amused by our encounter. I defiantly said, 'Somebody will know something!'

Damon said, 'She was a servant girl. Not anyone of note.'

'She mattered to her sister.'

The odious man shrugged. 'It's been a long time. People forget.'

'How long?' I asked. 'A few months?'

His answer was completely unexpected. 'It's been five years.'

'Five years?!'

His teeth gleamed in the dusk. I was right. He was laughing at my surprise. 'Yes. Five years. I don't think searching for her will really help, do you? I suggest you do not persist. It might be unwise.' He brushed past me and walked into the darkness.

Missing for five years! How Alice expected me to find her was beyond me.

Well, I have learnt my lesson. A writer should not be distracted. It is important to be selfish, or people are just waiting to fritter your time away. I am not here to hunt up lost sisters. I am here to write a work of great literary merit.

Tomorrow morning, first thing, I will tell Alice I cannot help her.

I could hear Alice's voice long before I saw her. It was raised in a piping off-key rendition of *Onward Christian*

Soldiers. The singing was mysteriously punctuated with grunts. I discovered that this was because Alice was playing hopscotch as she sang. With her leg banded and barred in metal, each jump took an immense effort. She stopped mid-hop when she saw me and asked eagerly, 'Did you find her?'

All my irritation flooded back. 'You didn't tell me she's been missing for five years! How on earth was I supposed to find her?'

'But you *said* you would!'

'I can't! It's going to take a lot of time and effort and I have work to do.'

'But you said *promise*!'

It is no use at all arguing with children. They never really listen. Alice's eyes were filling with tears and she was sniffing to stop her nose from running. I tried not to look. 'She's been gone five years. That's a very long time. I don't think she will come back.'

Alice shook her head. 'She *said* she would come back. She told me to wait. She *will* come!' She was fierce in her defence of her sister. 'Sara never breaks her promises. She doesn't break her promises—not like *you*!'

She climbed back into her corner and turned away from me. I could see her shoulders shaking. I stood there for a moment, undecided, before I remembered my resolve. Nothing will come between my writing and me. I cannot waste this chance.

I walked away.

The End of an Affair

What could I have done to help Alice? There is no use thinking about it again and again. I must shut the question out and get back to work.

I have been here three days already and do not have even a sentence to show for it. If I do not write my novel there will be no second attempt for me. It will be accounts and ledgers and an office every day. I know it is a matter of great prestige to be the Irani heir, and my mother cannot understand why I should wish for anything else. She blames it on my father and his inordinate love of poetry. Perhaps it is the poetry. But I find myself longing for a life apart from the one that has been meticulously charted for me.

No more trying to help orphan girls. I shall just sit and write.

It is inordinately difficult to extricate a bucket from a well. I have tried everything—hooks fashioned from coat hangers, twisted wire at the end of a rope, a bit of bent iron—everything. How do people take buckets out of wells? Or do they just let them be? I found my head filled with images of wells all over Goa slowly choking with abandoned, rusty buckets.

I intend to fish out the bucket, hand it to that girl

and make sure she does not come back. I cannot be distracted.

My visitor finally appeared in the early evening. I had just taken a sheet of paper out of my typewriter and was intently tearing it into little strips when I felt a presence. I turned in my chair and she was standing at the door watching me.

'I've come for my bucket.'

I couldn't admit that, try as I might, I was unable to fetch it out. 'Maybe I'm not ready to return it to you yet— Constania.'

She considered that a moment. 'Where did you get the name?'

'Oh, I guessed. I'm a writer. We can tell things just by looking at people. I looked at you and thought— Constania.'

She looked at me for a bit, then pointed out through the window. An austere-looking man wearing a hat was going down the lane at a funereal pace. 'Guess who that is.'

I made an extravagant guess. 'Let me see. He is Sebastian Seramos Seratin the Third. He's a man who has seen much suffering in his life. It's made him sombre and silent. He spends most of his days on his knees, praying.'

Constania smiled. 'His name is Antonio. He plays the guitar in a band and gets drunk on Sundays and beats his wife.'

Another familiar figure went down the road. It was my madman from the graveyard. I quickly salvaged my reputation. 'His name is Augustus Cajetan Monteiro. He lost his wife in a tragic accident twenty-five years ago and he has mourned her every single day since.'

'That is Crazy Charlie. He's never been married. His childhood sweetheart was married to someone else and he went crazy. She died in labour with her first child. So now he sits by her grave all day long.'

Suddenly, Constania's expression changed and she stepped behind me to hide. I looked to see who was passing. It was my elegant visitor of the evening before.

I announced his name with great pomp. 'That is Damon Casimir. Heir of the Casimirs. Steeped bone-deep in pride and arrogance. Dona Alcina's grandson. Flesh of her flesh, the blood of the Casimirs running blue in him.'

Constania said nothing for a moment. Then she whispered, 'If he sees me here ... I'd better go!'

All my resolutions not to be distracted deserted me. It had been a long day of absolute solitude. After a day of silence and blank pages, I needed someone to talk to. 'Don't go yet!'

'I have to. Sister Ursula says that a single girl should not be alone with a man at any time.'

'Who is Sister Ursula?'

'She is the principal of the orphanage. She says men are not to be trusted. Sister Ursula says, never let them touch you. If you do, they turn into beasts.'

Well, really! As if I am to be judged along with everyone else. I think half of what the nuns teach these orphans is out of spite. 'I'd like to meet this Sister Ursula and tell her a few things.'

Constania regarded me with a look of mischief. 'Are you not a beast?'

'I am Parsee,' I said. 'And I am an Irani.'

Neither meant anything to her. I am not surprised. She is a little village girl living in the middle of nowhere. She cannot be expected to know much of the world.

Constania giggled at my solemnity and then ran for the door. I followed and caught up with her at the well. A quick step and she was on the ledge, poised for flight.

I quickly baited her with promise of a mystery. 'I found a secret room yesterday. Perhaps you'd like to see it.'

'Secret nice or secret horrible?'

'Very nice. Listen! Can you hear that?'

The feet hesitated. A timely shimmer of notes hung on the air. 'What are those sounds?'

She was hooked. I reeled her in—'Come with me and I'll show you.'

'Sister Ursula says—'

'Sister Ursula talks rubbish. You have the word of an Irani.' She looked with me without understanding again. I amended my words with a smile. 'We are never beasts. Our mothers don't allow us to be.'

That drew a grin from her. The feet wriggled uncertainly on the ledge. Then they climbed down. 'All right.'

I led her through the endless rooms and she trailed behind me wide-eyed. She was entranced by the lion, never having seen one outside of a book. I had difficulty dragging her away and had to bribe her with the story of the real live lions at the Bombay zoo. She wanted to tarry in the music room and spent fully five minutes admiring the mermaid.

Finally, we arrived at the broken panel and squeezed through the door. Constania was delighted with the hall and its wind chimes. She ran from one to the other, cataloguing all that they were made of. 'Cowrie shells and driftwood. And teesro shells. Mangrove seeds. You find them on Morjim beach. Those are palm seeds. They wash up on shore during the monsoons. That is the seed case from the gulmohar.' She closed her eyes and listened intently to the cascades of sound. 'Who made these?'

'That's the secret,' I said.

The rainbow that dropped on the floor from the stained-glass panels delighted her as much. She laughed as she hopscotched from shade to shade. She spun around with her arms outstretched. It was only the piano she regarded doubtfully. 'It looks so lonely. All alone in this room.'

She went back to playing hopscotch by the windows. I sat in a bay window and watched her. She suddenly became self-conscious and came to stand demurely nearby. I realised I knew nothing about her at all.

'I only know your first name. What is your surname?'

Constania shrugged. 'I don't have any. None of us orphans do. The nuns choose the names for us.'

'I have five,' I said. 'Jamshed Fali Hormazd Ratan Irani.' The string of names made her giggle.

'Jam for short?' she asked.

'My name has never been shortened. I don't think anyone would dare,' I said. 'My mother says that we are the original immigrants from Iran which is why we have the surname. Even the housekeeper who has watched me being born calls me "Mr Irani".'

'I have never heard a surname like Irani,' said Constania doubtfully.

'I am a Parsee,' I said. 'That's where my ancestors came from. We stayed, thanks to a spoonful of sugar.'

'Sugar?' said Constania.

I told her the story that every Parsee child knows by heart. Fleeing after the fall of their earlier home in the Persian Empire to the invading Muslims, the Parsees arrived at the court of Jadhwa Rana on the west coast of India.

When the Parsees asked to stay in his kingdom, the Rana handed their spokesman a cup brimful with milk, to show that his kingdom was already full to overflowing with people. There was no more place for anyone. Add anything to it and it would spill over. But the king had counted without the canniness of the Parsees.

The Parsee priest who had been chosen as spokesperson stepped forward and put a spoonful of sugar in the milk. He handed it back, saying that the Parsees would be like the sugar, adding sweetness but not causing anything to spill.

'So charmed was the Rana, he allowed us to stay. In a couple of decades, we were running all the businesses there and lending him money!'

'Do you lend people money?' asked Constania doubtfully.

'We do lots of things. The family has a string of businesses.'

She looked even more doubtful. 'Are you very rich?'

'Well—yes,' I said. It did not seem to impress her at all. Quite the opposite.

'Jamshed Fali Hormazd—why do you have so many names?'

'I am named after two of our most important ancestors, the man who slipped the sugar in the milk, and the grandfather who made the first fortune for our family. We Parsees pride ourselves on our sense of history.'

'I'll never remember all those names,' said Constania. 'I like Jam.'

I had never had a nickname. I found myself charmed by the idea. 'Then you may call me Jam,' I said, 'and I will call you Tania.'

We sat quietly side by side in a bay window as the colours began to fade from the floor and day slid into dusk.

'Why are you always barefoot?' I asked her. 'Don't your feet hurt?'

'People give away shoes less often than clothes. So, sometimes I have shoes, sometimes I don't.' She wriggled those expressive toes. 'I like being barefoot. I like feeling what I'm walking on. If you blindfolded me, I could tell where I was just by the feel of what was underneath my feet.'

I gazed at her feet in admiration. From as far back as I can remember, I have possessed an inordinate number of shoes. Shoes to go out in, shoes to play tennis, shoes for the fire temple, special shoes for special occasions. And in the house, soft slippers for wearing in the bedroom, rubber slippers for the bathroom and sandals for the lawns. I kicked off my shoes and stretched my bare feet out beside hers. The dry boards rasped underfoot.

The chimes above our heads sounded and attracted Tania's attention. 'Look!' she said. 'This one is made up of old keys.'

They jangled together in a clatter of metallic clinks. All shapes and sizes of keys. Keys to chests that were dust, to doors that had long ago crumbled. I stood on the window ledge and tapped the chime. The strings were frail and a sudden shower of rusty keys rained on Tania. She dodged them and laughed as they cascaded onto the floor and scattered in every direction. I bent to gather them. Fumbling for the keys on the floor, my fingers brushed against something trapped between two warped floorboards. I eased it out.

It emerged into the light and we both stared at it. It was a folded note, yellowed and crumpled. I unfolded it and read:

Dearest,

It can never be. Our worlds are too far apart to meet. I wish you well—always and forever.

Felicidade seja sua sempre.

'I wonder who wrote that and to whom?' I said aloud.

'What does *"felicidade seja sua sempre"* mean?' she asked.

'I think it's Portuguese,' I ventured. I regarded the note I held. It was the End of an Affair.

Tania said, 'I wonder who he wrote it to.'

'He? It could have been a "she" as well.'

'It's a Goodbye Note,' said Tania, as if that explained everything.

'It's not only men who leave women!' I said indignantly. 'Women leave men as well.'

Tania said nothing. It was too dark to see her face, but I had a sudden moment of insight. Leaning forward I asked, 'Who left you, Tania?'

There was no answer. Just a sudden movement and the sound of bare feet swift on the wooden floor.

'Tania! Don't go!' I tried to follow, but her feet could see in the dark and fled ahead of me. My feet had been too long confined and were blind. I blundered in the dark and stubbed them on a variety of painful objects.

By the time I got to the well she was long gone. But her bucket was still bobbing in the water and she would have to return.

I wonder who broke Tania's heart and left her. I am rather pleased with my insight into the human heart. I am a writer. We can do these things.

I travelled back by lamplight through all the cluttered rooms. I had to collect the shoes I had left in the hall of wind chimes. The Goodbye Note was still lying where I had dropped it, a scrap of white against the dark floorboards.

The hall was silent, all the chimes unmoving. As I picked up the note, a sudden ripple of sound from the chimes washed through the dark. When I turned to go, it repeated itself more urgently. I hesitated. The chimes ran down the hall like a leading question. I walked to the end of the hall. A giant tapestry depicting *The Last Supper* hung in tatters from the wall at the far end. I had presumed that there was nothing behind it. But now, like an apocalyptic double vision, through the rents between Christ and the apostles, I could see that there was a door. I tugged at the tapestry and it ripped and fell, releasing a tidal wave of dust and musty smells.

It revealed a door that was triple-locked and barred. It stood solid and unmoving. I put an eye to a crevice, expecting darkness. Instead, I saw a slant of moonlight. It fell on a face twisted in a rictus of agony. Blood. A man exhausted and tortured to the edge of endurance. Strangely, it was a face I knew.

I stood there frozen, heart thudding—until I pinned down the familiarity. It was Christ, hanging from the cross. I had found the family chapel.

I put the Goodbye Note into my diary. As I did so, I was struck by a thought. I held a story right here in my hands.

The idea took hold of me and I found myself turning the words of the note over and over in my mind. I lay awake late at night, with suppositions and scenarios ricocheting through my head. Who wrote it? Who left whom? Why? How did the note come to lie upon the floor, abandoned in an empty house?

I think I can make a story of this note. One that only I can tell.

A False Note

I laid the Goodbye Note on the table, sure that today would be a day of beginnings. I put a new ribbon in the typewriter and laid out clean sheets of paper.

I am sure I have my story. Speculations have stirred through my head all night long. I am not going to rise from the table until I have something—anything at all!—down.

No sooner had I sat, facing the crisp new paper, than every single thought that had rampaged through my head the entire night vanished.

The bells rang. The children learned their lessons by rote all morning. Then the deep silence of afternoon smothered all sounds. In the hush I could hear Alice's voice echoing up from the ruins, calling, 'Sara … Saaaa—rah!' It quite ruined my concentration.

Sheet after sheet of paper found its way to the floor, as I struggled with my beginning.

It was almost dusk when I rose from the table. Tired of silence and, thinking of a way to break it, I walked through the darkening house.

I think I am beginning to understand how to clean things. You have to scrub a whole lot harder than you thought would be required. The gramophone is all cleared of grime and I have even managed to get a bit of a gleam on the horn.

I found a disc under the table and rescued it from cobwebs and dust. The label was printed in an elaborate font, all curly tails and serifs.

Limited Edition for Presentation Only
Lisbon Miranda Rose
In Concert
Solo Violin

I wound up the gramophone, hoping it would work. It would be nice to have some company. The turntable began to spin. I put the needle down gently and the sound of a lone violin called hauntingly into the room. Its plaintive voice was oddly appropriate to the air of sadness and neglect that hung thick in every room.

I sat back in a chair and shut my eyes. Slowly, the music unfolded and drifted through the silence of the house. When it came to an end, I opened my eyes.

Tania was sitting on the floor, head tilted, listening intently. 'That was beautiful,' she said. 'What is it?'

I had no need to consult the disc. My lessons had included studies of Western classical music. 'Bach's *Chaconne in D Minor.*'

'It made me very sad. It's like someone lost and lonely. Waiting for something. Waiting for years and years.'

Her words brought Alice to mind. Indeed, thoughts of Alice had not left me all day and had greatly interfered with my attempts to write. 'I know one little girl who has waited five years for someone to return.'

I wound up the gramophone again, lifted the arm and put the needle gently down. Sitting there, the violin keening around us, I told her the story of Alice and her sister Sara. To my alarm, her eyes filled with tears.

'Don't cry!' I said. 'It's not worth crying over.'

She scrubbed at her tears and turned on me so fiercely I was taken aback. 'How can you be a writer and write about people if you can't understand the pain in the heart of one little girl?'

'I tried to help her,' I said, a trifle stiffly. After all, she was accusing me of being unfeeling. When I had gone out of my way to help the unreasonable child. 'You can't find a girl who has been missing five years. It's impossible.'

'Do something!' cried Tania in distress.

Really! I don't know what she expected from me. 'What would you suggest?' I asked coldly.

'Write. You say you're a writer—then, *write* to her. Write from Sara, saying she still loves her. Alice has no one else in the whole world.'

I was about to laugh scornfully at the suggestion when I paused. With her quick orphan's heart, she had seen what I could not, surrounded as I was from childhood by the love and adoration of an entire family. With only one person to love you, the loss of that love is the loss of all your store.

Together, we devised the letter, sitting at my writing desk. Tania was shy and fumbled for words. I provided them with a flourish, pouring them out upon the paper, relieved at last to have a writing task as small as a flea. But she didn't appreciate my fine sentences at all. 'It's all so complicated.'

'It's *fine* writing!' I protested.

We argued over everything. Over words, meaning, intensity, intention. How much did Sara love her sister?

Enough to say 'dearly' or the more restrained 'very'? How about the sticky question of her return? Would she avoid any mention of it? Or make some sort of promise? What kind of excuse could she give for an absence of five years—surely little Alice would see past 'unavoidable circumstances'?

'If she understands the words at all!' cried Tania.

Matters came to a head over a fine sentence I had crafted about the bond between two sisters. I refused to part with it. Tania simply covered the piece of paper with her hand and looked at me. Then she spoke:

> *'Dear Alice,*
> *I know you have been alone and unhappy a long, long time.*
> *If I could have been there with you I would have. Because*
> *you are the one thing I love most in all the world. I pray*
> *every night that we can be together. You are always in my*
> *mind and my heart. I will keep my promise and come to you*
> *as soon as I can.*
> *Your sister who loves you forever,*
> *Sara.'*

Later that night, I was falling asleep when the thought came to me. I have finally done my first piece of writing. And it is not mine at all. It is a bit of ghost writing.

Remember

Even though it was early in the morning, the heat had set all the cicadas in the ruins singing. The air was thick and every breath was heavy. The trees stood, unmoving, their every attempt to converse stifled by the blanket of heat.

I inserted the letter in a crack in the wall, and it made a shining new flag among the tatters of all Alice's pleas. I sat down to wait for her, but the morning was hot and the little bird was singing again. My eyes closed.

When I opened them again, Alice was standing intent at the wall, reading the letter, pausing with frowning brow to spell out some of the words. She came to the end of it and her face was sunshine. 'Sara wrote! My sister wrote to me! She remembers me.'

'I am glad,' I said, sudden guilt staining my heart. I had been so focused on writing the letter, it was only her happiness that brought home to me that it was a lie.

She folded the letter carefully and tucked it into her dress. She held both hands over her heart where it was stored.

'She will come back for me!' Alice smiled at me and was off.

I could hear her making her way through the ruins. She was singing, 'Praise ye, the Faaaa—ther,' in time to the clicking of her brace. Her joy made the guilt I was feeling even heavier. I have allowed Tania to talk me into doing something unfair and immoral. For all Alice's joyful singing, I am not sure the outcome will be a happy one.

I was turning to go, when a flicker of movement caught my eye. Lorso was standing in front of the angel he so adored. He was fumbling with the base of the statue. He caught my attention because he looked around so furtively.

'Lorso!' He started at my call, but refrained from flight when he saw that it was me.

'I wanted to talk to you,' I said. 'I wanted to know a bit more about Sara.'

He was suspicious, his hands shaping questions.

'I want to know what happened to her. I want to know why she left her sister behind.'

He began to back away from me and I cast around for a means to hold him.

'Please!' I said. 'Just tell me about you and her. You're her friend. How did you meet?'

He sat down on a bit of broken wall. I sat beside him. His hands began to move, and I interpreted the story they told.

'You became friends because … you were always … punished?'

Theirs was a friendship forged in adversity. They always found themselves punished in the corridor together, the class Idiot and the Bad Girl. The nuns had decided that Lorso was Slow, and Sara was Bad.

'Why did they think that?'

Lorso shrugged, his hands signalling his mystification. The nuns thought that both conditions could be cured by enough punishment and catechism. Standing in the corridor with hands striped by weals, the two of them were forbidden to talk. But that was no hardship to Lorso who had never trusted his voice. His sore hands telegraphed to Sara and she learnt soon enough to sign back. They discussed why they had been so chosen.

One of the first signs that Lorso had learnt from Sister Ursula was 'try'. His hands flipped upwards and out again and again. Try. Try. Try. That is all he ever did. But he never got any faster. It was the same with Sara. Even the best of her actions somehow became Bad under the eye of authority. She set out with good intentions and found herself in a muddle of evildoing, the gold somehow turning to dross. Only on one day of the week was she tolerable. That was on Sunday, when she sang at mass.

A look of hopeless longing came over Lorso's face as he tried to describe her voice. It was—'... like birds in the sky ... like moonlight ... like a river talking to God. The most beautiful thing ever.'

He would sit beside her as she practised, soundlessly mouthing the words, imagining it was from his own mouth that the birds flew.

'Sara told you that ... everything has a voice ... there are voices everywhere ... one day you'd find yours ... it just wasn't where other people kept their voices.'

Lorso smiled sadly and shrugged. He was still searching. His head tilted, he mimed listening. Then his hands swayed and skittered and were still. The gestures conjured up the sounds so delicately that I could almost hear them. Wind chimes.

'Wind chimes? *Sara* made the wind chimes?'

'She said that there were voices in the wind.'

'Whose voices?'

The hands were slow and elegiac. 'Those that have left us … saying … Remember … remember … remember …'

Sibilant shells from the seashore; long, rattling pods from the gulmohar trees in the ruins; bits of glass from the rubbish heap behind the refectory; scrap wood and string from the timber yard in the village; broken porcelain from dustbins; bottles from the taverna; old keys and safety pins and hangers. Lorso foraged far and wide, carrying his finds back eagerly to Sara. Together they knotted the wind chimes, talking about forgetting and remembrance.

'She was your friend. Your friend first. Before … someone came? … Who came, Lorso?'

But anger made Lorso inarticulate, choking his throat and flinging his hands into tumult.

'Spell it, Lorso,' I said.

Lorso took a twig and scratched the letters in the dust. N.I.N.A.

'Nina? … they were best friends … they made a promise to be best friends forever …'

Lorso sat there, the sadness of betrayal slowing his hands. 'Sara didn't have time for you anymore … Nina didn't want you around … you tried to follow them but they wouldn't let you …'

Lorso got up and went to the statue. He gazed up at it, his hands upon the broken brickwork plinth. He turned around and looked at me as if he was trying to make up his mind to convey something. His fingers twitched. Then he firmly tucked his hands into his armpits, a shuttered look coming over his face.

'What is it, Lorso?' I asked. 'Tell me. I am trying to find Sara.'

He stood there, swaying from foot to foot, trying to decide. His eyes skipped to the angel and back. Then he abruptly turned and ran into the ruins, his footsteps stuttering away into the distance. I was left there, sitting on a wall, thinking of Sara and Nina. Friends forever.

I found myself gazing at the statue of the angel. The base was crumbling, the brickwork cracked and worn. A dark wisp caught my eye. Something was snagged in a crevice. I got up and bent to the wisp. It was a strand of hair. I pulled at it. The brick moved. I pulled the brick out, and a long braid of hair slithered from its hiding place and fell to the ground.

I picked up the braid of hair and stood looking at it. It was a long length, tied at one end with a bit of string, unravelling into strands at the other. Waist-length hair. I was bewildered by my find. The braid dangled from my hand like a question mark, with its dark suggestion of violence. Where had Lorso got it, and why had he hidden it? Was it Sara's? What had happened to her?

Until Death Do Them Part

The light leaves an old house reluctantly. It lingers in the cracks. Slides long fingers under the doors. Hangs suffused in the dim air, held in cobwebs and dancing motes of dusk. I watched the day slowly seep away. It was dark before I heard the noises at the well, and Tania appeared. She hesitated and said demurely, 'I've come for my bucket.' But I could see the laughter in her eyes. Then she noticed my expression. 'What is it?' she asked.

I held up the length of hair. It hung from my hand, swaying gently like a pliant snake.

'Where did you get that?' she asked, puzzled. I told her of my discovery and she was appalled. Her hands flew to her mouth.

'I think it belongs to Sara,' I said, and she voiced the heavy thought that had weighed me down all afternoon.

'Do you think he hurt her?'

'I don't know.'

We both stared at each other, neither willing to voice the surmise that was in our minds, as if saying the words would make the worst come true.

'Did he have something to do with her going missing?' said Tania at last.

'I don't know,' I said. 'And it's difficult to make him tell.'

Tania reached out a hand and ran it down the braid. 'She had long hair. All the way down to her waist, I think.'

'Like yours,' I said. Tania self-consciously flipped her long plait back over her shoulder.

Her voice was soft in the dark. 'I keep it long because I like combing it. That's all that I can remember of my mother. Her combing my hair and singing to me.'

'I like long hair,' I said, and discovered it to be true as I said the words.

She ignored my words. Instead, she looked at the braid and shuddered. 'Put it away, please.'

I put the plait away in a drawer and lit a lamp. Tania stood shyly at the doorway of my room, refusing to come in. Awkwardness lay between us. 'Let's go hear the wind chimes,' she said. We were both glad for something to do.

The stillness of the day had given way to a rising wind in the evening. We could hear the chimes calling frantically.

We walked to the wind chime room with me leading the way and the lamp making the shadows swell and shrink around us. When we stepped into the hall, a breeze made puppets of the chimes and they danced and jerked upon their strings.

Tania grew uneasy. 'It's eerie,' she said. 'Why are there only chimes in this hall? Why is it empty otherwise?'

'There is a piano,' I pointed out. It stood marooned in the middle of the hall, an occasional waft of breeze reaching out and teasing dribbles of dust from it.

Tania regarded it solemnly. 'Can you play?' she asked. My education had included lessons in both piano and violin, but I had proved to have no talent for either. Nor did I have the patience to practise when I could be reading a book.

'Yes,' I said, 'but the piano is entirely out of tune.'

Tania looked around and shuddered. 'I don't like it,' she said, taking a few steps towards the door. Hastening to stop her from leaving, I said—'Wait! I'll play something.'

I raised the lid, and, laying my hands on the keys, I picked out *Happy Birthday*, the only tune I remembered how to play.

Tania laughed aloud at the choice of song. However, the notes were off-key and two lines of the chorus proved impossible to play since the keys made no sound at all.

'They're stuck,' I said, banging away and getting nothing. I went around to the back of the piano and raised the lid that gave access to the strings. Sheets of dust slid from the lid and cascaded onto the floor. A thought struck me. 'It could be a rat's nest.'

Tania hastily retreated before the onslaught of dust and the threat of rats. I apprehensively raised the lamp and peered into the interior of the piano. I was not sure exactly how one deals with rats.

Something was stuck in the strings. But it was not a rat's nest. I put my hand in and found I was holding a crumbling diary. I prised the cover open with care. The first page was addressed in careful copperplate. '*Sara. My Diary,*' it said.

'Oh,' said Tania, peering over my shoulder. 'Sara's diary! What is it doing in the piano?'

Another mystery. A gun. A goodbye note. And now a diary. This house is so full of mysteries that I feel I will have no choice but to write a novel of that sort.

Sara's diary was battered and curling soggily at the edges. The damp had made the ink run in some places. In parts the writing had faded, and in others it was indecipherable. But I had never regarded any other book with as much expectation.

I was all for starting at the last page and solving the mystery immediately, but Tania would have none of it.

'We start at the beginning,' she said firmly. 'There's no point starting a story at the end. You should know that. You're a writer.'

Stung, I withdrew my suggestion and we started at the beginning. Which, as it turned out, was the first day that Sara left the convent.

Today is the first day of my new life. Sister Inga gave me this book to write my prayers and good intentions in, but I am going to use it for a diary. There is so much to tell and I have no one to tell it to so I shall write it down.

Nina is my best friend. But I used to hate her.

Nobody sat next to me in school because the nuns said I was bad. I didn't care. If they were stupid enough to think I was all bad, I didn't want them for a friend in any case. But one day Nina came and sat beside me. I hated her. Miss Ancy-Fancy Casimir. The nuns never shouted at her. No teacher ever had anything but soft words to say to her. And she never got punished no matter what she did because she was a Casimir. I told her to go away. Nina said she was going to sit where she liked. So, I got up and shifted to another bench. Nina came and sat next to me again. Sister Ursula came in and said maybe Nina would be better off sitting elsewhere. Nina said she was fine, thank you. Sister didn't say a word, though I could tell she was furious. I think Nina likes tormenting Sister Ursula.

She began sitting next to me every day and Sister Ursula's face got sourer and sourer. I waited for Nina to get bored and go away but she just wouldn't. We just sat there, side by side, ignoring each other and not saying a word. I think I would have hated her forever, except for Lorso.

All the boys had Lorso cornered one day during lunchtime. It was Zuze who led them. He is the butcher's boy and a fat pig. He told everyone that he was going to teach Lorso to sing. They all surrounded him, shouting at him to sing.

Lorso tried but all he could do was grunt. Those boys were laughing and hitting him in time to the grunts by the time I got there.

They wouldn't let me through the circle, no matter how much I shoved and pushed. Finally, I got on my hands and knees and managed to crawl in. But it only made them jeer louder.

Zuze was shouting for Lorso to sing the Lord's Prayer. Lorso was crying, with snot all over his face, so I took his hand and began to sing the Lord's Prayer for him. Those bastard boys began to pull us apart, but I wouldn't let Lorso's hand go and I wouldn't stop singing.

Then Nina arrived and she fixed them. She smacked and pinched and kicked her way through the circle. She looked at me and Lorso standing there, hand in hand. Then she turned to Zuze and butted him in the stomach with her head. He sat down in the dust and began to cry. Sister Ursula arrived and wanted to know what happened. Nina smiled sweetly at her and said that she knew nothing. It must have been the boys playing rough.

Zuze, bastard butcher boy, pointed at me and said I did it. He didn't dare say that Nina had. He said Sara hit me! Sara is a bad girl!

Sister Ursula gave me eight stripes on each hand. I've had more without crying. I went back to class and sat down next to Nina. I didn't look at her, but I put a bit of tamarind on the desk. When I looked again, the tamarind had gone and there was a sharpener on the desk. A pink one. A sharpener all to myself and all fancy!

The next morning, she came and sat beside me again. I didn't look at her, but I put my hand on the desk. I had something special in it. Nina put her hand on mine to take it and her eyes became big when it tickled. It was a baby squirrel I had found in the ruins. Nina gave me a huge smile. I smiled back. And then we were friends. But we weren't best friends forever yet. That happened the next day.

Zuze, the bastard butcher boy, hadn't forgotten what had happened the day before. Neither had I. At break time I ran to the graveyard, thinking he would not think of looking for me there.

But he and his gang came searching through the gravestones, shouting my name. I had nowhere to run so I stood up. Zuze laughed and said he only wanted to give me a present. He held up his hand and he was holding a knife. Must have stolen it from his father's shop. It was big and looked sharp, and I looked around to see where I could run. There was nowhere to go. All the boys had surrounded me.

Zuze came grinning up to me. He said I loved Lorso so much that they were going to make me match. He was going to cut out my tongue. He waved the knife and two boys tried to grab me. I fought them. I kicked and bit and struggled and fell, and they sat on me to hold me down. My face was in the mud so I didn't see Nina arrive, but I heard her.

She called Zuze a stupid butcher boy and an idiot and told him to put the knife down. When he told her to shut up, she said she would have his father thrown out of the village. His father was a pig like him.

I think maybe Zuze had only been trying to scare me, but Nina made him really angry. He said he was going to make her take those words about his father back or he was going to cut her tongue out too.

I managed to move my head and see through the tangle of arms and legs that were holding me down. He began to swing the knife around and it made a singing sound. Nina swung her hand and hit him hard under his ear. Zuze staggered back, then sprang forward at her again. There was a shout from Zuze and a sudden silence. All the hands holding me down loosened and I could see properly. There was a worm lying in the middle of the road. Zuze was staring down at his hand. It had one finger less. In the silence you could hear the patter of blood falling.

Nina shoved the boys aside and hauled me to my feet. She told me to run and we both ran. Behind us we heard Zuze give a gargling howl.

We ran all the way to the ruins where we sat down, trembling. Nina said she didn't mean to do anything. It just happened. We stared at each other. Then Nina began to giggle. I began to laugh too. It was awful. We were laughing out of fear and horror. And because we had no idea what else to do.

We stayed in the ruins until we could hear the bell for the final lesson of the day. Then we went back. There was nowhere else to go. Nina said not to worry. She would tell them it was all her doing. Nothing would happen. But she held my hand tight as she said it.

Sister Ursula was waiting for us, standing in the corridor. Nina told Sister Ursula that it was she who had cut off Zuze's finger. She said it again and again. She insisted it was her. But Sister Ursula refused to believe it. No matter how many times Nina swore it was her, Sister Ursula smiled and said it was very noble of her to try to take the blame. But she knew who it was. She knew it was me.

I will never again tell the truth. Nobody believes you. Because you are poor, your truth is not the same as the truth of those who are rich. They never hear the words. They only see you and that is enough for them. You are bad. You are not to be believed. You are to be punished.

I took the punishment. I was locked in a room for a week with a prayer book. Every day I got twenty stripes. Sister Ursula hit me again and again and she said that I didn't have any tears in me, because the devil was in me. That I was a bad, unnatural child who wouldn't cry. I didn't cry a single tear.

When they finally let me out, I had to go to class. Nina was waiting at the door. She ran down the corridor and took my hand. I winced and she turned my hand over and saw the state it was in. She put it to her lips and kissed it. Then she held it and we walked into class together.

She kissed my hand. Other than Alice, no one has kissed me since my mother died.

There was a sniffle at my left shoulder where Tania was peering into the book. She quickly turned her face away from the light so I couldn't see.

'Are you crying?' I asked.

'No,' she said in a voice that was marred by a wobble.

'Are you crying because you're happy or because you're sad?'

'Both. I'm happy because Sara found a friend. A true friend. But I'm sad because what she wrote is true. No one believes you if you aren't the right kind of person in their eyes. If you don't fit into their idea of a person who tells the truth.'

'That's unfair,' I said. 'But it doesn't mean you don't tell the truth just because no one will believe you.'

'If they don't, what are you to do?'

I considered that. 'Maybe you show them the truth. So they can see it for themselves and believe it.'

'Would you believe me?' asked Tania in a soft voice.

'Of course,' I said. She looked at me for a long moment. Then she returned to the diary.

Zuze is gone. His father has taken him out of school. Nina did that. I don't know how. Now everyone is afraid of us. No one will come near us. So we are left to be our own friends. And we are. Best friends who would do anything for each other. Best friends forever.

Carefully pasted on the next page was a scrap of paper. The writing was Sara's best copperplate.

> *Nina Casimir and Sara*
> *Swear that they will be friends*
> *Until death do them part*
> *So help us God*

Two signatures scrawled across the bottom. The ink was wine-dark. They had written the oath in blood.

'Best friends forever. What does that mean?'

'It means that you look after each other and help each other and keep every promise to each other that you ever made,' said Tania immediately.

'Do you have a best friend?' I asked Tania. There was a long silence. 'I don't either,' I offered. She peeped at me, shyly. I cleared my throat. 'We could be each other's, if you like.'

'Do we have to write it out in blood?' asked Tania. 'I don't like blood. It makes me feel funny.'

'I don't like blood either,' I said. 'We could just promise.'

She raised her hand and said solemnly, 'I promise to be your friend forever.'

'I promise to be your friend forever. And I promise to always believe you,' I added. I hesitated before saying the next words, they were so very solemn. 'Till death do us part.'

'So help us God,' she whispered quietly.

We looked at each other, both of us a bit shy now that the words had been said.

Then she said, 'Thank you,' and I said, 'You're welcome,' and we went back to reading from the diary.

I am going to live in Nina's house! The last year of school is over and I had nowhere to go. Sister Ursula said in front of the whole class that I was best suited to be a servant. She meant it as an insult, but Nina smiled and said then I could be a servant in her house. Nothing the nuns said would make her change her mind.

The nuns say it is a great opportunity and I am not worthy of it. I mean to work very hard and save all my money so that Alice and I can be together as soon as possible. She has to stay at the orphanage until I have a place to take her. But I am going to Nina's house!

Sara's writing was beautiful, but damp and age had made the ink fade until I had to almost put my nose to the page to decipher what was written on it. I sat back to give my eyes a rest.

'I am afraid,' Tania said in the silence. 'I am afraid to read the rest.'

'Why?'

'Because she sounds so happy. And now she's gone and no one knows or cares and all we have is her hair.'

'Maybe she still is happy. Somewhere.' But it sounded like hollow reassurance, even to me. I opted for a more prosaic approach. 'Let's keep reading. How else will we know what happened?' I asked, turning over a limp and stained page.

It is the first time I've stepped into the Casimir house, and it makes me feel like the nuns were a little bit right. It is too good for me, larger than the church. And more solemn. I feel I should genuflect.

Tania whispered, 'I felt like that a little bit too when I saw the house for the first time.' It made me recall that she was a servant girl. I had quite forgotten.

Nina has shown me things that have come from all over the world. There is china that is actually from China, and silver from Venice, and marble from Italy. The mirror frames are covered in gold, real gold, and have come from Paris.

I never knew there were so many forks and knives in the world! I thought one was all you needed. But there are knives for fish, and knives for meat, and knives for butter, and forks for a dozen different things. And there are dishes enough to use all the cutlery on. I have to help carry dishes into the dining room and at the first meal I gaped. They had chicken and pork and fish all on the table at the same time. And it wasn't even a feast day. All we orphans ever got was chicken on a feast day three times in the year.

We servants get the leftovers, so I now have fish and meat both at one meal and try not to feel guilty. The cake I hide away for Alice.

I had never wanted much before this because I never knew there was so much to want. Covetousness is one of the Seven Deadly Sins. But my greed is not for myself, it is all for Alice. I want everything for her. We meet most afternoons in the ruins and her eyes grow big when I tell her about the house. She keeps telling me not to get lost in the house, to always come back to her. I promised that I would always come to her in the ruins.

'Alice is still waiting,' said Tania.

'Maybe Sara forgot the promise,' I said and was roundly scolded for my remark.

'Don't say that!' said Tania. 'Don't you dare say that. How can anyone forget a promise? Or their own sister?'

Chastened, I resumed reading.

The cook dislikes me.

She put me to work washing the special dishes. It is a job that is never given to new girls. To break one would cost me two years' salary. They all have the Casimir 'C' on them and are seventy years old. I thought of Alice and was very careful, and now the dishes are clean and the cook's face is a sight to behold. She was hoping I would break one.

Nina's cousin Damon looks fierce all the time and frightens me. He notices none of the servants and does not know I exist for which I am glad.

There was a blank page that turned to reveal a neat list.

Lilac ribbons
A yellow petticoat
Blue satin shoes (Where am I to wear them? But they are beautiful!)
A necklace of silver beads
Eight red glass bangles

Nina has given me all these things. If I were to wear them all at once the nuns would start novenas to save my soul. I am keeping everything but the satin shoes for Alice. Satin shoes! They feel like milk on my feet.

I've known all along that Nina is rich, but now I begin to understand what that means.

She has so many clothes I could not count them. She has seventeen petticoats alone. Her shoes are specially ordered from Bombay. Her hair smells of roses because of some special soap sent from Portugal. One afternoon all the servants were set to work sewing rose petals into muslin bags to put in her cupboard. We sang hymns as we worked, although the cook made me stop, saying a voice like mine was pure showing-off.

Sara's cousin has noticed me. I didn't wish him to.

I had been set to cleaning in the library. There are so many books! And none of which anyone has read because most of them have their pages uncut. My arms are still aching from pulling hundreds of books from shelves and dusting. And then putting them all back exactly.

I was in one of the aisles when someone came into the room. It was Nina's cousin. He looked as fierce as usual and I didn't want to be seen so I stood behind the shelves. But then he settled down at a desk and began to work and I didn't know how long he'd be. When I tried to leave I bumped into a table and a lamp on it fell down and was shattered.

He called out asking who was there. In my hurry to gather up the glass, I cut my hand badly and when he came around the corner I put my hands behind my back. He asked who I was, looking at me like he had never noticed me before. I told him I was the new servant. He noticed my hand behind my back. He told me to hold out my hand.

When I hesitated, he was very angry, saying I was new in the house and already stealing. He twisted my arm out and forced open my fist. He got blood all over his hand for his efforts.

He looked at my face and asked what my name was. He then put his handkerchief in my hand and ordered me to go down to the kitchen and put something on it. I think he was sorry for what he had thought of me.

When I turned the page it fell into pieces, dismaying me. The next entry was written haphazardly, with obvious agitation.

There has been so much trouble! Nina is starving herself. Dona Alcina is furious. And I am the cause of it. Me and the cook.

Then came two pages that had entirely faded away. Only a few scattered words were legible which I struggled to read. 'Marzipan … starving … nothing will soothe the agony … a beggar and a thief.' The last had been underlined fiercely.

Tania was not content with these broken bits. 'I want to know what happened! What do you think happened? Why is Nina starving?'

But all we got was the ending, not the story.

The cook is gone. At the evening prayers in the chapel I lifted my voice and sang so joyfully that Dona Alcina turned and glared at me. I didn't care. The cook is gone! Praise the Lord, Alleluia. Amen.

'Oh,' said Tania.

We both sat there for a moment, minds busy with speculation. A little wandering wind came in and fluttered the flame in the lamp. The electricity has not been turned on yet.

'What time is it?' cried Tania. 'I have forgotten the time and stayed too long. I will be in trouble!' She started to her feet.

'Don't go!' I said. 'The story has just begun.'

'I have to. But you are not to read any of it while I am gone.' She stared earnestly down at me. 'Promise you won't read it without me.'

I protested. I tried to get her to stay. I promised her that I would not tell her what I had read, but she was determined. So, I promised, and now the book lies upon the table. It is a treasure house filled with riches. It is a box spilling over with promises. It is a torment like only an unfinished story can be.

Forbidden to read and my head filled with speculation, I found that I could not assuage my hunger for what came next. I sat down to write it myself and found myself inventing a cook.

The Incident of the Cook

The cook is enormously fat. The secret joy of her heart is marzipan. There are tins of it hidden behind the spices in the cupboard—fragrant with vanilla, sharp with cinnamon, redolent of lemon. She has perfected a recipe that turns almond and egg-white into pink and white bites of perfection. All through the day the cook takes secret bites of marzipan and dreams pink-and-white dreams at night.

The cook has a niece she has hoped to get employed in the Casimir household, and so is against the orphan from the start. She has heard from her niece already what they call her in the convent—'Bad' and 'Liar'. She is determined that the tainted one will soon be shunted out of the house if she has anything to do with it.

The assistant cook is her cousin. While the cook is fat, she is very thin. But a marked family resemblance makes her a reduced echo of the cook herself. She has accepted her role and developed a trick of agreeing with the cook by parroting all that she says.

'That orphan will bring ruin to this house.'

'Ruin,' says the able assistant, 'ruin.'

The cook fulminates, 'She is an unholy disgrace.'

'Unholy,' sighs her cousin over the onions. 'Disgrace.'

Sara, sewing at the dining table, is told to be quiet when she raises her voice to sing. The dishes she has washed are handed back to her again and again until her hands are red and wrinkled with scrubbing. Late at night, after everyone has retired to bed, Sara cleans the kitchen, sweeping out the corners, and getting down on hands and knees to gather every crumb in case it catches the cook's insatiable eye. To Nina she does not say a word, determined to make her own way in this hostile world.

Matters come to a head when a pig is killed. The cook gathers her forces to tackle the mountain of meat that is delivered to the kitchen table. The gardener is set to cutting the difficult joints. Several maids mince meat. The housekeeper cures large slabs in salt. But for Sara is reserved the grinding of the masala for the chorizo sausages.

The mortar is a hollowed circular stone and the pestle is a large monolith. The cook pours in the three kinds of chillies, vinegar, spices, measuring them with care. The combination bites so hard that it can leave your hands stinging for days.

The cook well knows what she has set Sara about. The pestle grazes her hands. The vinegar and salt sizzle in the tiny cuts, and the masala is hellfire and damnation. Sara grits her teeth and grinds for hours. She holds her battered swollen hands under the garden tap the whole evening, but nothing will soothe the agony. All night long she is crouched in the bathroom, her hands in a basin of water.

Still, she does not say a word. But the next day, Nina takes her hand in easy friendship and Sara winces. Nina turns her hands over and stares, dismayed. Sara begs her not to say anything. She is a servant now and this is part of her work. For a whole day Nina is silent, but with a look in her eye that Sara knows only too well.

That evening the cook follows a line of ants and discovers Sara's cache of cake. She is loud in her denunciation of Thieving Orphans. The assistant cook assists her as a solo Greek chorus. 'Untrustworthy ... upstart ... beggar and thief ...'

In the middle of all the righteous indignation, Nina walks into the kitchen and smacks the cook hard across the ear.

The matter is taken before Dona Alcina. Nina's defence is Christian virtue. 'You taught me we should never speak ill of our friends and fellowmen. And the cake is Sara's share, to do with as she pleases.'

Dona Alcina regards Sara and says, 'No blame attaches to Sara. People who are deprived all their lives and have never had a decent meal cannot help thieving. As Christians we should be forgiving, and understand.'

Sara writes later in her diary: 'She called me a thief and a beggar in the same breath as she claimed to be Christian! I did not say a word. But I forgot my burning hands because my heart burned so much.'

The cook is made to apologise to Sara for her words, which she does through gritted teeth. Dona Alcina tells Nina to apologise to the cook for the slap. A mutinous

Nina tells Dona that if she makes her apologise, then she will not eat a morsel cooked by the woman. Dona Alcina insists. Now Nina sits through every meal stone-faced, refusing to eat. Dona Alcina pretends not to notice, but she is worried.

The cook is determined she has the answer—'Fish Caldine! Chickens stuffed with fresh pepper and lime! Sausages with coriander and butter!'

'Butter!' cries her assistant. 'Butter!' Surely butter will do the trick. Surely the cook's skill with food is more than enough to break the will of one stubborn teenager.

Lamb is sautéed in butter and dressed with lemon. Chicken Cafreal cooks in large pots. The cook even sacrifices one of the prized litter to roast succulent suckling pig. In desperation she brings out the marzipan and dresses it in sugar-frosted flowers. All day long siren smells drift out of the kitchen. It is all that the rest of the household can do to wait for mealtimes. But on Nina there is no effect.

Damon has pleaded with Nina to eat. With her still refusing, he declares that he too will not eat until she does. He is as stubborn as she is, and sets his will against hers. Little does Nina care.

Meals are dismal affairs now, with only Dona Alcina putting up a brave front and pretending to make a proper meal. Damon sits courteously through the meal in silence. Only Nina enjoys the affair, humming gaily to herself and interestedly inspecting each dish before pushing it away. Sometimes she will even pick up a spoon and let it hover over a dish as if deeply tempted, then put it down with a sigh. It is all play-acting and it makes Dona Alcina almost as furious as she is worried. She knows Nina's stubbornness from when she was a child.

The cook is in floods of tears in the kitchen and takes to wailing loudly and beating her breast as each rejected dish is returned. She spends her time abusing Sara in an undertone, now that she dares not do it loudly. Her plaints reach Sara in a series of fading repetitions—'Hussy ... devil's curse ... chendi!'

The cook's tins are empty of marzipan and her life empty of consolation.

Sara is now really a thief, taking what is no longer her portion. She makes sure to take plenty from the dishes that Nina hesitated most over. Both of them make their meals secretly in the attic. Nina has chosen a spot where they can look through the floorboards at Dona Alcina at her rosary below, praying for Nina to eat a morsel. It makes Nina giggle to see her fumble her way through novena after novena.

So, the only one who really starves in the house is Damon.

It takes four days before Dona Alcina gives in and sends the cook away. The woman departs in a cart piled high with belongings and surrounded by empty tins. She bewails Ingratitude, Treachery and Deceitful Orphans as she goes lamenting down the lane. This time there is no echo. The cousin has been promoted to head cook, choosing Advancement over Family Love.

Nina tastes every one of the fourteen dishes the new cook prepares and declares them excellent. Damon waits until she has served herself before reaching for the food. Nina takes his plate away and declares that he must starve one more meal before she will let him eat. He says, 'As you wish.' In the very next moment she is running around the table laughing, piling his plate high with every delicacy.

He accepts Plenty from her hands as he had accepted Famine.

I regarded the number of pages I had written with surprise, the writer in me satisfied, the novelist disturbed. Why can I not write my novel with the same ease?

Ave Maria

With the first light, I sat down at my desk. I worked to the sound of a koel singing as if seven summers had arrived all together. A veritable forest full of birds joined it as the light grew stronger. I wonder how people living in villages ever get any sleep.

I typed up all the pages we had read from the diary. When I had finished, such a temptation came upon me to turn the page and keep on reading! I had to turn my back on the diary and take a walk or two around the house to rid myself of the longing.

The story intrigued me. Only one thing held me back from throwing myself into writing the story into my novel. I did not think anyone would care to read the story of a servant girl. People have certain literary expectations, and I must meet them.

The diary lay on the desk and whispered temptation to me. Refusing to give in, I went and prepared for Tania's evening visit. I laid out candles in a circle on the floor of the hall and all the time the chimes clicked and whispered around me.

I waited a long time there in the hall. I watched the slanting sun turn the windows into great mosaics of living colour. The shadows of the wind chimes stretched gnarled and knotted fingers upon the floor. Then the light seeped away and the chimes became strange skeletons of disjointed bones silhouetted in the windows.

She finally came. 'I wasn't able to come earlier. I just wasn't. Say you haven't read it without me!'

I was able to virtuously say that I hadn't.

'Why haven't you lit the candles? Why are you sitting in the dark?'

'I was thinking. Sit with me a while.'

Tania curled up on the floor. In the dark the chimes spoke softly to themselves. There was only enough of a breeze to coax from them a series of clicks and murmurs and whispers that sounded like conversation.

'Do you believe in ghosts?'

Tania said severely, 'If you're going to scare me, I'm leaving.'

'No. I really want to know. Do you believe in ghosts? Does something stay behind when people die? Why would people linger on after they died?'

'Perhaps,' said Tania, thinking carefully, 'they left something undone. Or they haven't got something they longed for. So, they can't leave without it.'

A soft shiver of notes came from the chimes. 'Sara made these wind chimes.'

'She did? Why?'

'So she could hear the whispers in the wind. She thought when people die their voices remain in the wind.'

Tania listened to the muted chatter of the chimes. 'What do they say?'

'Remember … remember … remember …' In the silence the chimes mimicked my three words in soft, branching voices.

Tania said, 'Stop! You're making it all eerie and terrifying. My hair is standing on end.'

Another sibilant ripple travelled from one end of the hall to another. It was so dark now that we could see each other only in outline. I leaned over to whisper in Tania's ear. 'There is something left behind in this house. I feel its presence late at night. I keep looking over my shoulder to see if something is there.'

Tania looked hastily over her own shoulder.

'It goes around the house, whispering. It is waiting for something. I don't know what. But it is sad and lonely and yearning.'

Tania whispered, 'What is it waiting for?'

'I don't know,' I said. 'I only know something is in this house. Something that cannot rest.'

'What is it?' breathed Tania.

I lowered my voice even further, 'The wind.'

Tania was indignant. 'You're just laughing at me!' I denied it roundly, but my voice gave me away.

Tania pointed out, 'But you're the one who thought I was a ghost and got scared when we first met.'

I denied it hotly. 'I laughed! *You* were scared.'

'Certainly not. *You* were.'

I reached for the matches. We squabbled in a comradely manner until the candles were lit. Then I opened the diary with great anticipation and resumed the story of Sara in her own words. The page was closely covered with writing. Sara had used a pen that blotted and I picked the words out from between great spots of ink.

I have been thinking about Sin. Covetousness can only be number six or seven on the list. Surely number one on the list.

is Pride. And Dona Alcina has a lot of it. You should have seen the pride she took in being the first in the village to acquire a gramophone. All the servants were called to the great hall so that we could see with our own eyes how the instrument worked. Nina wound it up and played a record. It was something of Handel's. Dona Alcina had told us she would not have frivolous music in the house. Everyone gave a chorus of acclamation except me. She must have noticed my expression because she asked me what the matter was. I told her that I had already seen a gramophone. Miss Miranda has one which she plays when I go to visit her. She even lets me wind it for her.

Dona Alcina said she did not know what Miss Miranda could want with one, being deaf now. I told her Miss Miranda could hear with her fingers and Dona told me not to be impertinent. But it is true.

There is only one gift I have. I do not know why God gave it to me. Sister Ursula thinks that he made a mistake. The very first time I sang in the music room she made me stop and forbade me to sing a single note again. But Mother Superior's office was just beside the music room and she came to find out who it was who was singing. She said I was to continue. That there must be a reason God gave me this gift, she said, and it was our duty to let me use it to praise him.

So I sang in church. And Miss Miranda heard me. And my life changed forever.

Sara's voice is birds in the sky. It is moonlight. It is a river talking to God. Lorso's description comes back to me the next morning when I sit down to write. I find the voice singing in my ears and the words come bubbling from me.

The Voice of an Angel

Sara is a devil six days of the week. And on the seventh she is transmuted to an angel. She stands straight, hands by her sides, hair neatly combed, and opens her mouth to sing. The orphans are making their first holy communion and, for the first time, Sara has been allowed to sing in church. Mother Superior herself made the request and so Sister Ursula could not deny it.

Sara sings the *Ave Maria*. She is thinking of her mother as the words wing out of her mouth and rise to the gilded beams. It is for her she sings and so her voice is filled with tenderness.

Ave Maria Gratia plena
Maria Gratia plena
Maria Gratia plena
Ave, ave dominus
Dominus tecum

Benedicta tu in mulieribus
Et benedictus
Et benedictus fructus ventris
Ventris tui Jesus

O Maiden hear a maiden's pleading
O Mother, hear a suppliant child

Such is the longing in the voice, that all the orphans sitting in the last two rows will weep into their pillows that night. But the voice has touched others in the church as well. Cecil dozing in the front row, Jose who is so steeped in feni that he is in an eternal pickle, Mrs Mascarenhas working out the Sunday menu in her head, Pia Menezes dreaming of a sunny afternoon and a hidden hollow in the rice fields, all of them are suddenly aware of a yearning that sweeps through them and moves them to inexplicable tears.

At the very first note, Miss Miranda takes a deep breath. It takes all her self-control and awe of the sacredness of the mass not to crane her neck to see who is singing.

The next day Sara is called to Mother Superior's office. A tall, thin lady dressed in black is waiting for her. Miss Miranda has come to hear the voice for herself.

'Sing!' she demands of Sara. She leans closer and closer as Sara sings.

'Wonderful!' she cries. 'She will have lessons with me. Straight after church every Sunday.'

Sister Ursula is furious, but dare not protest too much. Miss Miranda has been very generous to the orphanage indeed. And so, Sunday becomes a day of miracles for Sara. She sings her heart out in church, sending her voice soaring up to the rafters. Straight after the service she takes Miss Miranda's hand and they walk the long path up to her house.

Miss Miranda seats herself at the piano. 'Let us begin!' she says.

Miss Miranda teaches Sara how to use her voice. Sara learns how to make it trip up and down scales, how to send it out from deep within her, how to breathe so that her voice can rise up into impossible notes and sink to unbelievable ones. And with every note Sara sends up a fervent prayer, thanking God for Miss Miranda.

Together they leave hymns behind and start exploring varied musical landscapes. They traverse the vast ranges of music that rise to hold the Latin Mass aloft. They cross the great rolling plains and passions of opera. For rest, they use the little-known compositions written by devout musicians to praise the Lord, meant to be sung in the voices of young boys. Sara sings them all, her voice ranging through centuries and traditions, going from the sacred to the profane. What are all the great songs at the end but love songs? They sing of love for God, love for a lover, love for a mother, love for life. Love is the great sea to which all the winding songs flow.

As the years pass, Sara has to stand closer and closer to the piano. She sings louder and louder for Miss Miranda to hear. One day Miss Miranda lifts one hand from the piano and places it on Sara's cheek. It is a frail hand with a tremble in it. Miss Miranda has grown old without the child noticing it. A terrible fear clutches Sara's heart. What will she do if she loses this, her only happiness?

The candles ring us with mystery. Only the sound of the wind chimes come slipping into the golden circle. Inside we are spellbound, held by the light and the words and the story I read, one difficult page at a time.

Dona Alcina gives the servants a half-day on Sunday. I run all the way to Miss Miranda's house. We sit in the music room and she winds her gramophone and plays it. And she enjoys every note. Then we go to the piano. Miss Miranda has had it placed all by itself in the hall. She says it sounds best in this room. And she likes to play to the wind and the night.

'This room!' says Tania in delight. 'The room right here. This piano. Sara sang here!'

'That is why the wind chimes hang in this hall!' I say with equal wonder. They are gifts of love that Sara has carried to her teacher. She has listened for sounds wherever she went. Chosen the little voices with care. Knotted them together so that each will sing its own song for a woman who can no longer hear.

Miss Miranda places her fingers along my cheek and makes me sing and knows perfectly well when I have changed the tune, which I do sometimes, just to check if she can really hear.

This Sunday she was very excited. Her grand-nephew from Portugal has sent her some recordings of him playing the violin. She played them to me. She said he had fine training but is a trifle shallow. His playing sounds fine to me but very sad and lonely.

'The same that we heard!' says Tania. The story has come to live in the house with us and both Tania and I are gripped.

I thought I was all bad and there was nothing good in me until Miss Miranda came.

She tells me to sing because even the angels in their flight will pause to listen. I sing because it makes me happy and makes me remember. It is the only thing I remember of my mother. Her singing to me. All the rest has somehow gone away.

Miss Miranda died today. I sang her to heaven.

The Music of the Spheres

Sara sees Miss Miranda for the last time on a day that is not Sunday. She is woken up early in the morning and told to hurry. Miss Miranda is calling for her. She hurries up the hill, barely able to see for her tears.

The priest is with Miss Miranda, but she turns her head and smiles when Sara comes through the door.

'Don't go!' begs Sara. 'Please don't go.'

'Don't worry, child,' says Miss Miranda. 'I have taken care of you.'

But Sara's tears will not stop. Miss Miranda struggles for breath to console her. 'Do you know what waits for me in heaven? Music! I know the Lord loves music. Or he would not have given me my gift for playing the piano and you your voice. Such music we shall hear together one day! Great choirs of angels! I have always wondered what the music of the spheres was like. Now I shall know.'

She places a cold and shaking hand on Sara's cheek. 'Sing, my dear child,' she whispers. 'I need your voice to waft me to heaven.'

It takes every lesson that Miss Miranda has taught Sara across the years for her to control her shaking voice and sing. She sings the song that first brought them together. *Ave Maria* rises like a staircase of crystal and leads Miss Miranda to her very own heaven.

Sister Ursula sent for me to come to the school. She told me that Miss Miranda left me her piano. Miss Miranda also left me a key to the house so that I could go there and play and sing whenever I wanted. Sister Ursula held out the key and I took it. I held it so tight. I have never owned anything at all in my life.

She held up a letter and told me Miss Miranda had written it to the bishop. It was a request to send me to Portugal so that I could train my voice at the conservatory for music there. She had left money for the education. Sister Ursula said that the bishop had better things to do than concern himself with unworthy orphan girls, and that the money was better spent on more worthy things. She tore the letter into pieces as I watched.

She said that there were things in the house too valuable for unreliable girls like me to have a key to. Then she took the key from me. She had to hit me across the hand with her ruler to make me let go.

I dared not look at Tania. I knew she would have tears in her eyes. I hastily turned the page, and read the next entry.

I have been to the house, sat at the piano and sung. I didn't need a key. I climbed in from the well window. The piano is mine. Miss Miranda gave it to me and it is mine and I shall play it.

I sang for Miss Miranda. All the songs that were her favourites. I sang exactly as she taught me to and I thought of her and I was both happy and very sad.

I shall come and go as I please. So there, Sister Ursula!

'Oh!' says Tania, her eyes going bright with delight. 'She came in the same way I do!'

'But she never came for sweet water,' I said.

'Neither did I,' said Tania softly. 'The water is only an excuse. I come just to get away from that house. From all that I am in that house.'

'What are you in that house?'

'A servant,' said Tania simply. 'Nothing more.'

The next few pages reveal that Sara too is a servant, nothing more. Tania reads them in a soft voice.

Sister Ursula has taken my only chance from me. Now there is nothing I can be but a servant. I begin to understand what that is. To pick up their dirty dishes. To scrape away what they have left on them with your hands. To wash the dishes and set them out to dry and know that these are dishes that you will never ever eat off because you are a servant.

Tania's voice faltered and stopped.

I must confess I have never thought how servants must feel. I thought they were paid and therefore happy to do the work they were assigned. It has never occurred to me that they must feel the difference so very much.

Tania resolutely read on.

Everyone thinks they can do anything at all to you. As if by being an orphan and poor you were less of a person. As if being no one's property you could be anyone's property at all, and anyone could lay hands upon you.

I run past the taverna. They shout such things after me — things they would never shout after the sisters and wives and daughters of rich people. If any of the men see me alone on the road I have to dodge their eyes, their dirty words, their hands. Always their hands. Groping, reaching out, grabbing at you. I hate their hands.

Tania broke off reading. All unthinking, I reached out a hand of sympathy. Immediately, Tania shrank away from it.

I understood why she was always a hand's breadth away from me. I was appalled. Surely she does not equate me with the boors from the taverna!

'I'm sorry,' I said stiffly, much offended. 'I mean—my intent was just to comfort you.' Tania stared at a candle, not turning to look at me. A glint on her chin showed a tear, trembling before it fell. As it slipped free, my indignation fell from me.

'I am so sorry,' I said, 'that you have had to suffer such insults.'

A second tear dripped off her chin. 'Stop!' I said. 'Please don't cry.'

The smallest sniffle sounded as she turned her face away. Impulsively, I said, 'I am not like those men. I'm your friend. I promise you that I won't touch you. I won't lay a hand on you ever, unless you want me to.'

I cursed myself for that last sentence with all its sudden suggestion. 'I meant, I will simply never touch you if that makes you more comfortable. Ever.'

Just when I had a sinking feeling that I had said all the wrong things, she dragged her hands across her eyes and gave me the smallest smile. I put one hand on my heart and the other over a candle. 'Promise.'

My new resolution immediately proved to be a torment. No sooner had I sworn never to touch her, than my hands became great awkward implements swinging out of my control, bent on a collision. I reached for the next page at the same moment that she did and nearly broke my newly pledged vow on the spot.

Tania said, 'You read.'

Damon met me on the stairs and stepped in front of me so that I could not hurry past. He wears a gold ring and a gold watch and has been to Portugal twice on business. He asked me if my hand was quite all right. I nodded, keeping my hands behind my back.

He said he will try not to startle me and I must try not to break anything. I nodded. He offered to shake on it and held out his hand. I have never had a hand held out to me to shake. I did not want him to touch me but I could think of nothing else to do. I held out my hand, trembling lest anyone saw us. He held on to my hand and turned it over. The cut had healed. He released it and smiled at me, saying he was sorry to have fooled me, but I always put my hands behind my back whenever we met. Then he went up the stairs. I do not know what to make of it.

I knew perfectly well what to make of it. I am sure Sister Ursula would have known too. I didn't dare say a thing in case it came out all wrong again. When I went to turn the page, Tania said, 'Enough. I have to go now.'

I protested. I hate a story told in instalments. 'Stay just a little longer.'

Tania turned her head to look straight at me. Her voice was soft. 'I am a girl who comes secretly at night to a house where a man lives alone. What do you think they will say in the taverna if they know?'

I did not have to guess. They said it already about Sara.

'Will you come back tomorrow?' I asked.

'I will try,' she said. She stepped outside the circle of light. Her voice spoke from the darkness. 'Thank you.'

'For what?'

'For the promise.' The whisper came from the darkness and then she was gone. It is the third promise I have made to Tania. I also promised to be her friend forever and to believe her. I am determined I will not break any of my vows.

I walked back with a candle through the rooms. I stopped in the music room where the light from my candle danced in all the photographs that stood in silent rows on the wall. I stood in front of the collection that held Miss Miranda's story.

The first photograph showed her as a child standing on the piano stool in a dress of silk, her mother smiling as she held her. The last photo showed her as an old lady, holding on to the piano, head tilted as if listening intently. She was gazing with great sadness out of the photo.

I went to sleep wondering if God truly loved music.

Mother, Hear a Suppliant Child

I woke to the sound of a koel stitching great loops and whorls of song across the dawn. Words began to come to me. I rose from my bed and went to my typewriter. The day fell away and it was almost noon before the flood stopped. I sat back and regarded the neatly typed pages scattered across the table. It was the story of the serried ranks of photographs I'd seen that had spilled from me.

Ave Maria

Late at night when Miss Miranda cannot sleep, she wanders through the house. Always, her feet lead her here. She stands before the photographs and stares at them as if they show a life that somebody else has lived. She has found that memory is a treacherous thing. To try and remember is to find yourself lost in a treacherous topography that has changed shape. It is to traverse a land that you barely recognise, to visit someone who has grown to be a stranger.

Locked in her house, in her silence, she walks through the pathways of her past. She finds her way by the photographs, though they are a faulty compass, never pointing true north.

The first photo shows Celine and her mother. It transforms into black-and-white the most vivid yellow of her mother's dress, embroidered all over with butterflies. It has also somehow muted the joy that Celine felt, standing on the piano stool, arms around her mother. The photographer was quite smitten with the young mother and wanted her to pose by herself, but she insisted that she would be photographed only with her daughter.

There are several photographs of her mother at the piano. Seraphina Miranda had been a promising young classical pianist when Celine's father first saw her perform in Lisbon. It was her first concert, and his first time abroad as an attaché to the Portuguese Embassy representing the state of Goa.

Their courtship was conducted in cities across the continent. She travelled to give a series of concerts and he drummed up diplomatic concerns in each place that she went. Finally, she fell in love with the tall, good-looking Indian, and agreed to marry him. They had Celine within a year, travelling back to her husband's ancestral home for the birth. He managed an appropriate posting and for the first six years of Celine's life, it was in Goa that the family lived.

It was her life in Portugal that the homesick Seraphina recreated. There were dinners and dances and recitals. She had such a court of admirers that the house was always filled with flowers and overflowing with people and laughter and music. Above all, music.

Celine was allowed to stay up late for the parties and only required to go to bed after her mother had played. She stayed with her nurse on the edges of the party until her mother got up to walk to the piano. Then she would run ahead and slip into the space under the keyboard.

Celine would sit huddled close to her mother's feet, surrounded by the music. When her mother pressed the pedals the notes became shivering fingers that ran up and down her spine. Her mother played a repertoire that was meant for concert halls around the world, and the little girl drank in every note. From time to time her mother would lean down a hand and gently caress her hair. Celine's hair was her mother's delight. She insisted on brushing it herself, winding it around her fingers, until Celine's head was a riot of curls.

But Miss Miranda's favourite memories come from when she wept. At the first sign of tears her mother would sweep her into her lap and sing for her. Always the same thing in the original Latin, *Ave Maria*. By the age of three, Celine could play the original arrangement by Schubert, her small hands searching out the keys on the piano.

Miss Miranda struggles to remember her mother. She wants to remember the piano, the music, the love. Instead, strange new memories are drifting through her mind. One particular memory has suddenly surfaced and taken her peace of mind.

She is five. It is the day after a party. The servants are cleaning up and are busy shifting furniture and scrubbing the floors. No one goes into the hall where her mother sits at the keyboard, her hands not moving. Celine is at the door watching her mother, but she knows she must not go in. Her mother sits unmoving for a long time. Then she picks up her glass and slowly and meticulously pours her wine into the keys of the piano. She picks up the sheaf of music on the rack and flings it in the air. Then she sits there very still, hands folded in her lap, as the music falls in sheets and drifts aimlessly across the floor.

When Celine is seven, her mother vanishes from the photographs. Her mother had arranged a picnic to a waterfall. Celine was left at home because she had a heavy cold. The monsoon was just over and the waterfall was full and fast. Her mother slipped and fell into the pool beneath and was drowned before anyone could reach her.

Miss Miranda knows that her mother lay in the house for two days before being buried, but she cannot remember it at all. It is a dark hall in her memories, unlit and empty.

Her father is not so lucky. Everywhere he turns in the house, there are memories of his wife. Finally, he locks up the house, takes his daughter and begins to travel. Paris, Rome, Madrid, across Europe, as far as Brazil, three short months in China. Further and further they go from the music room where Celine once sat beneath the piano and trembled to her mother's playing.

With each shift she becomes a more and more difficult child. She has screaming fits and temper tantrums. She rolls on the floor, wild with grief and anger. Nothing can tame her until, in Paris, her father sends her for her first piano lesson.

That memory Miss Miranda has managed to keep shiny and un-fingermarked. She walks into the room and sees the piano sitting in the late afternoon sunshine. She runs to it and places her hands upon the keys. Without playing a single note such joy wells up in her that she begins laughing hysterically. Then she plays. How she plays! The days aren't long enough. She longs for the summers when the light allows her to stretch her quota of music out into lingering evenings and slow dusks. Suddenly, she is no longer a problem child.

Hers is a prodigious talent. By the age of twenty-two she has debuted with the Orchestra de Madrid. By the age of twenty-seven she has her own billing on every performance that the orchestra gives. When she plays solo, the halls are filled. At thirty she does a tour of Europe that is deemed a triumph.

Miss Miranda stands before the photographs from that time and tries to remember the full houses, the applause, the music. Brittle photographs stare back at her, images empty of remembrance.

The photographs show a thin girl with eyes that take up all of her pinched face. There is no sign of the wild girl who screamed and kicked her nurses. Only her hair is still untamed. In photo after photo, it hangs down to her waist in a great riotous mass.

Even when she played at the Royal Albert Hall and was told that etiquette demanded that she present herself formally and correctly dressed, she refused point blank to tie up her hair.

Love comes to Miss Miranda late. She is thirty-two when she concludes a concert and steps out of the theatre into the rain and finds him waiting for her with an umbrella. He has just heard her play and her music has swept him into love. They talk into the night and when they are walking back, his umbrella blows away and they walk on in the rain.

She is foolish. It takes her six years of hotel rooms in various cities to discover that he is married. He says that he cannot leave his wife. The day he tells her that, she walks to the door and out into the cold. Then she travels. Seven countries in seven days. A night in each city. Choosing an eighth city, she finds herself saying, 'Panjim. India.'

She arrives late one afternoon. When the caretaker opens up the house for her, she realises for the first time just how unreliable memory is. The house is shrunken and dusty, the walls spotted with mould. When she enters the music room and sees the piano, she knows why she has returned.

Passing neighbours hear the piano play for three days and nights. Then it stops. They break open the door and find Miss Miranda lying in the space underneath the piano, curled up like a child. She is in the hospital for two months. Her father flies down to be with her. In the tiny courtyard of the hospital he sits beside her and winces as he gently touches her head. An outbreak of lice has led the nurses to shave the heads of all the patients. Her great mane of hair is gone and it will grow back thin and grey. He takes her hand and speaks to her.

Miss Miranda wishes she could forget his words. They are a strong acid that has eaten into her childhood, that has stained all the photographs, that has spotted and smeared her memories so that she cannot any longer recognise them.

'You are old enough to know the truth. And I think I have been wrong in shielding you from it all this time. Your mother's death was no accident. She killed herself. She was never happy without the concert halls and the applause. We had fought. Again. We fought so much. She was standing right next to the waterfall. All it took was one step.'

Miss Miranda will not believe him. In her excess of anger, she strikes him again and again. He sits there with his head bowed and lets her hit him. She does not see her father again. He dies two years later in Spain and she never leaves Goa once she has returned to the house. She never gives a public concert again.

Late at night, when it is difficult to sleep, Miss Miranda walks the long corridors hung with photographs, slipping down the pathways of her family's history. Stopping at her own story, she stares at the photographs, willing them to stay still. When they slip and slide, she goes to the piano and plays for hours.

Then, in her forties, the music begins to sound distant. She sees a doctor who does strange tests with a tuning fork. When she returns from the doctor, she shuts the door and sits at the piano. She puts her hands on the ivory and begins to play. She feels the notes shiver through her and she weeps. She tries to hold the music in her body and in her hands, tries to stop it slipping away.

After that, she stays in the house, leaving it only to go to church on Sundays. And then, one Sunday, she faintly hears a voice. It calls across the river of silence that has slowly been growing between Miss Miranda and the world. Each note is like unclouded crystal. As the voice touches the second verse, it is so tender that Miss Miranda is moved to tears. It is singing the song that means her mother, and happiness, and comfort—*Ave Maria*.

Tania came in the early dusk. 'Quick!' she cried. 'Let's read!'

I was ready, book placed on the floor, candles lit ahead of time. I turned the page we had last read, to find myself faced with a blank one. The page after that was entirely faded. I squinted in the candlelight, but could not make out the words.

Tania gave a sigh of disappointment, but I had waited an entire endless day. I was not going to be denied. I

pulled the page from the diary—'Oh! Be careful!'—and
held it against the candle. Faint writing showed against
the glow.

*Someone has told Dona Alcina they saw me with Damon. I am
sure it was the new cook, spiteful thing that she too is. The Dona
called for me in the evening before prayers.*

*She was sitting still in her chair, waiting like a black spider.
She said the nuns had warned her I was bad but she could not
get Nina to change her mind about taking me in. She said she
knew what girls like me were and warned me to stay away from
Damon, or she would put me out on the street. She said I was
an ingrate, trying to return Nina's kindness by stealing her
betrothed. She went on and on but I barely heard her.*

*Nina is to marry Damon! She is to marry Damon and she
never once said a word about it to me and I am her best friend.*

*Nina says that the marriage was arranged when they were
children. Damon is not Nina's cousin at all. He is adopted. He
is an orphan, just like me. Dona adopted him when he was little
so that there would be someone to carry on the Casimir name.
Cook says she'd heard that, when he first came to the house, he
was barefoot and couldn't read his own name.*

*I met Alice in the ruins and told her about Damon and she
said she will pray every night for us to be adopted. I told her I
am too old. Then she said that no one would want her, with her
crooked leg.*

*I have been thinking about it. Imagine—someone just comes
and adopts you and in one day, suddenly, you can eat chicken
and fish and pork all at one meal. You are wanted and loved.
Just like that.*

As I turned the page it crumpled into bits in my hand. I
shook the pieces loose and they flew away. The next page

was so thick with mould that I had to put my nose to the page to read it at all.

Nina told me a secret. She doesn't want to marry Damon. They've been engaged all their lives. But she says she doesn't love him and he is marrying the house, not her. She wants to be in love. She says nothing will stop her when she is in love. She will do anything at all for it.

It seems to me the rich can buy so many things. Love is one of them. One more thing that the poor cannot have, like meat every day, or plates that are of china. We cannot afford love.

It is not love that men offer servant girls. And who could love an orphan who has nothing at all and who everyone calls Bad?

I think she is wrong to spurn Damon's love, for I am sure he loves her. If love of any sort were offered me, I would not spurn it. I asked her what would happen to me if she got married. She said I would stay with her. Nothing would ever separate us. We have promised to be friends forever.

'Where is Nina?' I asked, the thought coming suddenly into my head. 'Has she married Damon?'

'No,' said Tania. 'No one will ever speak of her in the house. And Damon does not wear a wedding ring.'

'Is Nina missing too?'

'I don't know,' said Tania.

'Did she go away with Sara?'

'Nina Casimir of the House of Casimir and the servant girl?' said Tania sadly. 'I don't think so.'

I ran out of guesses. Another mystery. The place is thick with them. Who would have thought that a simple Goan village could hide so many secrets? Trying to solve just one has led me so far astray from my original ambitions that I am quite sure I will never have a novel to show for my time here. All I have are pages and pages of writing about a story that I do not wish to tell.

'I have to go,' said Tania and got to her feet. I reached out a hand to stop her and hastily converted the gesture to a wave.

'Tomorrow,' I said.

'Tomorrow,' said a soft voice from the darkness and she was gone.

A Fine Stew

I have been trying to remember the number of servants in my parents' house, and find that I cannot. I have never been involved in the running of a household. That has always been my mother's territory. It is she who appoints the servants and makes sure the house runs smoothly. Since my father's death, she has been making sure the business runs equitably as well. As far as I know, there are the servants in the kitchen, the houseboy, the odd-job man, two gardeners, the driver—I forgot the housekeeper. I would make it nine people. Or more. To wait upon only my mother and me.

I find myself feeling slightly ashamed for all the demands that I have made so thoughtlessly until now. I have thought nothing of sending a dish back to the kitchen if I didn't like it, or shouting at the houseboy if my clothes had a crease in them. I do not believe that I have ever thanked a servant for anything they did for me.

I thanked the caretaker's wife as she was serving lunch. I was most courteous and thanked her profusely. She gave me a look of black suspicion and banged the plate down in front of me. I think no one has thanked her before.

I have been restless the whole day. No writing has come to me and I cannot bring myself to read. I pick up books and then fling them aside. There is only one story that I wish to know. The story of Sara has me in its grip. I am in an agony of waiting.

I have read a page—but it is not cheating. When I picked up the diary to rearrange my table, a page slipped from it and fell to the ground. I am forbidden only the diary, not anything that falls from it. I might still have resisted, but Lorso's name caught my eye.

I never thought I would be afraid of Lorso. But I am now.

He has been upset with me for some time. He says I have forgotten him and I am no longer his friend. I keep explaining that I cannot get away from the house. And the little bit of time I get, Alice is waiting for me. But he doesn't listen. And today he terrified me.

He had brought me things to make wind chimes with. I told him I no longer have time to make them. All I do is wake up at dawn and work work work. He kept trying to show me what he had brought me and when I said I had to go, he became angry. There were glass pieces among the bits and pieces he had gathered. He grabbed my hair and held a glass piece to my throat. He stuttered that I was his and he wouldn't let me go.

I didn't know what to do, so I sang. I sang his favourite song with a knife of glass against my throat.

He began to cry and dropped the glass. But he wouldn't let me go. He told me he loved me and I had to be his. He held my arms. I had to fight and fight to be free. There are bruises on my arms and shoulders and my heart is broken. He was my friend. And now he has spoilt it all and I am afraid of him. I am so afraid of him.

I sat back and thought about those entries. The braid lay upon my table like a dark question mark. My conviction that something bad had happened to Sara grew. I feared the worst.

I put the braid in my pocket and went to find the police station.

The police station was a little cottage groaning under the weight of a creeper that had smothered the porch. The front door opened into a single large hall. A couple of rooms led off from the hall. A barred door on one end indicated it was the jail. Somebody was sprawled within it, snoring loudly.

When I enquired, a skinny man pointed a lazy finger to a desk. Behind it was a man with a large moustache. I introduced myself to him.

'Inspector? My name is Jamshed Irani.'

'Jamshed Fali Hormazd Ratan Irani?'

I was so astounded that I just stared at him. 'I was coming to see you,' he continued.

'Me? Why?' I could not think of one earthly reason why an inspector should wish to see me.

The inspector pulled open a drawer and fished around in it. 'I have here a letter from a Mrs Dilnaz Irani.' He held up a letter. I recognised the firm hand that had addressed it to: 'The Police Chief—Chimbel Village'. My heart sank.

'I am not a police chief, but merely an inspector,' said the inspector. 'Perhaps you could correct your mother on that front.'

'Why is my mother writing to you?' I asked, already knowing the answer.

'Your mother wishes me to keep an eye on you.' The

inspector unfolded the rather long letter. 'It seems that you are all alone in a strange land with no friends.'

'I am fine!' I said. 'I have friends. Many friends.'

The inspector referred to the letter. 'And your health—?'

'Is fine, thank you!' I said.

'Your mother says here—'

'I am perfectly all right,' I said. 'And I intend to stay that way.' I glared at him across the table, daring him to enquire further.

'I am glad,' he said mildly. 'I am an inspector, not a doctor.'

'I shall mention that to my mother,' I said. 'She worries too much. Unnecessarily.'

The inspector folded the letter and regarded me standing there in a great fluster. 'And what exactly did you wish to see me about?'

'It's about a missing girl.'

'One of your many friends?'

'No,' I said. 'I don't know her at all, actually, but someone has asked me to try and find her.' I sat down in a chair without being invited to, took a deep breath and launched into my story about Sara and how she was missing.

The inspector listened to me, stroking his moustache occasionally with a forefinger. My narration was most annoyingly punctuated by the man in the jail. He had stopped snoring and begun singing, completely off-key.

I ended by placing the plait of hair upon the table. 'I found this. It was hidden by Lorso. I am afraid he has done something to her.'

'He told you it was hers?'

'No,' I said. 'I found it hidden behind a brick.'

'And how do you know it belongs to this servant girl?'

'I don't. But it couldn't belong to anyone else.'

The inspector regarded the long curve of braided hair that lay upon his table. 'And you say this girl went missing five years ago?'

'Yes,' I said.

'So, a servant girl went off five years ago. Then you found this bit of hair that may or may not be hers. And now you want to make a police case.'

Put like that it did not sound like much. 'She was afraid of Lorso. He threatened her! She wrote it in her diary.'

'Which you have also found. What a lot of things you have been finding, Mr Irani.' The inspector stared at the hair for a long time. Then he sighed. 'Mr Irani, what are you here in Goa for, exactly?'

'It is a private matter,' I said.

'You are an Irani,' said the inspector, 'of the Navsari Iranis.' The inspector had done his homework. 'You are the sole heir to a large business house. There is turmoil in India. Factories are shut. Business is suffering. Perhaps you are considering an investment in Goa?'

'I am not here for business,' I said firmly. 'I am here to write a book.'

'Ah,' said the inspector. 'Not a man of business but one of letters. I am a great admirer of authors. Such great imaginations.'

'I am not imagining things!' I said. 'Something could have happened to Sara.'

'And it could have not,' said the inspector. He smiled at me. 'Why don't you get on with the writing of that book so that you can return safely to your mother as soon as possible?'

It is the letter. He thinks me a hysterical mama's boy. He refuses to take me seriously. 'But Sara? The missing girl?'

'Ah,' said the inspector. 'No one has reported her missing for five years. If she was truly missing, someone would have.'

'That is because no one cares!' I said heatedly. 'But they should! I know she's a servant girl but she should matter! She is missing!'

There was silence in the police station. The few people there were staring at me. I realised that I had jumped to my feet and had been shouting. A snatch of off-key singing meandered through the pause.

The inspector gestured. 'Sit down, Mr Irani. Do you know what sorpotel is?'

I had to confess I didn't. I had no idea at all what he was talking about.

'It is a pork curry. I make an excellent one. Do you know how best to eat it?'

I shook my head, wondering if he was making a fool of me with his sudden talk of food.

'Leave it in the pot for a week. All that time, it is stewing and stewing. The longer it stands, the stronger the flavours get.' The inspector pointed a finger out of the window. 'The people in this village, they have been stewing for decades. Nobody leaves the village. Nothing changes. They live next to each other and they stew.'

He leaned forward and I could smell what I had come to recognise as the alcohol called feni. All the villagers exuded it.

'I know you are a big city man and you see this as a simple village. You're wrong. It's full of people. And there is nothing simple about people. There is nothing one man will not do to another if he's stewed long enough.'

His eyes watched me as he talked. 'Take two neighbours. One thinks the other has built his fence wrong and fenced off two coconut trees that belong to him. They argue for fifteen years. Stewing all the time. Then one day, Jose is cutting open a coconut and he ends the argument with a *koita*. It's a sharp curved blade. Slices open coconuts, and sometimes—human heads.'

I stared at him in silence, quite deprived of words.

'Piedade the butcher. Gets drunk every day and beats his wife. She takes a long long time to come to full stew. But one Sunday the wife decides, enough! And she uses the cleaver on the butcher. Tells everyone he has gone off drunk and she has no idea where he is.' The inspector suddenly beamed. 'And I, *I* solve the case because suddenly the sorpotel at the Tinto tastes different. The word that people use is "delicious". She has fed him to the pigs. And the pigs have gone into the sorpotel.'

My horror must have showed on my face. The inspector stabbed a finger in the direction of the singing. 'Take Leroy, who we have locked up. He gets drunk and angry and rides his neighbour's pigs. He does it because he believes his neighbour stole a piglet from him. I lock him up, because I know he is well stewed. Full flavour. And he could go out there and give his neighbour an indigestion that neither a doctor nor a priest could cure.'

'Really, Inspector, I do not see what—'

The inspector raised a hand to silence me. 'Young people? They do not stew. They run away. The young girls? They find someone and they run away. Gone! Haven't you noticed how few young people we have?'

'Sara didn't find someone and go away.'

'How do you know?' said the inspector. 'You bring me a length of hair and a whole lot of stories.'

'But something could have happened to her!'

He shrugged. 'I like cooking. And I am a policeman. Surprisingly, the two of them go together.' He smiled at me. 'I know very well all the ingredients that mix in the pot. My job is to keep the pot from coming to the boil.' He stabbed a finger at me. 'You are stirring things up.'

'I am just trying to find a missing girl!'

He waved his hands dismissively. 'Go home and write your book, Mr Irani, and I,' he said meaningfully, 'will tell your mother that all is well.'

In the silence that followed, Leroy's voice rang out, untuneful and wandering. I stood up, clear that I was going to get no help here. I stretched my hand out for the length of hair.

'You can leave that,' said the inspector.

'Why? You don't think anything at all has happened to Sara,' I said.

We both smiled most politely at each other, straining at the effort. I picked up the length of hair. The inspector didn't stop me.

A Love Note

I walked back to the house, deeply disturbed. The horrors that lie under the peaceful surface of a village! I had not suspected them at all. Far from dissuading me, all the inspector had done was convince me that something had happened to Sara. Something really bad, to judge by all the things the villagers seemed to do to each other when they got well and truly stewed.

Lost in my thoughts I was passing through the ruins when I stopped. Lorso was standing at the base of the statue of the angel. His back was to me, his hands desperately searching the empty niche in which I had found the diary and the braid of hair.

'It's with me,' I said. 'It's Sara's hair, isn't it?'

Lorso jerked around. His mouth fell open, his hands paddled the air.

'It's all right,' I said. 'I just want to talk to you.'

He began to back away, eyes wide, his hands beating the air in utter panic.

'Stop!' I said. 'I just want to find out what happened to her. What happened, Lorso? Why did you keep her hair?'

Lorso shook his head repeatedly. His mouth sawed and small creaky noises fell out of it. He looked petrified.

I stepped forward, one hand held out reassuringly. 'I just want to talk. What did you do to her?'

Lorso's hands jerked and jittered. Suddenly, there was a flash of silver, and his left hand was holding a wicked curved blade. I recognised it from the inspector's story as the blade that cuts both coconuts and heads.

He swung at me and I stumbled back. As I fell, I felt the blade snicker against the skin of my arm. I opened my mouth with some idea of shouting, but terror sat like a frog in my throat and only a croak came out.

Lorso leapt towards me, the blade a shiver of silver in his hand. I closed my eyes. There was nothing else I could do. A strangled cry from Lorso made me jerk them open. Somebody had grabbed Lorso's arm. It was Damon. He wrenched the blade from Lorso's hand.

They faced each other across my prone body. The rage went out of Lorso and fear stiffened his features. He looked desperately from Damon to me, then turned and ran as fast as he could.

I lay there listening to my heart thud, until Damon knelt beside me and asked, 'Are you all right?'

I sat up. Frantically, I began to search myself. 'Is there blood?' I asked. 'Can you see any blood?'

'No,' said Damon. 'You are not hurt.'

I continued my search, running my unbelieving hands over my body. 'Are you sure? No blood?' I knelt there, unable to believe my reprieve.

I looked up to see Damon looking at me with contempt. I got to my feet, still running questing hands over my arms and legs.

'You do not have even a scratch,' said Damon, a sneer in his voice. Then he walked over to the maw of the well that lay hidden between the long grass. 'Go home. Back to Bombay. You will be safe there.' He flung the blade into it and turned and walked away. I was unsure whether to be furious with him or grateful.

I hurried home, half-running. If I had been cut! I could not bear to think of it.

Back in the safety of my room, I pulled my clothes apart, searching. I had not been in such a panic for a long time. I could not believe that I was unscathed. Again and again I passed my hands over my body, sure that somewhere there was a cut. Somewhere there was the slow trickle of blood.

'What are you doing?'

Tania was standing at the door, watching me curiously. It was just sheer luck that I had not removed my trousers. I grabbed for my shirt.

'Lorso attacked me with a sharp instrument. I am checking that I am not hurt.'

'Stand still,' she said. I did, and she walked around me.

'Is there blood?' I asked, anxiously.

'No blood anywhere.'

'But he attacked me!' I put my shirt on and buttoned it with shaking hands.

'Calm down,' she said. 'You aren't hurt. Nothing happened.'

'But it could have!' I cried. I flung myself into a chair and tried to get my jittering heart back under control.

'Why are you so upset?' asked Tania, watching me curiously.

'It's nothing,' I said. To divert her, I told her the story of my visit to the police station. I must say, I felt all my frustration come flooding back as I told the tale. 'The inspector is going to do nothing at all.'

'Then we must do it,' said Tania. 'We must find her.'

'I think Lorso did something to her,' I said. 'He is dangerous. He tried to kill me! It would be foolish for us to continue.'

'You can't stop now!' cried Tania.

'He attacked me! I could have been hurt!' She didn't seem to comprehend what that meant. She just stood there looking at me, not saying a word.

I put into words the thought that had been bothering me. 'I really need to work on my book,' I said. 'Already, I have wasted so many days. All these distractions! I came here for peace and quiet, and those are the last things I am getting. Instead, I find I am attacked by maniacs with enormous knives!'

Tania continued looking at me. I steeled myself. 'I really think you should go as well, so I can get back to work,' I said.

'And the diary?' she asked softly.

I really could not stand it. Why do girls cry? Even worse is when they try to hold it back, but you can hear it right there in the voice.

'Take it,' I said. 'Read it. Let me know what happened.'

Tania just stood there. I did my best not to look at her.

'All right,' she said. From the corner of my eye, I saw the small movement as she brushed a tear away.

I knew I should have just let her go. I blame it on artistic sensitivity. It is part of the artistic temperament. What is one to do, really?

I sighed and picked up the diary and said, 'Come on. Let's read it together.'

We went to the hall of chimes. They were silent, their shapes hanging unmoving in the windows. When we lit the candles, the flames stood upright, as if frozen. My voice was loud in the night. The page I opened to held a surprise.

I have had a note. And such a note! Someone slipped it under the door. It has left me so bothered and confused.

A note was folded between the pages. I took it out and smoothened it. The writing slanted across the page. I read it out.

Dear Girl with the Beautiful Voice. Your voice is joy. Please sing again. I wait to hear you.

There were more notes tucked in between the pages. I unfolded a few and read them out.

How does it matter what you do? Love cares nothing for position. Do servants not love? Do not kings? I know only I heard a voice and now I cannot sleep at night. I must see you. Come to me.

Open the door. My heart has listened for so long at this door. My whole world waits here, outside a door that will not open. Come to me. Do not be afraid.

I was delighted. 'Look!' I said. 'Someone loved Sara!'

I riffled through the pages for more notes, but Tania leaned over and shut the diary abruptly, saying, 'We won't read any more tonight.'

'Why not? Sara has found someone who will love her. We can't stop now!'

Tania placed her hand on the diary when I went to open it again.

'What is it?' I asked her, but she did not reply. 'You don't believe that Sara found love? Why? Why are you so bitter?'

Tania said softly, 'It is not love that men offer servant girls. No.'

'What happened to you?' I asked, knowing that any moment those feet would be up and flying. 'Who broke your heart and took away all your trust?'

Tania turned her head and stared at me.

In that loaded moment, a breeze snatched at the pages of the diary and it tore open, gusts of paper flying all over the room. I tried to hold the diary from disintegrating completely. Tania sat there unmoving, the still centre of a blizzard of pages. I got to my feet and frantically gathered bits and pieces from the farthest corners of the room.

Tania looked at the untidy heap that I was holding. 'It's completely muddled up.'

I tried to sort a few pages but soon realised that it was almost a hopeless task. What with the faded writing, and the pages eaten by white ants, and no dates on the pages, there was no real hope of putting them back in the right order.

'But how will we know what happened to Sara?' I looked at Tania in dismay. Impossible to tell what was beginning, middle and end. With that untimely gust of wind, the story had become an enigma, a riddle. We had lost Sara again in its convulsed pages. Just when love had come to her.

Tania got to her feet. 'You will write it,' she said, before slipping away into darkness.

She is right. It is not my story. It is not even my business. I do not wish to write it. But it will not let me go. I will have to write it to be free of it.

Thou Shalt Not Steal

Early the next morning, I flung open all eight windows in my workroom and was rewarded with a panoramic view of trees. In the distance were the first smoky smudges of gathering clouds. They slowly condensed across the day.

I laid out the snarl of papers that was the diary on the bed. I know that I will get nothing at all done until I am done with Sara and her story. I must get through it as quickly as I can. I shuffled through the pages, trying to make sense of the tangle. I matched tears and smears and edges. I guessed at combinations and sequences. It was a task of patience that took me all day, and my labours were without reward.

Reassembled, the diary still gave me no clear idea of what really happened to Sara. I sat down to type up the last few pages.

The day grew to be the hottest I had known till then in Goa. The keys of my typewriter were warm under my fingertips, and my mind would not stir itself. I could scarcely bear the clothes upon my skin. Not a leaf moved and even the insects appeared to be struck dumb by the suffocating blanket of heat. The hush grew denser as the afternoon progressed and the light seeped from the sky with excruciating slowness. I waited for inspiration. I waited for rain. Finally, I could not bear the inertia anymore and headed down to the ruins.

I listened for Alice's voice, or the clicking of her brace, but no sound stirred in the broken stone. I walked through it, my footsteps falling dead and hollow upon the air. The grass in the graveyard was unmoving, and it felt eerie without its constant susurrus.

Charlie sat bolt upright beside the grave of his beloved. His head was tilted and he was listening intently. He turned at my approach. 'I was listening for the rain.'

He gestured to a gravestone opposite. 'Do join us,' he said expansively. 'And how does the writing progress?'

I confessed it did not progress at all. Crazy Charlie looked at me keenly. Then he leaned forward and whispered, 'Fall in love.' I recoiled from his musty old-man's breath. 'Fall in love, young man,' he said again. 'Break your heart. Only those who have known loss can ever make anything of value.' The cobwebbed eyes shone with fervour.

A shadow fell across the graveyard. I looked up. The darkness was suddenly spilling across the sky with frightening speed. The first stir of wind rustled through the grass. Then the air was full of currents that pushed and tugged at me, snatching at my clothes and hair.

'Fall in love,' said Charlie, raising his voice to shout above the wind. 'Break your heart. Understand pain. Like he does. *He* understands pain.' He gestured to the far edge of the graveyard. A figure was standing there that I had not noticed before. It was Damon.

Dressed in his usual sombre black, he was standing in a fenced-off portion of the graveyard. He was staring down at the grave at his feet. The first rumbles of thunder announced imminent rain. Dark clouds boiled over the last band of clear horizon. Lightning flared and flashed.

The wind rose and rampaged through the graveyard. I struggled to get to the grave, through knee-high grass that was whipped around and furrowed by the gale. Overhead, crows were screaming as they were blown about like tattered scraps. In the half-light, the flowers on the grave were a splash of unreal colour. I had to kneel to read the inscription.

Nina Casimir

1921–1942

Beloved of her Grandmother and her Fiancé

We wait only till we are reunited with you

Rain began to spatter down. I looked up at Damon, standing there unheeding of the rain. 'You never told me she was dead!'

'You never asked. She died five years ago.'

'Of what?' I asked.

'Of betrayal,' said Damon, his voice bitter.

The sound of peacocks crying came through the rain like the voices of children screaming. Damon didn't notice. He stood there, rain slashing at him, eyes upon the gravestone. I could not tell if there were tears upon his face. I turned and walked away.

The rain was a deluge now. The monsoon had arrived a week early.

Nina is dead. The news has shaken me deeply. I cannot understand it. I was fearing it would be Sara's death I would stumble upon and instead it is Nina who has been dead for five years. And Sara? With her only friend gone, what happened to her? Did Dona Alcina drive her out of the house? Where did she go? I walked back to the house, bent against the battering of wind and rain, my thoughts as disordered as the weather.

By the time I reached the house I was soaking wet. I changed my clothes to a cacophony of sounds evoked from the house by the downpour. There were great rattling surges of rain upon the roof and an uproar that rose from the tossed trees around it. Water shouted in many voices as it spouted down to earth. Small drips and large ones tapped impatient fingers everywhere.

To my dismay it was raining even inside the house, dribbles and small cataracts falling in every room, a fine spray misting down everywhere from above. I ran to the kitchen for my hoard of utensils. But the leaks in the roof were numerous and my store of pots and pans meagre.

Tania came searching for me on happy feet. Harassed to the extreme, I told her to find something to hold the drips in. 'Quickly! The rain is coming into the house!'

She said, 'Let it!'

The rain for her was a delight. She danced between the leaks, dodging them. 'Listen!' she said. 'Everyone is singing!'

The air was filled with trills and chirrups and fluting. I wondered what birds could be out in weather like this.

'Not birds. Frogs!' said Tania, laughing. 'It's frog-song. They're singing because of the rain.' A thousand frogs were sending their delight upon the air in myriad notes.

She paused under one small waterfall and demanded of me, 'Taste it!' I demurred that it would be unhygienic to do so. I could well imagine what my mother would have to say about it. Her eyes dared me, and I hesitantly stuck my tongue under the spout. The water was cold. I could taste the mustiness of mud in it and the sweetness of green leaves. I nudged closer, closed my eyes and let it run down my face. I understood the impulse that had set all the frogs to singing.

I opened my eyes to find Tania laughing at me. 'Come on!' she said. 'I want to hear what the chimes have to say about the rain.' We ran through the house, making a game out of dodging the small showers.

Every window in the wind chime hall was open and the length of it was one shout of wind and driving rain. The chimes were spinning and shivering in the windows. Lightning threw brilliant fragments of colour on the floor.

Tania climbed onto a windowsill and settled down to watch the rain. I sat opposite her. I watched the delight she took in the downpour almost as much as I watched the rain. Sheets of rain came slanting in at us. In the valley below stands of trees heaved and tossed like waves. We could hear the shrieking fall of branches. Lightning revealed the tower in the ruins like a bony white finger of warning.

Slowly, the storm passed overhead, the thunder reduced to muttering, the rain abruptly ceasing. We made our way back to the workroom, splashing through puddles, breathing in the deep evocative smell of wet earth in every room. The smell transformed all the others in the decaying house, so that every breath was filled with musk.

I lit a lamp and its quiet glow was balm after the storm.

'I have to tell you something I learnt today. She's dead,' I said.

'*Sara*?'

'No. Nina. She died five years ago. I've just seen her grave. Damon was standing at it.'

'Oh,' said Tania, 'that is why he wears black. That is why they never talk of her in the house.'

Frog-sound was loud in the stillness. The dripping from the roof was a series of disjointed percussions on timber and tile. 'How did she die?'

I had watched Tania becoming more and more fiercely protective of Sara as we read her diary together. I pushed my explanation forward, fumbling. 'Perhaps … perhaps she killed herself. That would explain many things.'

'Why would she do that?' asked Tania, shaking her head in denial.

'Because maybe her best friend and her fiancé—'

'Don't say it!' said Tania. 'I won't listen!'

I did not argue. I took three sheets of paper from the pile that made the diary and placed them before Tania.

I took the old Bible in the chapel, closed my eyes and opened it. My finger was on a verse that said, 'Take not the harvest from the field that is not rightfully yours.' I cannot go. I cannot.

I think of him all the time. Standing at the door and listening. It has been seven days, and every day there is a note under the door. I am so confused. Should I go to him or not?

He still waits for me. I will go. For once in my life I will not think and think and think. I will reach out my hand and take what is offered. I will go.

Tania said nothing. She reached out a hand and re-ordered the three pages.

He still waits for me. I will go. For once in my life I will not think and think and think. I will reach out my hand and take what is offered. I will go.

I think of him all the time. Standing at the door and listening. It has been seven days, and every day there is a note under the door. I am so confused. Should I go to him or not?

I took the old Bible in the chapel, closed my eyes and opened it. My finger was on a verse that said, 'Take not the harvest from the field that is not rightfully yours.' I cannot go. I cannot.

The story lay in the eye of the beholder and each of us had felt out the story we believed in when we reconstructed the pages. I had spent hours trying to piece the diary together. Matching inks, mould spots, sequences. Searching for clues in the condition of the pages. Tania had read the pages and felt the words in her heart.

We found that the interpretation of the story hopelessly divided us.

'Who was it who put notes under her door?'

'It can only be one person,' I said. 'Damon.'

The name hung between us. Tania shook her head in stubborn denial.

'There is no one else, Tania,' I said. 'He stopped her on the stairs. He held her hand.' I borrowed Sister Ursula's words to try and convince her. 'Some men are beasts.'

'No,' said Tania. 'She would never have betrayed Nina. They promised to be friends forever!'

'Damon said that Nina died of betrayal. Maybe he mourns at her grave because he feels his guilt.'

'Maybe she never went,' said Tania snatching at explanations. 'Maybe it was someone else who wrote the notes. It could have been another person altogether.'

She was as distressed as if it were to her that the accusing finger pointed. As if she herself was accused of stealing her best friend's fiancé.

I shook my head. 'She went.'

'No! They were friends. Friends forever! They promised. You don't break a promise you make in blood.' Tania got to her feet. Lightning flung the shadows of the wind chimes on the floor and lit up her anger in abrupt white flashes.

'Listen to me, Tania—' I said, but she would not.

'You are just like the rest. You are happy to believe the worst!'

'What else can I believe? Everyone talks ill of her. Besides, these things happen. He was the master of that house. And she was a servant,' I said. And, even as the words left my lips, I knew the mistake I had made.

Tania looked at me with such mingled hurt and scorn, I wished I could have burnt my foolish tongue. Cut out the words. Taken them back.

'You swore to believe me,' she said softly. 'But I too am a servant, aren't I? You never will.'

'I'm sorry! I'm sorry. I take it back!' I cried. 'I said the wrong thing. I never meant it like that. I don't know what to say!'

'There's nothing else to say, is there?' she said softly. And then she left.

A Knocking in the Night

I lit my way to bed. Rimmed by lamplight I went down the long corridor. I found myself looking over my shoulder. The sense of a presence came powerfully upon me. I had a feeling that something other than rats and wind was in the house. The sense tugged at the edges of my perception. Wind that was almost voices … shadows that were almost substance … something moved restlessly in this house. The words I had once uttered in jest suddenly began to ring true. I was glad to come to the bedroom and shut the door.

As I put the assembled pages of the diary on my bedside table, one of them slipped and flew from my hand. I started after it and had just seized it when my sense of unease suddenly coalesced into something concrete. I listened intently.

Someone or something was knocking deep within the house.

Loud, imperative knocks. Hard stones of sound that fell rattling through the darkness. I could not tell if it was something knocking to get out or get in. Silence fell. Then came the sound of a distant door shrieking open on stiff hinges.

Even in my fear, I knew I would rather go in search of it than have it find me. I grabbed the lantern. Then I picked up the gun from where it lay beside my bed. I was not quite sure how to use it, but it felt good in my hands.

The knocking began again. Now there was more than one knocker. Overlapping castanets of sound clattered through the house. It did not surprise me that they were coming from the direction of the wind chime hall.

The wind chime hall was empty. It was a dark funnel reverberating with the sounds that dropped into it from the open door at the end. The chapel door stood open wide. The sounds that echoed from it suddenly ceased. Even the chimes were mute. In an intense silence I walked the long length of the hall.

I paused at the door and made the sign of the cross as I had seen Tania doing. Then I stepped in.

At the far end of the chapel was the altar. It was incandescent with silver light. Puzzled, I looked up. Strangely enough, I could see the moon above me. There was a sudden crescendo of voices … a snatch of stars … and then darkness.

Blackness.

Light.

Blinding light. My eyes hurt with the cauterising glare. Slowly, shapes formed and floated through the whiteness. A slow drizzle of red landed lightly upon my face and hair. For one blinded moment I thought showers of blood were raining on me. Then I realised that they were petals floating down from a blue sky. I was lying on the floor staring up at a gulmohar tree through a gaping hole in the roof. Each gust of wind shook free fresh drifts of carmine and scarlet.

A face intruded on my vision. A large moustache stared down at me. I cleared my dry throat and whispered, 'Who are you?'

'Police,' said the moustache phlegmatically. Of course. I recognised that moustache. It was the inspector.

A hand hauled me upright. 'Who did you think I was?'

I felt silly admitting it in the broad light of day, 'A ghost.'

The moustache twitched. 'The only ghosts I ever knew gave up haunting after a spell in jail.'

I was dusted down and seated on a box bench. I put my hand to my head and winced at the size of the bump. Fear seized me. 'Is there blood? Is there any blood?'

The inspector said, 'No.'

'Are you sure? Look carefully!'

The inspector said, 'I know what it looks like.'

He watched me without comment as I checked slowly and thoroughly to see if he was right. He was. Other policemen were busy in the chapel, searching methodically through it.

'Robbery,' said the inspector when I finished checking. 'Got in through the roof. Usual way that they rob in this part of the world. Seem to have emptied the chapel. Was there anything of worth in here?'

'I don't know. I've never been in here,' I said. 'Ask him.' The caretaker was hovering agitatedly in the background.

The caretaker was loud in his lamentations. He had no idea of what was in the chapel. This part of the house had been locked up since he started looking after it. 'Mr Miranda Rose locked it himself. Mr Miranda Rose is going to be very angry! He told me never to let anyone into this part of the house.'

The inspector recommended that he immediately inform Mr Miranda Rose of what had happened. The caretaker protested that he would have to travel all the way to Panjim to book a call to Portugal and there was only one bus in the day. The inspector told him to waste no time in that case, and turned to me. 'And I suggest you go and lie down.' I nodded and regretted it immediately as my head was shot with bolts of pain.

I felt my head again. 'Is there any blood?'

The inspector shook his head, 'No blood. Bloody big lump.' He hefted a large crucifix which had one arm broken off. 'Hit you with this. No respect. Are you sure you can tell us nothing of help?' His eyes stayed sharply on me. 'You will let me know if you suspect any more—er—ghosts?'

I promised I would. 'Inspector,' I added hesitantly. 'Could you not mention this to my mother?'

'I am terrible at correspondence,' said the inspector promptly. 'I dislike letter-writing and avoid it as much as I can.' I was grateful for his circumspection. Just a mere hint of what had passed and my mother would be on the next steamer to Goa.

The policemen sealed the hole in the roof and assured me that the robbers were unlikely to come back. When the police left, I inspected my surroundings. In the light of day, the chapel was just an ordinary room, dusty and neglected. Damp had seeped through the rafters. The walls were peeling. Jesus in the daylight was mere plaster, his agony an effect of garish paint.

No ghosts.

The Wishing Well

There were gaps in the monsoon now, when the rain paused and a hundred shades of green intensified in every direction. The monsoon had filled the eye with a wash of new growth. Even the mermaid's withered wisteria was budding in tiny tender leaves.

An orchestra of frogs piped me to sleep every night with bassoon and flute and fife. They were everywhere— hopping ponderously though the house, taking up residence in dark corners, crowding into the spaces between my row of books. I even found one small specimen with tarnished gold eyes who had taken residence in my typewriter. I ousted this unlikely muse and put fresh paper in its place.

It has been three days since the robbery. I must confess I find the nights a little difficult, coming wide awake to every sound. In an old house like this, that creaks and groans all the time, that means I get very little sleep. I have, however, gained some consolation from the pistol that I now keep next to my pillow.

Tania has not come to visit. It has rained endlessly. I have stayed at home, trying very hard to get on with writing. I have put aside all the work I have done so far. I am not going to write the story of Sara. It is going nowhere.

Instead I have gone back to one of the ideas I was toying
with earlier. A rather clever satire about the British rule in
India. If published, it is likely to get me arrested. But I am
running out of time and I must write *something*.

I have typed for three full days with only minor breaks.
It seemed to me that the novel was coming along well.
Then this morning I read it through and it is tedious and
pretentious. A thumping dull read that is nothing at all
like what it was inside my head. I flung the entire wad of
papers at the wall and went down to the village.

There was a break in the rain and a pale sun lit the raindrops
on the leaves so they looked like scatters of broken glass.
The news of my little adventure had clearly travelled
all over the village. I was standing at the corner shop
buying bread and eggs when I realised that the attention
of the entire taverna was fixed upon me again. Several
men were falling back with contorted expressions, hands
outstretched and shivering. For a moment I wondered if
they were drunk so early in the day, then I realised they
were miming being afraid of ghosts.

'Oh, mother of God! Ghost!'

'I see ghosts as well. Especially after the fourth peg.'

'Holy water is the answer. Here! Have some more.'

I waited impatiently for my purchases to be wrapped
up. I walked away with gusts of laughter and raucous
sallies following me.

'Ooooh. I'm so scared.'

'Baptism is the answer. Here, pass the holy spirit.'

By the time I reached the shortcut through the graveyard
I was hot and sweating. Crazy Charlie was sitting in his
usual place. His battered black umbrella let in as much rain

as it kept out. The weak and fitful sun made a patchwork of sunspots dance all over him each time he moved.

'Good afternoon,' said Crazy Charlie. 'I hear you saw one of our departed.'

I gritted my teeth and said, 'It was robbers.'

'What a disappointment,' said Charlie. 'You know, I have never seen one of them—I only hear them. They are very quiet today. Listen.'

I caught myself in the act of listening and told Charlie firmly, 'It is only insects. Anything else is imagination.'

Charlie, however, had the last say. 'As a writer, that is your most precious possession, isn't it? Imagination?'

I made my escape cursing my overactive imagination and wishing perversely I had enough of it to write even a single book.

I came back to the house and it welcomed me with the now-familiar smell of musty decay. I sat on my bed and wondered what exactly I was doing here in this mouldering pile, moss on the walls, dust everywhere. Instead of my grand novel I first wrote the wrong story, then produced a work that proved insipid and worthless. I have been distracted completely. I have twice put my life in danger. This had been my only chance and I have nothing to show for it. I have become obsessed with a story that has no conclusion.

And yet, I found I could think of nothing but Sara's fate. I am held prisoner by the story. I am shackled to it and drag it around all day long. I pry at the mystery with sharp questions trying to force it open. I need to be free of it.

Plagued with restlessness and obsessed with the untold tale, I found myself returning to Sara's diary again and again. I thought we had read whatever was there, but I found two pages stuck together and peeled them apart with a great sense of anticipation. Faint writing trailed across one page. I had found another bit of the story.

I wandered through the empty house aimlessly, then discovered that my feet had a mind of their own. They led me to the wind chime hall. A handful of candle stumps marked the magic circle where we read Sara's story. Tania has not been here for three days and the hall seems even emptier than before. I stood in the hall wishing she would return. Wishing my stupid words unsaid. Wishing I could share the bit of story I had found with her.

The wind had been blustering all day, and the chimes were so loud in their chatter, I never heard the footsteps at all. I turned and she was standing there like a sudden apparition. It gave me such a start!

'Tania!' I gasped.

'I'm sorry,' she said. 'I'm sorry I quarrelled with you. I just heard. Are you hurt? Did the robbers do anything?'

'They hit me on the head,' I said. 'But there was no blood.'

We stood there, staring at each other, neither sure of what to say.

'I am glad you are unharmed,' she said finally.

'And I am glad you came back.'

Her smile dimpled out at me and she seated herself in a window. I sat opposite her.

'I am a fool,' I said abruptly. 'My stupid tongue is foolish. The words I said were foolish. I am sorry I hurt you. Forgive me.'

Tania lowered her head and didn't meet my eyes. 'I am sorry I quarrelled with you.'

'Friends again?' I asked softly.

She nodded.

I broke the awkward silence. 'I hope Sara found happiness wherever it is she went. Whoever she chose. I hope she found love.'

Tania shook her head. 'Love? Sara knew that love is not for girls like us.'

'Why not? Surely you intend to find a suitable man someday to spend your life with?'

'And what would be suitable for me? The men from the taverna?'

'Certainly not those boors!' I said, appalled.

'Then who? Who is suitable for an orphan and a servant?' asked Tania softly.

'I don't know. But surely you have a right to love as well.'

'Do you know the matches the nuns find for their orphan girls? Cripples. Blind men. Older men. Widowers. That is all we can hope for.' The bitterness that I hated to hear had come back into her voice. 'Love is for people like you. Who are rich enough to afford it.'

'We can't afford it either!' I said. 'Do you think I will be allowed to marry whomever I want? My father—' I stopped abruptly.

'What happened to your father?'

I didn't answer her question but spoke forcefully. 'I don't know who you will find. I don't know what your fate is going to be. But that doesn't mean you are not deserving. First, you have to believe you deserve love.'

There was silence from Tania. It exasperated me. 'What does being a servant have to do with it? It's just a job.'

'There is nothing wrong with being a servant. It's what being a servant makes you.'

'What does it make you?' I asked.

'Untouchable,' said Tania.

'But you're Christian!' I said. 'They have no caste!'

'Do you really think everyone here put away caste when they converted? Do you not see that I am thrice as lowly? I am an orphan. And a servant. And a girl.'

In exasperation I put out one hand and then dropped it.

'I am untouchable in many ways,' said Tania softly.

I took a deep breath. If I had not, I would have broken my vow on the spot by shaking her. I knew my words would not sway her. I pulled out the page I had been carrying in my pocket ever since I read it. I held it out to her.

Nina comes with me to Miss Miranda's house. She dances in the hall while I play. Today she wanted me to play only love songs. Then she insisted we make a wish. For love. She laughed at me when I said it was a foolish wish and took my hand and dragged me to the well. She says wishes made in wells come true. We threw in coins and wished.

Nina wished for true love to come and find her and take her far away. I whispered my wish so she couldn't hear. I don't want a grand love of the kind Nina hopes for. I would be content with a small one. At least once. I wished to be loved at least once in my life. Everyone deserves to be loved at least once.

'Sara thought everyone deserves to be loved at least once.'

Tania turned away from me. Her face was shadowed. The smell of earth was rich in my nostrils. It was ancient and primal and heady. It made me reckless. 'Tania— everyone deserves that. You have to believe it. No matter how rich or poor or ugly or stupid, or anything. At least once!'

She would not turn around to face me.

'Come on,' I said fumbling in my pocket.

Her voice was small and uncertain in the shadows. 'Where are we going?'

I led the way. 'To the well. To make wishes.'

By the well the smell was a high tide of musk and wet leaves and clay tiles long in the sun. The receding rain had left behind soft mutterings of water easing into the earth, swirling in drains, splattering into the well. A sibilant curtain of sound shifted and swayed around us.

I placed two coins on the ledge of the well. Tania watched me. I carefully took one coin and held it over the well. 'I wish that I find Sara.'

The coin fell glinting into the darkness and disappeared into the mouth of the well. Tania hesitated. Then her hand inched forward and she picked up the second coin.

Her voice was soft in the laden air—'I wish that I am truly loved at least once.'

I willed her to drop the coin in. She paused—and in that moment there was a tremendous knocking on the front door.

The sound smashed through the moment, leaving it in fragments. Tania closed her fist around the coin. She thrust her hand behind her back.

'Who could it be, so late?' I wondered.

'Maybe it's the police again. I better go. They shouldn't see me here.'

'Don't go! You haven't made your wish.'

Tania looked at me a long sad moment. 'Perhaps it's never meant to be made.' She climbed onto the ledge of the well.

'No!' I said. 'You have to make it! You have to take the chance.'

Tania took three quick steps and vanished into the wet night.

I fetched the pistol from the bedroom in case it was not the police, and went to answer the door.

I kept a firm grip on the gun as I opened the door. On the doorstep was the caretaker, sodden with both rain and drink. He stood swaying in the doorway, giving off the reek of feni. He had come to deliver a Dire Warning. Beside him stood his wife, dressed all in black and weeping loudly.

The caretaker swayed closer until the stink of his breath forced me to take a step backwards. 'Go away!' he said. 'You must go away. Terrible things will happen if you don't.'

'More ghosts I suppose,' I said.

'No, no,' said the caretaker. 'You must leave this house immediately.' His bloodshot eyes went wide, his hands windmilled terrible prospects. Beside him his wife let out a babble of Konkani and clutched her hands together in supplication.

'Go home,' I said irritably. 'I'm not going anywhere.'

'You must!' insisted the caretaker. 'You must leave immediately!'

I put a hand on his chest and firmly pushed him backwards out of the door. Then I showed him the gun. 'If anything is going to happen to me—I'm prepared.'

His wife left off her wailing, her eyes going wide in fright. She grabbed his arm and hauled him away.

I shut the door on a last glimpse of the caretaker struggling to get his voice back, his eyes wide in panic, rain dripping off his nose. His wife was clutching his arm, fat tears rolling off her face, a stream of agitated Konkani issuing from her.

Really. I cannot imagine what all the dread and drama is about.

Someone Else

I woke to unusual silence in the early dawn. The steady rain had ceased, leaving sodden silence in its wake. And in the silence, something was moving about in the house.

I could hear footsteps as somebody walked about, then hesitated. I reached for the gun under the pillow, picked it up and hefted its reassuring weight. Then I went in search of the sound. I was determined that I would not be ambushed again. And I was quite clear that it was not ghosts. There are no such things as ghosts.

I came around the corner of the corridor that led to my workroom, gun held before me. A young man was standing in the doorway, with his back to me. He turned, and shock bleached his face.

'My God!' said the man. 'You're not a ghost, are you?'

'NO, I AM NOT!' I said. I had had enough of ghosts. If anyone said the word again to me, I would have hit them. My arm ached. Guns are devilishly heavy and very difficult to hold steady.

'Who are you? What are you doing here?' asked the man, not moving. His voice was highly accented with the lilt of a habit of talking Portuguese.

'The question is, rather, what are *you* doing here? You are a trespasser. I'm within my rights to shoot you.'

The man said slowly, 'Trespasser? I thought this was my house.'

'What? Who are you?'

'Lisbon Miranda e Cabral.'

I lowered the gun. 'Solo Violin,' I said.

'What?' Lisbon looked pale and disoriented. He was a young man, weary with travel. He was slim and dishevelled. A white scar ran from his eyebrow into his hairline.

'You're the violinist. I heard the records you sent your aunt.'

'Who *are* you?'

'Jamshed Irani. I'm writing a book. I'm your tenant.'

Lisbon looked even more disoriented. 'I don't understand. How can you be my tenant? I never leased the house.'

I understood at last the dread of the caretaker.

Half an hour later, terrible things were indeed happening. The caretaker blustered, apologised, whined, and called upon the pantheon of saints to support him. I grinned as I listened to Lisbon Miranda e Cabral pithily summarise the caretaker's lineage and scathingly review his future prospects. He informed him he was lucky he was not in jail for leasing the house behind the owner's back.

Taking my eyes off the thoroughly enjoyable tableau for a moment to glance out the window, a movement in black caught my eye. Damon was standing across the road, staring up at the house. The look in his eye made me back away from the window.

Having dealt with the caretaker, Lisbon turned to me. 'Perhaps you will show me where the robbery took place?'

Lisbon hesitated in the music room for a moment before the photo of the old lady standing by the piano. He hurried through the windblown courtyard with the scorched walls. He paused, but did not comment, at the white ant-eaten door with all its futile locks. We traversed the wind chime hall trailed by little trills of melody and stopped at the chapel.

Lisbon took a deep breath and said, 'Here?'

He stood a long time at the door, hesitating to go in. I watched him curiously. Once again, to my eyes, it was a dusty, ordinary little room. I had no idea what Lisbon saw in it that so filled him with reluctance. Finally, Lisbon made a furtive sign of the cross and stepped over the threshold.

The roof had been inexpertly patched, and the floor was wet with rain. Lisbon walked around the chapel slowly, pausing by the broken crucifix, running a finger over the dusty box bench. He paused at the altar.

I said, 'I have never been in here so I do not know what was taken. What's gone?'

Lisbon replied distractedly. 'All the silver. There were silver chalices ... a silver cross ... some icons, which I suppose must be expensive. I don't really know. I've only been here once, five years ago, when I inherited the house.'

He stood near the altar for a moment longer, then turned to me. 'Look, I don't really know how to say this—but you'll have to leave.'

'But I have nowhere else to go! And my book is not finished—'

'You will have to go!' said Lisbon.

'The house is big,' I argued. 'You will want to stay, but we both can—'

Lisbon shook his head vehemently. 'No. No.' He looked quickly around the chapel once again, then hurried out of the door. He waited for me to step out and slammed the doors shut behind me. 'I'm not staying here. I'll stay at the guest house in the seminary. You'll have to go. Sorry. But the caretaker had no business to lease out the house behind my back.'

I made another effort to avoid eviction. 'I understand, but this is really inconvenient! I've just started on a novel and—'

'You will have to go!' said Lisbon, echoing himself. 'I want to lock up the house again. It should never have been opened.'

'But at such short notice!'

He ignored my protests, walking swiftly back through the house. I trailed behind him, dismayed. At the door he paused. 'Tomorrow.'

I bowed to the inevitable. 'Tomorrow.'

I watched Lisbon go down the lane from my eyrie in the round room. I was puzzled by his hesitations, his unmistakable sense of dread, of sorrow almost. A sudden thought came to me.

Even as the idea took hold of me, I saw a figure in black step out from behind a tree and start to follow Lisbon. There was a purpose and motive in Damon's tread. It worried me. I hurried to the door.

I was running by the time I took the bend. Lisbon and Damon were standing facing each other. Damon grabbed Lisbon by the shoulder. 'Where is she?' he demanded.

Lisbon tried to fend him off as he said, 'Who? I don't know what you are talking about.'

The path was slick with mud, and, as he struggled to get free of that hand, Lisbon lost his footing. Damon went down with him, grabbing at his throat as he fell. 'Where is she? What did you do with her?'

Lisbon fought to be free. They slipped and skidded in the mud and went rolling over and over. Damon still had his hands at Lisbon's throat. He asked the same question over and over again with gritted teeth: 'Where is she? *Where is she?*'

Lisbon could not answer, with the life being choked out of him. I flung myself on Damon and tried to pull him off. For all the notice that Damon took, I might as well not have been there. Slipping and sliding in the mud, I edged around and grabbed Damon's hands, trying to pry them from Lisbon's neck. *'Where is she?'*

All the veneer of sophistication and pride was gone from Damon. His teeth were bared in a snarl and his eyes were wild. Lisbon's laboured breathing stuttered and stopped. His eyes began to roll in his head. In a surge of panic, I leaned over and sunk my teeth into one knotted hand. Damon turned his head and seemed to realise for the first time that I was there. The wild look in his eyes flickered out. The hands unlocked. With a grimace of distaste Damon removed them from Lisbon's skin. He got to his feet and stood there a long moment staring down at Lisbon. Then he spat on him. The gobbet of spit slid down Lisbon's face.

Damon glanced at the crescent shape my teeth had left in his hand and gave me a black look. Then he turned and stalked away.

I spat on the ground in my turn. I could not bear the taste of that man on my tongue. I turned back to Lisbon.

He was lying on the ground, eyes staring blankly at the sky. His face was white and he made no effort to breathe. Rain drizzled into his open eyes.

'Breathe!' I shouted. 'Take a breath!'

I panicked completely and hit him sharply on the chest with both fists. His mouth opened and he swallowed great wheezing chunks of air. I helped him sit up, feeling his tumultuous heartbeat shaking his whole body as I did so. We both just sat there in the mud, too shaken to move. Lisbon wiped the spit from his face with a shaking hand.

'He tried to kill me.'

'Yes,' I said. There was nothing else to say.

The wheezing settled. Lisbon turned blankly to me. 'What was he saying? Who was he asking for?'

I said, 'I suppose—Sara.' The idea that had entered my head had taken full form as Damon shouted his question again and again at Lisbon. Here was Tania's speculation in the flesh. This was Someone Else.

'Sara?' said Lisbon. He turned and stared at me.

'You're the one, aren't you? The one that Sara loved?'

Lisbon said nothing, just looked at me in a daze.

'Where is she?' I asked. 'What happened?'

'What do you mean?' asked Lisbon, his eyes suddenly focusing. He grabbed my arm. 'Has something happened to Sara? Where is she?'

I told him, 'She has been missing for five years.'

Lisbon looked as bewildered as a child. 'She can't be. I have come all this way for her.'

The Open Door

The Gift

In every generation of the Mirandas, one child is born with The Gift.

Lisbon was the first child born to a very young mother. His parents lived in Paris then, but they named him after the city he had been conceived in. Therese Miranda was lost without the large family that surrounds any first birth in India. Her husband was too junior a diplomatic employee for them to employ a nurse and so, exhausted and weepy, she struggled all by herself with the infant. Putting the child to bed was a task that left her worn, each mealtime was a prolonged test of competence, and a touch of colic became a calamity. Still, she managed to powder her face and greet her new husband with a smile when he returned from work every evening. Until the day when Lisbon refused to stop crying.

He started as soon as Inacio left for work and continued without pause through the day. He shrieked until his mother feared he would damage something permanently. Surely the heart of something so tiny would burst with these despairing wails. She tried gripe water, hot fermentation, every single remedy she could think of, but nothing would make him stop. Finally, she found herself gritting her teeth, trying to hold back screams as violent as those of her child.

Her husband came home to find Therese weeping in the rocking chair with the screaming baby in her arms. The tears dripped off her face, the child shrieked and she made no attempt to soothe it, having come to the end of her ability to cope.

Inacio had no solutions but he realised that, for his young wife's sake, he had to think of one. Somewhere, a hazy quotation about the soothing effects of music came to mind. He put his violin to his chin and began to play silly tunes to distract Lisbon. And miraculously, the infant stopped crying and turned his head to listen intently to the sound. After that Therese never had a problem getting Lisbon to stop crying. Inacio bought a gramophone and a selection of classical music and the very finest composers lulled Lisbon into serenity.

By the time he was two, his father's silly tunes bored Lisbon, and he stubbornly indicated that his favourite composers be played again and again. He listened with an expression of concentration when his father played Mozart and Liszt. By three, his father was smiling ruefully and saying, 'The little critic is going to tire of me soon. He wants more complex fare.' At four he had his own violin and attended his first class. By the age of eleven, it was his father who sat listening as his son played Brahms and Bach and Dvořák.

Unwilling to disturb his son's classes, his father went to his last posting in Venice alone. At a diplomatic reception he let slip that he was searching for a master's violin for his son who was currently studying under Maestro Castriani. When his tenure came to an end, he was diplomatically presented with a Guadagnini violin. It was Lisbon's delight and he was never far from it.

For his twenty-first birthday his father arranged for Lisbon's very first recording. Father and son chose the selection together. Nothing too thrusting or ambitious— humbleness is the necessary foundation to greatness—but with a range wide enough to show his virtuosity. His mother carefully prepared the list of relatives and friends to whom a copy of the record would be mailed as a Christmas gift. From ambassadors to aunts, she forgot no one. Someone remembered that Grand-aunt Miranda was the one who had The Gift in her generation, though hers led her to the piano.

A mother's pride carefully prepared a package that would withstand the long journey to India, and she enclosed a note that, without descending into boasting, hinted that this was only the first step for a great talent. *'We have high hopes for Lisbon. He has applied to the London Conservatory to study under Sir Edmundson and we are sure he will be accepted.'*

Lisbon received a thank-you note in elegant handwriting. *'Dear Nephew, I enjoyed your gift …'* What Lisbon and his family did not know was that by the time the record reached Grand-aunt Miranda, she was completely and utterly deaf. She had laid a hand against the phonograph and listened with her fingertips. *'I appreciated your particular interpretation of …'*

The record did more than elicit a thank-you note. It made Grand-aunt Miranda quite determined that Lisbon would be her heir. Two months later, another letter in Portuguese arrived informing him of her choice. Enclosed with it was a note from the parish priest telling them that Miss Miranda had died peacefully in her sleep.

Lisbon decided to go to Goa in the face of his parents' open reluctance. He should not disturb his studies, he should be concentrating on preparing for the entrance test to the conservatory—but Lisbon knew their reluctance had deeper roots.

It had to do with the Family Secret. He had no idea what it was, but for a long time he had known there was something the family edged carefully around. As a child he had found hints—a conversation among grownups, terminated as soon as he entered the room; an aunt bursting into hysterical tears in the middle of a family reunion for no apparent cause; significant looks that passed between various members of the family from time to time; and of course, whispers. Whispers that buzzed just above the level of the children and left them tantalised and guessing. A Family Secret and an Unexpected Inheritance. The two together dazzled him and made him withstand all the gentle pressure his parents brought to bear on him not to return to the ancestral home.

Lisbon was to fly, becoming the first member of the family to try the newest method of transport. He boarded the plane amidst his father's reminiscences of how it once took twelve days to travel from Lisbon to Bombay. He did it in twenty-two hours. A train from Victoria Terminal thereafter, and he was in Goa, just three days after he started out.

The house sorely disappointed Lisbon. He had been brought up in the opulence of diplomatic accommodation. Imitation rococo palaces could scarcely interest someone who had lived in the real ones almost all his life.

He wandered through the many rooms, noting their contents with distaste. It all reeked of backwardness and decay and rot.

One bored evening he took out the large bunches of
keys the lawyer had handed him and opened every lock
and door he could find. So far, his inheritance had proved
disappointing. Perhaps in one of the many cupboards he
would find something unexpected enough to make this
trip worth something. He found nothing less than the
Family Secret.

It lay in a triple-locked cupboard in his aunt's room—
piles of ancient ledgers with dates marked on them. They
went back seventy-five years. He didn't know it but he
was looking at a detailed record of the Miranda family's
rise to fortune. It was based on trade out of Africa.

Portuguese was Lisbon's mother tongue and he could
read the trade ledgers so carefully maintained generation
after generation.

Male	*20 years old.*	*Branded on right buttock.*
Male	*11 years old.*	*Diseased.*
Female	*14 years old.*	*Pregnant. Previous branding. Re-branded.*
Male	*18 years old.*	*Troublemaker. Punished with Silencio.*

Later, back in Portugal, obsessively researching the slave
trade and its links with Goa, Lisbon will trace down the
Silencio. In the Regiao Sul library he will find a matter-
of-fact account of the slave trade written by Miguel
Fernandes. The writer devotes half a page to the Silencio.
Slaves who talked too much and fermented revolt had
their lips stitched up with wire and were left without food
or water until their spirit was broken. Fernandes points
out that it was a wasteful punishment, killing nearly all
those subjected to it and reforming few. Lisbon will sit in
the silence of the library, tears falling down his face.

Now he piles the books in the courtyard and sets fire to them. The fire is not easy to start. The ledgers are thick and their covers made of cured hide. Lisbon begins to tear them apart, to fling slabs of papers into the flames, fanning them frantically until the fire catches. Pages and pages of neatly itemised merchandise; rivers of black gold that flowed through the family's homestead in Nigeria and out; whole families and villages and mothers and brothers and sisters and lovers—all go into the fire. The smoke gets in his eyes and is bitter in his mouth. The ashes rise in the hot air and fly everywhere.

That night he dreams of singing. It wells up from somewhere in the house. Long, undulating voices flow through the rooms, seeping under every door, ebbing and returning. He does not understand the words but knows that they sing of loss. A great rising tide of grief fills the house and he is drowning. He wakes with his face wet.

He cannot wait to leave the house behind him. He wonders how he is ever going to pass the days that remain till his return journey. But then he hears the voice.

It rises up out of the dusk air. It is a flute, a pipe of silver. Each note is wrought of crystal and inlaid with pearls. He goes in search of the voice.

'It was coming from within the house. From the large hall. Someone was playing the piano and singing. And such a voice!'

Lisbon's face holds a reflection of the wonder he felt the first time he heard that voice. 'I followed the singing. It led me here. I stepped through the door and had a glimpse of two girls seated on the piano stool. I got just a glimpse.

Then they were both screaming and running.' Lisbon's smiles ruefully. 'They thought I was a ghost.'

The chimes in the window chortle and laugh to themselves. We are sitting in the wind chime hall and Lisbon is telling me the story I have held bits and pieces of, but have never been able to piece together whole.

'I tried to follow, but they were too quick. I had no idea who they were. But I couldn't get that voice out of my head. So, I left a note for them. For the girl with the voice actually.'

Dear Girl with the Beautiful Voice,
Your voice is joy. Please sing again. I wait to hear you.

It is Nina who finds the note, a small square of sudden whiteness on the floor. She reads it to Sara and they both break into giggles. But it is Sara who bars the door. All the warnings of the nuns ring in her ears.

Then she sits at the piano and sings. She sings for the man who caught them by surprise and so terrified them the previous day. She sings for happiness that he wishes to hear her again. She sings for the tingle that his note has set in her blood. And on the other side of the door, a voice replies.

Lisbon walks the length of the wind chime hall, restless, as he tells his tale. 'The next day I listened all day. In the late afternoon I heard the voice again, calling to me. I went to the door. But it was locked. They had shut it against me. I leaned against the wood and listened. I wanted to call through the door but I was afraid that if I said anything, she would stop singing. An idea struck me. I fetched my violin and began to play.'

The voice that calls through the door is filled with sadness. It is steeped in yearning. It cries out in its thirst. And a voice answers, slipping under the door like water.

The two voices run beside each other. They flow into a melody of such beauty that the whole house listens.

The music ripples through the house and laps at the feet of the mermaid, turned to stone in her forgotten courtyard. It pours down the corridors and washes past the rows of memories hung on the walls. It seeps away in an abandoned bedroom where mirrors gaze into infinity, knowing they are empty like never before.

Day after day the two voices undulate around each other, surging ever closer together. Soon, they are a single stream that runs towards the open arms of the sea. A sea that sings its way to the horizon.

But the door stays closed.

'I wrote another note and slipped it under the door,' says Lisbon. 'I wrote a dozen notes. I was in love. Shakespeare was wrong. Love does not come in from the eyes. It slipped in through the ears. I fell in love standing at a door and listening. Not at all how I had ever imagined it would be.' Lisbon gives a shrug. 'But when loves comes—what can one do?'

Dear Girl with the Beautiful Voice,
Your voice is joy. Please sing again. I wait to hear you.

Thank you. My music gives me much happiness. I am glad you share it.

Open the door. I stand here and listen and it is not enough. I want to see you. I want to know who the girl with the voice of an angel is. Why do you not open the door?

I should tell you who I am. I am a servant for the Casimirs. My name is Sara.

How does it matter who you are? Love cares nothing for position. Do servants not love? Do not kings? I know only that I heard a voice and now I cannot sleep at night. I must see you. Come to me.

You cannot fall in love with a voice. I cannot come.

False. Both false. I have fallen in love with a voice. And you can come to me. All you have to do is open the door. My love waits. All of our time together waits for you. Open the door. Beloved. Be loved.

Everyone deserves love once in their lives. Rich, poor, crippled, orphaned, it does not matter. Everyone deserves one chance. I asked the question that had so divided Tania and me. 'Did she come?'

'Yes. One day Sara opened the door and came to me.'

In the chapel I took the old Bible, closed my eyes and opened it. My finger was on a verse that said, 'Take not the harvest from the field that is not rightfully yours.' I cannot go. I cannot.

I think of him all the time. Standing at the door and listening. It has been seven days and every day there is a note under the door. I am so confused. Should I go to him or not.

He still waits for me. I will go. For once in my life I will not think and think and think. I will reach out my hand and take what is offered. I will go.

The song is done. There has been silence for a long time. Yet, Lisbon is loath to leave. He stands at the door, wishing it ajar. He leans his head against the door and it unexpectedly swings open. He steps through the door and there is a girl sitting at the piano stool. She raises her head to look at him.

Sunlight streams through the stained glass, throwing great lilies of blue and red upon the floor. He walks towards her on a carpet of flowers made of light. The wind chimes sing in the windows. He holds out his hand to her. At that moment her smile changes to fear. Someone is standing outside the windows, watching.

Lisbon's face twists with hate. He spits out the words. 'It was the first time I saw her. And even that moment he poisoned.'

'Who?'

'Damon. She turned her head and saw him. He was watching the house, standing in the shadow of a tree.'

Lisbon sees the face of love and the face of hate on the same day. Damon stands beneath the trees, watching the windows. He has stood for many days, listening to the two voices calling yearningly to each other. Now there is a silence that is more evocative than all the music that streamed from the windows.

She takes his hand and tells him to hide her! Quick! They hide in the space under the piano. They crouch in a tangle, knees against chin against arm against cheek. They watch his shadow upon the floor as he goes from window to window, a dark knife against the light. Sara is starting to giggle, the proximity making her nervous. Lisbon knows he must stop her, but he cannot move. He reaches over and places his lips on hers. Her surprised mouth opens and he tastes her.

'We met every night after that. She'd come to me after work. Late in the evening, when no one was about and could see. We talked. We walked through all the rooms. This was our kingdom. And we loved each other. Night after night.'

Across the bridge redolent with unseen jasmine. Then through the graveyard with its high smell of grass. The scent of mango blossom and jackfruit lying heavy in the ruins. Feet hurrying now through rich forest smells of mould and growth and decay. The door standing open, exuding candle wax and the faint fragrance of the wisteria trailing from the roof. And then the tang of him—deep and warm and easing into the breath.

Lisbon ran out of words and sat lost in his melancholy. I said, 'People noticed. This is a village. They notice everything. They began to talk. She got a reputation.'

'There was nothing underhand in my love. I meant to marry her,' says Lisbon. 'I swore on the altar in this chapel that I meant to marry her. I didn't want to go in that chapel again. It is where I made my promise to her.'

He leaned forward and spoke earnestly. 'I loved her and she loved me. We were to be happy together. I told her to come away with me and she agreed. She was to come to me on the night before I left. Both of us would leave together in the morning.'

The night is long—from the call of the nightjar to the first light in the sky. A wide river flowing from sunset shore to sunrise. He thinks he will never cross it. The first watch of the night is filled with the sound of sleep settling in. Birds bicker in the trees. Crows wing their way across darkening fields.

The second watch of the night is slower. The geckos call stuttering across the roof. There are frogs in the garden and some insect that scrapes its wings against the windowpane.

The third watch of the night is the longest. All sounds have faded to silence. The distant call of the heron in the paddy fields is cold and alone. The one persistent cricket which has kept watch with him falls silent. He crosses the deepest part of the river in this watch, knowing that there are endless depths under his prow and he is quite alone, and a man alone will soon be adrift. It is in this watch that the messenger arrives.

'She never came. She sent a message instead.'

'She never came? Why?'

'I don't know. She sent me a note saying that our worlds were too far apart to ever meet.'

I recognised the Goodbye Note.

The sadness that Lisbon seemed to be steeped in surfaced in his face and voice. 'I sent her back a note begging her to come. I waited. But she did not come.'

I could not believe that, yet again, I was to be left with no ending to Sara's tale. 'Where did she go, if not with you?'

'*I don't know!*' cried Lisbon. 'I never knew she was missing! I thought she had changed her mind about me. That she did not care for me anymore.'

Hurt and despair mingled in his voice. 'The woman I loved rejected me. I left without her. I thought I would forget her, but I have spent all these years waiting for her to come to me.'

All the nights have now become rivers flowing endlessly in search of the sea. Lisbon has found himself adrift and waiting every night since that longest one. He looks down into the water and sees his reflection, alone but for the pieces of the moon scattered in every ripple.

He turned to me and there was anguish on his face. 'I didn't care when I was informed that things had been robbed from this place. I came hurrying back only because the call gave me an excuse to come back to India. Come back and see her one more time. Maybe, this time, convince her that we could be together. Only to find that she has been gone all this time.'

I sat silent. Lisbon asked urgently, 'Where is she? Tell me!'

'I don't know,' I said. 'I know nothing about any of this. I never even knew Sara. I'm just trying to find her.'

'He knows!' said Lisbon bitterly. 'He knows where she is. Damon.'

'Then why did he nearly kill you trying to get that answer out of you?'

Lisbon put a hand to his blue and bruised throat. 'Lies! He's just pretending. He has something to do with her disappearance. He was jealous.'

Lisbon looked miserably around the hall. 'You wondered why I didn't want to stay here. It's because I can't bear the thought of it. This was our little world. I was happy here. I know I will never be happy like that again. Every day is an absence of her.'

He got to his feet and began to walk away. I hurried after him as he made his way through the many rooms and corridors to the front door.

'You can't go!' I said. 'There are so many unanswered questions.'

I got no reply. He paused at the door to say, 'Leave. Just leave by tomorrow.' He stepped into the rain and was gone.

All I can conclude is that neither of the men in Sara's life know what happened to her. Lisbon returned to find her gone. And Damon searched for her with fervour enough to kill for the answer. Why did nothing lead to Sara? No matter what turn the story took, it still wandered in a labyrinth. Sara refused to be found.

So that was that. And now I was to be ousted from the house with not even a page of a proper novel to show for the time I had spent there.

The best plan I could come up with was to go to Panjim and find a hotel room until I found another place in which to work. But where that would be, I had no idea. Some other little village—most probably. Perhaps, I thought, it was for the best to have a new setting, with no distractions. Time was running out, I reminded myself, and I had accomplished nothing. Absolutely nothing!

I packed with heavy hands and a reluctant heart. My books were the hardest to pack. I took them one by one from their hopeful row and put them into the trunk. And when it came to the little stack of writing that I had done, I stood there helpless, not knowing what to do with it. It was not a novel, nor was it the story I was searching for, nor did I wish to write it. I put the pages down beside Sara's diary. I could only think of giving both to Tania. I sat down to wait for her.

Those bare feet made no noise. I had no idea she was there until I turned my head and saw her looking at my packed bags. Her eyes were heavy with accusation.

I said, 'I'm only leaving the house, Tania. Nothing else.'

But she could see only one thing. 'You're leaving.'

'Listen to me!' I said. 'I found the man that Sara loved. He loved her truly. It wasn't Damon. His name is Lisbon. The man who played the violin on the record. He inherited this house. And when he came here he met her and fell in love.'

'She never betrayed her friend with Damon.' It was a statement. Tania had never believed for even one second that she had.

'No,' I said. 'She never betrayed her friend. I should have believed you. I broke my promise. Forgive me.'

Tania's eyes didn't move from my face. 'Her wish came true? She's happy with this other man?'

It was a question I didn't want to answer. 'She's not with him. He offered to marry her. He waited for her to come to him, but she never did.'

'Why?'

'Because she didn't believe love could be for her. She didn't even give it a chance.' Tania took a step backwards into the shadows.

I felt a surge of hopeless anger. 'You should have made that wish! A wish can't come true if you don't make it.'

My words never gave those bare feet pause. She continued to walk away. I followed her through the dark corridor. Tania paused at the well. Three more steps and I knew she would be gone.

'Make the wish, Tania!'

Tania was a shadow in the dark. I could not see her eyes. Did her hands stir into movement? Quietly, she said, 'My bucket is in your well. I think you should return it to me before you go.'

Three light steps, three beats of a heart, and she was gone.

I was running out of time. The only bus to Panjim would leave soon. But I could not leave without returning her possession.

I fashioned a hook from a bent coat hanger. A sliver of the bucket was visible in the well, like a half-moon. I managed to snag the handle, but the movement tilted the bucket so that the last inch filled up. It plummeted to the bottom and the rope unreeled from my hand. The thud and scrape of finding bottom travelled up the rope to my arm. I dared not move, afraid that the bucket would roll free of its precarious mooring.

Holding my breath, I looped the rope over the pulley and began to draw it in. The pulley screamed unbearably in my ear. I felt the heft of its weight as the bucket pulled out of the water. I was so relieved to have it safe, that it was a moment before I realised there was something more than muddy water in it. A white fish gleamed there. I dipped my hand towards it, and it came away holding a long thin bone. I had learned its name years ago, in a heavy tome on biology. I recognised it from a diagram that had been etched on yellowing paper. It was the radius, named for the Latin word for 'ray', one of two complementary bones found in the human forearm.

The Lonely Bones

Whose bones are these that have lain so long in the well? Gazing up at the far stars in twilight and deep night. Lain deep and quiet in silent water. Five seasons did the leaves drift off the trees. Five times did the rain fall down the throat of the well. Still, the bones lay dreaming. What did they dream of—these bones, as they lay in still water? They dreamed of their name. They hummed a song in the water, singing their name. They sang of grass they had once walked on, sun that had shone upon them. Solitary in still water, they crooned a litany of their memories lest they forget them.

In the first year, the water tasted of blood. In the second year it tasted of corruption. In the third year it tasted of distant seas and dark tides. In the fourth year it tasted of leaves and musk. And, at last, the water became sweet.

All the dross melted off them, the bones lay washed clean. They lay now in sweet water.

Whose bones are these that have lain so long in starlight in still water? What name is it they hum to themselves? Do they remember?

The kitchen floor was awash in water. There was a man in the well who sent up buckets that disgorged silt and slime and dull slivers of bone onto the floor. The pulley groaned and gave a mourning wail with each load.

The bones were white and clean. Two policemen assembled them on an old sheet, slowly fitting together knuckle bones and tibia and phalanges and carpals.

'Sara,' said the inspector, 'after all these years.'

'Why is she in the well?' I asked.

'For the usual reason that girls throw themselves into wells. She must have been pregnant.'

'Can you tell that from the bones?'

'No. But it's quite a favourite way to commit suicide around here.'

The inspector regarded the bones dispassionately. He had fetched quite a few desperate girls out of wells in his time. Some looking like they were asleep and dreaming, others when they had begun to return to liquid, a few dissolved into mud and mire. At least five years in the well had leached the smell out of this water and these bones.

The right hand was almost intact. The left hand, missing. The long curve of the spine was a broken trail, gapped and incomplete. The left foot was a scatter of fractured lines. The ribs were a tarnished cage breached in a dozen places. Scatters of bones were still being sorted, measured, slotted into place.

My eyes were drawn back again and again to the careful assembly. One more time, Sara was a puzzle to which the pieces must be assembled.

The news goes out swiftly into the village. It finds Lorso, on his knees in the taverna, picking up a scatter of fallen coins. It comes in urgent tones to the convent and disturbs Sister Ursula at her dinner. She pushes aside the second helping of pudding she was considering.

It finds Lisbon on the beach, sheltering in the lee of some fishing boats. It whispers up to him in an overheard conversation and is like a spear to the heart. He stumbles out into the pelting rain.

It knocks at Damon's door as he supervises the removal of books from the spot in his study where rain has found a breach in the ancient roof. He walks out into the dusk, leaving the door to slam back and forth in the wind.

It interrupts Dona Alcina in the middle of the private confession she makes to the priest every Friday. It terminates this most sacred of rites and brings the priest hurriedly out of the confessional box. But first, he asks Dona Alcina if there is anything else she wishes to confess, and she denies it.

By the time darkness has fallen, it is all over the village in whispers, conversations, shouts and speculations.

Evening calm came late to the house. The police finally left with instructions that I was not to leave the place while the investigation was on. The inspector said he would speak to Lisbon about it himself. The kitchen was still wet. The pulley at last silent.

I had my house again. I began to unpack. But, midway through, I stopped and picked up the diary. I searched its pages again and again trying to make sense of this unexpected ending. How had Sara come to this?

I raised my eyes from the pages and Tania stood in the doorway watching me. She had crept upon me unheard, as always.

'Did you hear?' I asked.

She nodded. I could see the gleam of tears in her eyes. 'What are you doing?'

'Searching. For Sara. Trying to understand why she did it. She had it all. She had love. And she chose to throw herself into a well.' I turned the pages, flipping blindly through them, letting them cascade from my hands to the floor. 'Why? I don't understand why.' The pages lay on the floor, mute.

Tania didn't move. Very softly, she asked a question. 'Has anyone told Alice?'

A Chapter of Revelations

The night was long, from the first call of the nightjar to the first light in the sky. My typewriter was metronome to the first watch. I typed letter after letter and flung them all on the floor. The second watch I marked with steady pace upon the floor. Still, no words came to me fit to break the news to a child, that she had waited five years in vain. The third watch was the longest and was frayed by rain and wind. The breeze took all the crumpled bits of paper that littered the floor and made playthings of them. All my fumbling explanations drifted whispering away into the house and were lost. The fourth watch ended with the wisps of smoky dawn on the horizon. With the light I put away any thought of writing a letter. For some duties, words alone are not enough.

Wind and rain had stripped the gulmohar trees, and I stepped out of the house on to a carpet of red blossoms. A tree had fallen across the path and I had to pick my way through the splayed branches. Wet leaves flapped past on the wind. Scattered and random rain spat down on me.

Alice was tucked into her little niche, folding a piece of paper carefully into a boat. She floated it into a large puddle, calling out to me, 'Do you know how to make boats? We can have a race.'

I stopped in front of her. 'I have to tell you something, Alice.'

Her face immediately lit up. 'You found her? You found Sara?'

I shook my head. 'There's something you should know. The letter that you got from your sister—didn't you wonder how that letter got in the wall?'

Alice turned the thought over in her mind. 'She must have come and put it there.'

I unburdened the guilt I had carried for days. 'No, Alice. I did.'

It only served to increase Alice's puzzlement. 'You met my sister? She gave it to you?'

'No, Alice. I wrote that letter. Your sister didn't. I made it up.'

Alice looked at me in dismay. 'Made it up? Why?'

'I just thought it would make your waiting easier.'

Alice came closer and stared up into my face intently. 'She is coming back, isn't she?'

I shook my head. 'No, she isn't. Alice—'

Betrayal made Alice's face crumple and her lips tremble. Anger held back the tears. The anger was on her sister's behalf. 'She will! She *promised*! Don't call my sister a liar! She's not a liar! I know what it is. You've been talking to people. They've been saying bad things about her. But they're wrong. My sister is not bad!'

I said, 'I know that. I know she was never bad. But she's not coming back. Alice, listen to me. She is not coming back!'

Alice's voice shrank and became small with dread. 'Why?'

I said it baldly—'She's dead.' Alice shook her head in quick denial. 'She's dead, Alice. She died five years ago.'

Alice dragged the hair from her face. Puzzled, she leaned close to me and whispered, 'But if she's dead—why isn't she here, with me?'

I didn't understand at all. Shaking her head, Alice backed into the niche she always hid in. And then there was nothing there.

A flurry of wind tore all the scraps of paper from the wall and they whirled about my head. The puddle held only a glimpse of dark sky. A breeze shivered the reflection and scattered it. The niche was empty.

There is a ghost in this story after all.

A Prayer for the Departed

I fell into a fevered sleep and understood that I was dreaming.

In my dream I went wandering through the house, opening doors. With each door that I opened, I set voices free. Long, sad voices that came flowing out of the opening doors, joining into one stream of song. I could not understand the words, but I understood that the slow, swelling songs were lamentation for things lost.

Frantic in my search, I opened door after door and the chorus swelled, calling through the darkness for things that were gone long ago and far away. In the voices I heard fathers, brothers, sisters—all gone. Through the doors I saw vast seas of golden grass, strange trees and villages under a lean sky. An entire land lost and gone. The voices keened around me, wailing for things that were no more.

Someone took my hand, and I saw that it was Alice. I held tight on to her hand for comfort as I stood waist-deep in the singing streams of loss and sorrow. I did not know how many doors I would have to open before I found Sara.

Alice tugged herself free. She began to comb her hair with a comb of mother-of-pearl. She spoke as she stroked it through her hair. Her voice came to me through the dark veils of the mourning songs. 'Who,' she asked, 'is in the coffin?'

A bell began to toll. Its slow, mournful voice was calling the faithful to pray for the departed. Almost the entire village had heeded the call. Unusual events were few and far between, and everyone was determined not to miss a minute of the current sensation. The priest's voice echoed in the church as he said the last rites for the dead.

'De profundus clamavi ad te Domine—Domine exaudi vocem meam.' *Out of the depths I have cried to thee, O Lord! Lord, hear my voice.*

I arrived at the door of the church, out of breath and with a stitch in my side from running all the way.

'Si iniquitates observaveris Domine—Domine quis sustinebit?' *If thou O Lord will mark iniquities—Lord, then, who will stand?*

'*Stop*!' I shouted. 'That's not Sara!'

The priest froze mid-benediction. Faces turned towards me. I saw outrage, bewilderment, blankness. A few familiar faces floated out of the crowd. The pale face of Lisbon shone in its grief through the crowd. In the special pew, marked with a family crest, the dark brow of Damon glowered at me. The simple bewilderment of Lorso stared at me from the last pew.

There was one more mourner whose presence no one had noticed. The inspector rose from his unobtrusive place in the shadows.

The priest recovered his sagging jaw and thundered, 'How dare you interrupt a sacred ceremony? Have you no respect for the dead?'

The wrath of God's representative on earth fell mightily about my ears, but I stuck to my newfound creed. 'That's not Sara.'

The inspector stepped up behind me and took a firm grip on my elbow. The priest came down from the altar in high outrage. 'Really! This is ridiculous. You disturb a sacred ceremony. Just walk in and—'

'I had to. That's not Sara. She is still alive.'

'My dear man, we are burying the dead. This is not the time to come bursting in here with some insane story,' said the priest. 'It's blasphemy to interrupt!'

'You're burying the wrong girl.'

Around us there were whispers, craning necks, a great susurrus of conjecture and excitement.

The inspector didn't let go of the firm grip on my arm. 'There are no other girls missing.'

'That is not Sara.'

The priest was incredulous. 'I've never come across anything like this in my life! It is outrageous! The archbishop shall hear of this!'

I looked around to try and find support and found myself facing the wordless speculation of the other mourners. Every face was turned to me. Every eye riveted. Lisbon was white in the face. Damon darkly silent. Wearily and stubbornly I said, 'That's not Sara.'

'All right,' said the inspector, 'that's enough. Time we got you out of here.' The grip was now inexorable and was turning me to head for the door. I saw a grey habit in the pews.

'Sister Ursula?'

The dour-looking nun was startled. 'Yes?'

'How long was Sara's hair?'

'Waist-length. She insisted on keeping it long. What is this about?'

A hank of hair and a huddle of bones lay in the coffin. The hair was still partially attached to the skull. It was matted and long. Hair survives long years under water.

'That's not Sara. That is not her hair.'

'What *is* this about Sara's hair?' asked the bewildered nun.

'I have it,' I said.

I fumbled in my pocket and held out the long plait. It slid through my fingers and slithered to the floor. A ring of bewildered faces stared down at it.

There was the sudden sound of bare feet running for the door. The inspector was quick for someone his size. He fielded Lorso before he could make it.

I slid into a pew and sat down. I was too weary to stand anymore. The keening voices had stayed in my head, and I still carried the grief they filled me with.

Lorso was dragged back into the church despite the priest's protests. The inspector dropped him in a pew and stood over him.

The priest was getting ready for a second round of displaying the displeasure of His representatives here on earth, when the inspector decided differently. He raised his voice and said—'Clear the church. There will be no burial today.'

A great sigh of disappointment echoed around the church. Nobody moved. The priest nodded at the sacristan who began to herd people towards the door. The church-goers left reluctantly, craning their necks to get a last glimpse of whatever they could. The taverna regulars lingered until the priest cleared his throat and glared meaningfully. The shuffling and muttering slowly receded and we were alone. Lisbon, Damon and the nun stayed on.

The inspector cleared his throat and asked Lorso, 'So—what do you know about this hair?'

Lorso shrank from the eyes fixed on him. He shook his head vehemently in denial. But the dash for freedom had damned him. The inspector grabbed him by his vest and slammed him against a pew. 'Speak up or I'll—'

'Remember where you are, Inspector!' thundered the priest.

The inspector quickly dropped his tone. 'Tell me!' he said, with far less effect. Lorso cringed, his arms paddling the air in panic.

Sister Ursula stepped into the breach. 'Speak up, Lawrence, like I taught you. Calm down. Use your hands.' They were an odd couple. His trembling, passionate hands shaping answers, and her clipped nun's voice assuming the imperative, 'I'.

'It's Sara's hair. I cut it off. But I did nothing to Sara.'

'Get him to tell us the whole story,' said the inspector.

The hands marked denial, trembled in explanation. 'I followed her because I loved her. On the night she disappeared I found her in the ruins. I had gone to visit the angel'—there was a slight delay while the interjection of the angel was satisfactorily explained—'I was in the ruins late. She came there, crying. She said she had to go away, because she had been thrown out of the Big House.'

The angel is serene in the moonlight. The girl who crouches at its feet weeps helplessly. She does not know what to do or where to go. She has no home. No one of her own.

The hands were eloquent in their urging. 'I pleaded with her not to go. To stay. To marry me.' The hands wove a dozen different pleas, each easing into the sign 'stay' again and again.

'She wouldn't listen. She tried to run away. Then I got angry. I wasn't thinking right. I had my koita from cutting rice in the fields all day.' One hand snaked out and grasped. The other arced through the air.

The crescent flashes in the moonlight. The girl twists and turns. Then she is free and running. Lorso is left holding a length of braided hair. He howls his inarticulate rage and grief but she has gone swiftly into the dark night. The angel continues serene in the moonlight.

There was silence in the church. A ripple of shock and distaste was widening on the faces turned to him. Lorso's hands began to shape frantic beats of denial.

'I only cut her hair. I didn't harm her. I just cut off her hair. And she ran away. For always.'

'All he did was cut off her hair?' asked the inspector.

Sister Ursula said, 'He says so. Yes.'

'But he meant to kill her.'

Great strangled moans of denial come from Lorso's throat. He shook his head again and again. 'I couldn't kill her. I loved her. I just wanted her to stay, and it went all wrong!'

The inspector said dryly, 'I'll get the truth out of him. You only cut her hair, you—'

'Inspector!' cried the priest. 'You forget where you are!'

The inspector hastily converted his gesture into an awkward sign of the cross.

I spoke into the silence. 'He didn't kill her.'

'How do you know that?' asked the inspector.

'Because she is still alive.'

'And how do you know that?'

I looked at all the faces around me and knew I could not tell them it was because a little girl still waited in the ruins past death for Sara to return.

Sister Ursula broke the silence, asking, 'So, if we believe Lawrence, which poor soul do we have here?' Every head turned to the coffin.

The bones lay in the coffin, inscrutable, holding close the secret of their name.

Alice

The grave was a humble one. A small whitewashed hump at the end of a long row. An equally small wooden cross had '*Alice*' carved on it. Just the single name and nothing else. A small statue of Mater Dolorosa, the Mother of Sorrows, smiled down at the rows of graves that stood lapped by great waves of grass that ran in ripples through their ranks, chased by the wind. The graveyard was enclosed within the grounds of the convent. Sister Ursula had unlocked the gate and let me in reluctantly.

Sister Ursula said, 'I brought Alice to the convent the night she was born. Her mother died giving birth to her. She was a tribal woman. One of those that come up from the south hoping to earn money here. A troupe of them passed through the village and left the mother behind. The woman was in labour. Perhaps they knew she was going to die and left her to her fate. From what I can gather, Sara was taken along by the rest of the group but ran away and found her way back to her dying mother and her infant sibling. The convent adopted them. I made Christians of the two children. I taught them to pray.'

Regard, then, Sara upon her knees. She prays to The Mother, remembering her own.

Holy Mary, Mother of God. Mystic Rose. Pillar of Ivory. Column of Gold. Help of Sinners. Pray for us.

There is a beast in the woods, howling, shrieking. Its agony cuts through the forest. She takes a deep breath and runs towards the howls. She has walked three miles in the darkness to find her way back here. When the caravan halted for the night, she had slipped away from the only people she had ever known and set off into the darkness.

Holy Mary, Mother of God. Anchor of the Faithful. Pray for us.

The beast lies on its back. It has clawed a shattered circle around it in its agony. It raises its head and howls as pain tears into its belly again. Pain has been slashing at it, worrying at it for the last four hours.

She steps into the circle, but the beast cannot recognise her, although she screams its name again and again. Something lies between the beast's legs. It gasps and moves blindly, mewling.

She backs away. She runs as fast as she can on torn and battered feet.

The bell at the convent door is loud in the silent night. The shrieks of the child at the door bring a crowd of nuns running.

Holy Mary, Immaculate Virgin. Pray for us sinners.

The howls have ceased and she blunders through the wood, running ahead of the nuns, fear sharp in her heart that she will never find her way back. Scratched and torn and frantic, she stumbles to the place where she left the beast.

The howls have become whimpers. The child kneels beside the beast. It is blind and cannot see her. The beast snarls but the breath is going out of it.

Now and at the hour of our death.

The blind beast scents the air. Turns a questing head towards the little girl. The eyes come back from far away and see her. The beast vanishes and once again it is her mother looking at her with the eyes that she loves so well. Her voice is torn into shreds and she can only whisper. She dies with Sara's real name upon her lips.

The girl puts her arms around her mother and burrows fiercely into her side. This is how the nuns find her a few minutes later when they come blundering into the clearing. When they try to take her from her mother she bites and screams and kicks like a little beast herself. One nun comes forward and slaps the hysterical child. She snarls and spits in her face.

It is a moment Sister Ursula will not forget, standing there with the spittle of some beggar brat running down her face. In that moment she has the measure of the beast.

Amen

Sara climbs into bed. She has buried these memories like she has buried her name. Alone in the dark she takes them out and turns them over and over in a litany of remembrance. She whispers to herself her own, her very own secret birth name. Her mother gave it to her. It is the name of the goddess of wisdom. Swan of purity.

Fortunate one. Watchful one. She who created words. Sweet of speech. Worthy of salutation. Saraswati.

Sister Ursula said, 'I chose their names—Sara and Alice.' The name on the grave was neatly printed. It was four years since Alice died. 'Sara at that time was seven. Alice newly born. We had never had an infant in our care before.'

Some of the nuns are of the opinion that they should let the infant die. It will go in all its innocence straight to Heaven. But Sister Gerta ascends from the kitchen. Her arms still hold the memory of the last of her many brothers and sisters that she rocked to sleep. She organises a bottle and stays up nights feeding the child carefully boiled milk.

Sister Gerta is the cook and, in her absence, the refectory is reduced to chaos, and the nuns pull long faces over unappetising meals. They grow lean and hungry, but the child grows fat and content. She is fed the finest that the larder has to offer. Woe betide any nun who dares to chastise the toddler. Her breakfast eggs will be mysteriously over-salted and her portion of pudding exceptionally small.

The nuns are having their share of trouble with the elder sister. Nothing can induce her to keep her shoes on her feet. And nothing can keep her away from her little sister. No sooner does a nun turn her back for an instant, than Sara is missing from class. Her shoes will be in the corridor, or just outside the window, and Sara will be running, on light feet, to Alice's side. She is caned regularly, and spends entire days with the shoes balanced on her head. But given the slightest opportunity, her feet unshackle themselves, sprout wings and are gone to her sister's cot.

When Alice is three she wakes one night burning with fever. Sister Gerta gives Sara a chair in the infirmary and she sits there for three days and nights. Sister Gerta soothes the child, gives her medicine, prays for her. Through the dark nights the two of them watch the little girl as she spins and floats further away from them on a burning tide. On the third night, Sara can bear it no more and begins screaming her name again and again. Alice hears her and fights the tide that is carrying her into the night. She returns.

Alice lives, but the fever has withered her right leg. The last thing Sister Gerta has done for Alice is give her back her life. She is transferred soon afterwards and Alice loses the protector who defended her as fiercely as a mother.

The other nuns have no idea what to do with the toddler. They take to locking her in the empty sewing room. It is far away enough for her wails not to disturb their matins. Sister Ursula decides that this is her one chance to break Sara in. She tells her she will not be allowed to see her sister until her love for Jesus proves satisfactory. Squads of nuns in telepathic coordination hedge off Sara at every attempt she makes to get to her sister. Despairing, Sara decides to give Jesus a try and writes him long misspelt letters, telling him about her sister and begging his intercession. These are dropped into the collection box at church and, finally, the priest comes to see Mother Superior and lays the crumpled notes in rows on the table.

Mother Superior buys peace and suggests that they let Sara babysit her sister. Sara loves Jesus in one joyous bound. Her shoes stay on her feet for months, and she does nothing whatsoever to bring the wrath of authority down on her head.

Alice learns appeasement much earlier in life than her elder sister does. She sits quietly under Sara's desk in class, holding on to one foot. Sometimes, she curls up and sleeps at her feet like a little puppy. At all other times she is carried around on Sara's hip like an extension that has grown there, a Siamese twin. At night she sleeps in Sara's bed and her bed-wetting ceases. Sara takes the withered little foot in her hand and kisses it again and again and again. She will not let Alice out of her sight for a minute. They are never seen apart.

This state of happiness lasts for two whole years. Then Mother Superior is transferred. No one else takes her place for some years. Sister Ursula becomes the superior in everything but name. She decrees that Alice is five now and old enough to tie her own shoelaces. She no longer needs to be babysat. All Alice's privileges are revoked and she is sent to the junior dorm.

On the advice of the doctor, she is fitted with a brace. It aches and chafes her baby skin till it bleeds. But five-year-old Alice will not cry. She thinks if she bears it all and prays a lot, then her sister will be given back to her.

'Two sisters, so completely different. One a good, biddable child. And the other—' Sister Ursula compressed her lips as if Sara was a bad taste in her mouth.

'What was wrong with Sara?' I asked, anger rising in me.

'She was just—*bad*. That girl was a liar. There were just so many incidents … I tried my best, but …'

'Maybe you should have left her alone.'

'Alone?' said Sister Ursula. 'It is my duty to bring these children to the Lord.'

'Punishing them repeatedly is perhaps not a good demonstration of the love of the Lord.'

'She deserved to be punished.'

'And maybe she deserved love as well. Isn't it in the Bible somewhere—love one another as I have loved you?'

'I know what kind of love that girl went looking for!' spat Sister Ursula.

'It is not a sin to be loved by a man. And not all men are beasts.'

I was so angry that I forgot she was a nun and would have said several things more. But Sister Ursula tightened her thin lips again, hastily turned and began to walk away.

I ran after her and stood athwart the gate that led out of the cemetery. 'Tell me how Alice died.'

Sister Ursula told me, coldly and cruelly. 'She died a year after her sister disappeared. Despite several warnings, she used to run away every afternoon to the ruins to wait for Sara. One day she got caught in a thunderstorm and got pneumonia. She was delirious. In her delirium she wanted to go to her sister. We tied her to the bed. I will never know how she got free. When I came to give her a midnight dose of medicine, the bed was empty. We found her in the ruins. She was quite cold.'

The rain is cold, the drops spattering against the window. A woman rain, weeping through the night.

The sick child dreams of comfort. Time and again she rises from her bed, determined that she will go to her sister. Finally, they bring petticoat-strings and bind her to the bed. Tethered and helpless, still she dreams of Sara singing, covering her withered foot with kisses. Her desire picks the knots free. It leads her burning, burning, out of the window and into the night

The searching torches go fumbling through the ruins. The nuns' voices are blown about by wind and rain. The white squares of paper in the wall are markers that beckon them to another crumpled patch of white.

A little child, curled head to knees, is lying in the niche in the wall. Curled tight into herself, but cold nevertheless. A child in her nightgown, one leg banded in iron. Curled tight and waiting. Cold. Quite cold.

An Angel Weeps

I walked back towards the house in the twilight, a light rain falling at my back, the birds winging their way home overhead. My heart was heavy with the thought of Alice, alone and cold in the rain.

In the ruins I stopped by the wall that had once been filled with the notes that Alice had written. The little niche that she had curled into was empty. But it was decorated with living gems. A handful of fireflies had made it into a box filled with treasure. I looked around. The damp night was spangled with their erratic light. They were everywhere, sparking sudden in the darkness. Whole trees were filled with hundreds of them blinking on and off in unison. I switched off my torch and stood there looking at the bejewelled darkness.

The statue of the angel caught my eye. Fireflies had made it into a thing of beauty, sprinkling it with cold fire. I walked over to it and placed my hand upon the base. 'I don't know where you are,' I said. 'I wish I could find you. I want to keep my promise to Alice. She loves you very much. She misses you even though she is gone.'

The statue trembled as if it had heard me. I was so startled that I froze. Then it was falling towards me, a white blur in the night. I leapt backwards. I was saved by a stumble upon landing that flung me sideways. I fell, and the statue fell beside me, shattering into pieces. Shards of white marble scattered into the night. I felt them spatter against me. One hit my head and set it ringing.

I shoved myself back to my feet. An explosion of broken marble lay around me. I looked hastily around for the cause of the fall, but there was no one there.

The angel's head had rolled and lay against my foot. I looked down at it. A single dark teardrop slid down the angel's face. It was a moment before I realised it was blood. My blood. I fumbled back my torn sleeve and saw a long gash that ran down my arm to my hand. Blood dripped from my fingers and fell like dark tears upon the angel's face. A sharp-edged fragment of marble had cut me without my knowing it.

I ran. I ran through the ruins and back to the house. If I hurried, I thought, I might make it to the bus to Panjim. I had to get to a doctor.

I ripped the sheet from the bed. I shredded it into strips and tied them with trembling hands over the cut. I tied them so tight, I had no feeling left in my arm. Awkward in my left-handed state, I dragged out the trunk and began to fling things into it. My mind was scarcely working. Randomly, I grabbed anything that came to hand. I slammed the lid of the trunk shut and realised that I would never be able to carry it one-armed down to the bus stop. With the remnants of the sheet I began to tie together a bundle.

I looked up to find Tania staring at me in puzzlement. 'Why are you packing? Where are you going?'

'Panjim. If I hurry, I will catch the last bus to Panjim.'

Tania asked, 'Why? What happened?'

I said, 'I've been cut. I'm bleeding.'

'Show me,' said Tania. I held out my arm. It was an alien limb that I could no longer feel. It was made of ice, except where the blood fell burning from it.

'It's just a cut,' she said. 'Are you going to leave just because of that?'

'Is there a doctor in the village?' I asked in turn.

'No,' said Tania. 'But we could bind that up ourselves.'

'You don't understand,' I said. 'It's the blood. I cannot stay.' I tried to draw the knots on my little bundle tight.

'You just keep saying that you won't really leave. But you are!'

'*You don't understand*!' I shouted.

My words drove Tania backwards. It was as if I had slapped her.

'Please,' I begged. 'You don't understand. I don't have time.'

Tania dragged a hand across her eyes. Then she walked away into the darkness.

I could not follow her. There was no time. I looked at the little clock that stood on my desk and all my hope dribbled away. It was too late. I had run out of time entirely. The last bus was gone.

I tried to figure out what I should do. I should go down to the village, I told myself. Try and find someone to help me. Instead, I sat down, losing my orientation, unclear what it was I was so intent on doing.

It was an hour later when she returned. I was sitting on the floor of the bedroom, unmoving, unable to even frame a notion of what I should do. She knelt beside me and whispered, 'I'm sorry, I didn't mean to be unkind.'

Her hand touched the floor and she realised it was wet. Her hand came away slick with blood. She turned horrified eyes on me.

'Haemophilia,' I said.

Haemophilia. I remember turning the word over and over as a child. It sounds like it should be the name of a fabulous jewel, an ancient bird, the palace of an eastern king. Instead, it names the taint in my blood that makes it eager to run free of my veins.

'It is too late now,' I whispered. The last bus for Panjim has left, and there is no doctor in the village. There is nowhere to go, no hope of help. We will have to wait the night through. Tania began to pray.

Time and again I replaced the bandages, tying them closer and closer each time, clawing at the knots with teeth and fingers to draw them just one bit tighter. Still, the crimson seeped swiftly through the cloth, and slow worms of blood crawled down my arm to drip on the floor.

It became too much trouble to stay upright. My eyes began to close.

'You must stay awake!' cried Tania. 'You have to. Talk to me!'

And so, with a voice that stumbled and whispered and wandered, I told her the story of my traitorous blood.

Haemophilia is the cage in which my life has been confined. Like a prince bound under a curse, I spent my childhood locked in a tower in a palace. The palace stood in the leafy lanes of Malabar Hill in Bombay. The tower room was perfectly round and was reached by an ornate staircase wrought of iron. The window framed a gulmohar, a jacaranda filled with crows, and a glorious laburnum. My first few years were spent entirely in the tower, attended upon by a regiment of servants and doctors. The garden was only to look upon. The grass seemed to be there chiefly to occupy three gardeners. I never dreamt of running upon it. I ran nowhere. My ayah led me everywhere by a finger.

The slightest bump was a calamity. A fall was a tragedy of vast dimensions, in which servants were dismissed, doctors summoned and special prayers read at the fire temple. I would watch the deep purple bruises unfurling under my skin with interest. It was the blood I was taught to be afraid of. Its treachery was immense. Given the slightest egress, it would flow copiously. Doctors would have to be called in to construct traps and dams to hold it, and still the outcome would be unsure. I wondered what would happen if it all ran out of me. My mother slapped me when I asked her.

The palpable fear of my mother and the army of servants sank deep into me and I became a careful child. One who never ran anywhere and who came down the stairs holding on to the banisters.

With little to do, rarely allowed out of the house, never allowed to play, I read. Reading seemed to be the only activity that my mother thought safe. At the age of four I tried to explain to my ayah the idea of Ahura Mazda. My proud father hired a university man to teach me.

Until the age of six, I visited my father every afternoon. I timed my arrival with that of his tea tray so that I could get all the biscuits. I remember my last visit well.

My father was reclining in his armchair, hands folded neatly in his lap. I climbed into a chair and busied myself with the biscuits. My father spoke to me. We always conversed like gentlemen, but today I could not follow what it was he was saying so wearily to me.

'I have tried very hard to do it, but it is a difficult thing, this business of living. I find that I lack the courage for it. I feel myself very keenly to be alone. No discredit to your mother. She has done the best that she can.'

I took a chocolate biscuit from the tray and wished there were more. My father continued with his careful, courteous conversation. 'I apologise. I shall not be here to teach you the things that are really important. Perhaps it is best, I know so little after all. All of it is other people's truths, other people's certainties. I have no truths of my own. There is only one thing I am certain of. That I know for myself.'

He leaned forward and compelled my attention. 'We do not choose to love. Love comes to us. We can only be grateful that it chose us.'

My father waited until I had finished all the biscuits before he said, 'Perhaps you should go now. I am growing cold and tired.' It struck me as I jumped off the chair that I had never seen my father dressed in red before.

Outside in the corridor, the ayah pounced on me and demanded an explanation for the blood that edged my cuffs. I was searched, my mother almost hysterical as she investigated me again and again, unable to find the source. The doctor had been called before they realised that one explanation could be that the blood was not mine at all. The doctor arrived to find he had been called to the wrong person and far too late.

I heard rumours in later years. Parsees never married anyone but Parsees. My father had contracted an unsuitable passion, unacceptable to his class or religion. The whispers said that she was a servant girl.

In my mother's later obsessive search for a perfect match for me, I recognised that there could never be an unsuitable passion for me. My mother would never survive a second such betrayal. I resolved to be a good son, and my resolve remained untried. My father's truth had remained another man's certainty for all these years.

I grew up in the tower, surrounded by books. Books were my friends, my solace, my refuge, my delight. Slowly, an ambition grew to create worlds of my own. It was stoked by my tutor who thought most highly of my abilities. It was he who first suggested that I consider a serious pursuit of literature. When I announced that I wanted to go away to write, my mother immediately took up arms against the idea. The battle raged for days. I ended it eventually, with a knife held against my wrist.

Our Goan cook, Maria, suggested a better solution. Her cousin and his wife were caretakers of a wonderful house in Goa. I could go there and they could look after my every need. Little did she know that her cousin had degenerated into permanent drunkenness and the house was a neglected ruin. When I discovered these developments on arrival, they suited me fine. To be alone, without a single person caring what I did! It had been a fantasy of mine from childhood.

I felt, at last, that I was free. Free to write. I was sure I would find a great subject. Write a great novel. Emerge from my retreat remade as a man.

The journey I embarked upon with such eagerness has lost its way in the wilderness. All my sureties have foundered one by one. And my traitor blood has brought me low at last. All through the night, it trickles through the egress that it has found.

I must keep awake. I must. But I am so tired. If only I wasn't so weary. I must close my eyes for a moment.

'Stay awake!' cries Tania in distress. 'Tell me another story!'

I tell her the story I have stumbled upon. The one I have not dared tell anyone yet. The story of a little girl who waits in the ruins for her sister to return to her, even in death. In the darkness, drifting towards death myself, I tell her my ghost story, hoping she will believe it, though she has made no promise to do so.

Tania gives me her belief. All she asks is, 'Alice is dead? And she is still waiting?' I can hear the tears in her voice.

'Sara made her a promise. And her love for her sister has lasted when all else has gone.' I turn my head with difficulty. I can barely keep my eyes open. My words are heavy on my lips. 'If tonight I die—'

'Don't say that!' cries Tania, and there are tears on her cheeks now.

I whisper, 'You must know that it will last. Even when I am gone.'

'What will?' she whispers back.

I close my eyes as I say the words. I do not know if I say them aloud because I am drifting away. But I know they are the truth.

'My love for you.'

Dawn found the two of us fast asleep side by side. Waking, I knew one breath was enough to bring me against Tania's sleeping shoulder. I lay there rapt with wonder as it came to me that I had been made anew. I felt like I was filled with light, a shell so transparent that the morning light shone through me. I carefully unwrapped the bandages and held my hand to the sun. I could see the veins in my right hand, the cut like a dark bridge spanning rivulets and tributaries. The bleeding had stopped.

I turned my newly minted eyes on Tania and she was wrought of gold. I understood that love had come upon me.

Among the row of books lined up on the windowsill is one that is bound in handsome red leather. It is a book of poetry, and the name on the flyleaf is written in an ornate hand: 'Hormaz Fali Irani'. The book falls open at a touch, to the page that I have turned to countless times. A wine-dark handprint lies across the words.

The poem is by an American author, Edna St. Vincent Millay. I do not need to read it. I know the words by heart.

> *Love is not all: it is not meat nor drink*
> *Nor slumber nor a roof against the rain;*
> *Nor yet a floating spar to men that sink*
> *And rise and sink and rise and sink again;*
> *Love cannot fill the thickened lung with breath,*
> *Nor clean the blood, nor set the fractured bone;*
> *Yet many a man is making friends with death*
> *Even as I speak, for lack of love alone.*
> *It may well be that in a difficult hour,*
> *Pinned down by pain and moaning for release,*
> *Or nagged by want past resolution's power,*
> *I might be driven to sell your love for peace,*
> *Or trade the memory of this night for food.*
> *It well may be. I do not think I would.*

I lay there, watching Tania sleep. Her eyes opened and she looked back at me. We lay there, our eyes upon each other, neither speaking. I did not know if I had said the words that had changed my world to her or not. I wanted to.

I broke the silence. 'Tania—'

'No,' she whispered. 'Don't say the words. Don't!'

'Make the wish in the well,' I whispered. 'Please. Believe in love.'

Tania lowered her eyes and turned away. 'Please,' I whispered.

Tania sat up abruptly, denying me a reply. 'I have to go. I have been gone an entire night! There will be so much trouble!' With those words the moment was broken and the world was back with us.

Tania looked at me anxiously. 'Will you be all right now that the bleeding has stopped?'

I told her I would be.

'Then I'll be going. I'll come back when I can!' She got to her feet and hurried from the room. Her bare feet were light upon the floor and made not a sound.

I wanted to run after her. Call her back. Tell her all the things that were running through my veins, tumbling through my head. But getting to my feet was impossible. I could barely move my head to watch those feet running away from me. I closed my eyes and drifted away.

When I woke, a full moon was in the sky. I had slept through the day. I wrote in the patch of moonlight cast on the table. I moved my chair and my writing followed the slow slide of the moon across the sky.

What is this love that is the secret wish in the heart of so many? I have never known it before. A man who died for love told me that you did not choose love. Love chose you.

I walked through the world not knowing that I was unchosen. That I was alone. I was unloved and didn't know its lack, never having known its touch. I was making friends with death, all unknown.

At last, it has pointed an eager finger at me. It is an unsuitable passion. Incongruous and unthinkable entirely. But I have been chosen, having no choice myself.

How sweet it is.

The smoke of dawn light was fuming on the horizon when I finished writing. The first birdcalls were threading the air. The morning was fresh and tender. I knew what I had to do. I gathered together the pages that told the story of Sara and Alice, the two sisters who could never be parted. Then I made my way down to the ruins.

I knelt beside the niche. The wall above was clear, unflagged by any papers. I took the white sheets and folded them over and over again and tucked them into the crevices. The white squares were new-minted silver in the first light that suffused the sky.

'I will find her,' I said. 'I am making the promise again, Alice. And I will not break it. I will find Sara.'

A Game of Hide and Seek

It has been an uneventful day. If you can count finding that you are unexpectedly in love as uneventful. To me the realisation was so enormous, it lay across my life. There was life before love and life after. I turned over every moment I had spent with Tania again and again, trying to find the roots of it. I had no idea when it had seeded, knowing only that it had grown and twined around my heart. I walked around the house and thought of her and understood that love is mostly uncertainty and great confusion. This is an entirely unsuitable love and there is nothing at all I can do about it.

I wanted to be left alone all day with nothing but the thought of her for company. But the housekeeper came in the afternoon and announced there would be no lunch today, unless I went shopping, because the larder was empty. The thought was absurd. Shopping, of all things! When you have just come back from the brink of death and discovered that you are in love and your life is changed forever!

I also did not wish to leave the house in case Tania came. But the housekeeper gabbled at me so fiercely that I finally fetched the basket and walked down to the village.

I had barely reached the shop, before I wanted to turn and run back just in case she had returned. I have no idea what it was that I hastily filled my basket with, before hurrying back. I had to take a long detour, because I was determined not to walk alone through the ruins. That tremble of the statue under my fingers stayed with me. I was not sure if the statue had fallen by itself, or had been pushed. The thought was a dark stain, soaking into the glow that had suffused my day so far.

I was halfway home when the rain came cascading down. So heavy was the downpour that I wondered if there would be air enough for me to breathe. I had, of course, forgotten my umbrella and my torch. A strange half-darkness fell swiftly and I hurried through the vast expanse of wind-tossed wilderness I had to cross before I got home.

A small pool of wet collected swiftly in my collar. A rivulet ran down each arm. A dozen tiny waterfalls dripped from my eyebrows and obscured my sight. As I blundered through the dark, I looked up at the house. Perhaps Tania was waiting for me. The rain felt suddenly light on my shoulders as I hurried home.

I opened the door to find Tania sitting by the doorway, a faint silhouette in the waning light. Her voice was a thread in the dark. 'I came to see if you were all right, and then it started raining, and I can't go back. Are you all right?'

With difficulty I found the voice and words to reassure her. My heart was thudding and I felt particularly odd. All the while, a small shower dripped from me onto the floor. She exclaimed at my state and urged me towards the bedroom.

I changed my wet clothes in the lamplit bedroom, while Tania waited on the other side of the door.

'Are you sure you are all right?' she asked again. 'Have your bandages got wet?'

I had dropped a button and did not reply immediately.

Her voice came anxiously through the door again. 'Are you all right?!'

I was light-headed with her closeness. A sudden impish urge seized me. I knocked over the footstool by the bed and the clangour was loud in the silence.

On the other side of the door, Tania heard the sound and paused. 'What happened? What is it?'

I held my peace.

'Hello?'

Silence.

I smiled as I imagined her confusion. The silence stretched until I had the sudden thought that she might have left and quickly reached for the handle.

Her voice came through the door, 'You better be dressed. I'm coming in.' The door creaked open to reveal Tania standing there with her hands firmly over her eyes.

I found it hugely funny. 'And if something had happened to me, how would you have seen—with your hands over your eyes?'

Tania was indignant that her concern was so maligned by laughter. She turned and ran into the darkness.

'I was only teasing!' I called, as I started after her with the lamp. The light undulated down the corridor. 'Come back, Tania! I'm sorry!'

Her pique and my remorse resolved themselves into a game of hide-and-seek.

The older odours of damp and decay in the house had become grass and leaves and clean wetness. The rain was ending. The thunder was receding, the flashes of lightning fewer between, the clashes fading further and further away.

I walked in a warm wash of lamplight within which I felt safe. Tania ran ahead, just beyond the circle of light. She was a shadow moving faster than the others, a shape that shifted, a sudden footfall further down the corridor.

'Tania!' I called. 'I'm going to find you!'

In the menagerie my lamp flared and glinted from dozens of glass eyes. In the room lined with photographs of the piano, each picture became a mirror reflecting the lamp, multiplying the circle of light endlessly.

A flicker of lightning rewarded me with a stutter of images as Tania ran down a corridor. She fled from me into the darkness. I followed, bearing light.

In the music room, lightning again flared into a vision of blinding clarity—Tania in the doorway, head turned over her shoulder to watch me. Her hand upon the door frame was so clear, I could even see the white half-moons under her nails.

The two of us played through the house in light and shadow. She fled from me down the meandering halls. And I followed on swift feet in her wake. The house was suddenly a wonderland laid out for us to delight in.

Our game took us to the wind chime hall. All the chimes were in a mad jangle as wind tore through every window.

A flash of lightning showed me a square of white spinning and swooping across the floor. I trapped it with my hand. Lowering the lamp to it, I discovered it was a page dense with Sara's handwriting.

'What is it?' asked Tania, keeping carefully away.

'A page of the diary. It must have got left behind when the wind mixed up the pages.'

'Oh,' said Tania, stepping into the light. 'Read it!'

There were only a few sentences on the page, but they bewildered us.

I deserve love. I made my choice. I opened the door.

I opened the door and waited and waited. No one came. I should have known it could not be true. I should have known it was not for me. Words on bits of paper, and I believed them.

I raised bewildered eyes to Tania. '*Nobody came?* But Lisbon said he did! That he loved her. That he wanted to marry her.'

I found myself confounded. Once again, the story had proved treacherous, rearranging itself to different ends.

'There's more,' I said. The other side of the page was covered with writing. The words were blotted but it was not age that had smeared them, but tears. 'Listen, let me read it—'

'No,' she said. 'I was right, wasn't I? Love is not for the likes of us.'

'Stop it!' I said. 'This has nothing to do with Sara being a servant.'

Tania turned her head away. I knew I had to stay her feet. 'You are not a servant to me. That is not how I think of you. I wish that you could believe in love. Just once! Give it a chance!'

She edged away from me as I spoke. Words found their way to my mouth but fell out hopelessly tangled. 'Love chooses you. Men make friends with death for lack of love alone! Tania, don't leave me!'

A gust of wind blew out the lamp. Yet another shiver of lightning showed Tania running away from me. She fled on feet too swift for me to catch up with, although I ran through all the rooms, calling her name, heart stuttering.

The words on the other side of the page were a cry of sorrow. The words were blotted. Sara's elegant writing had become an anguished scrawl.

Wishes don't come true. It is foolish to throw coins in wells and wish. I opened the door and waited. And nobody came. I stepped into the house. I wandered through all the rooms expecting to see him any moment. But the house was empty. I stood in the room that he has taken for his bedroom. His shirt was flung across the bed. I picked it up and held it and the smell of it made me start to cry. I threw it down and ran out of the house. I don't understand it. He sent me so many notes that I began to hope. But when I opened the door he wasn't there. I am a stupid, foolish girl. I dreamed of things I had no right to dream of. Was he just leading me on? Making fun of me? It was cruel and unkind of him. It hurts. It hurts so much. I shall not wish for love again. It is lies. Lies. All lies.

The Buried Truth

A string of puddles ran down the middle of the path, each holding a snatch of clouds. It felt like I was walking upon the sky, shivering it to bits as I passed. The wind rose as I approached the beach. Two fishing eagles were riding the wind, weaving about in a complicated game with each other, their long screams rising and falling on the wind. They flew in great, graceful entwined arcs. Sometimes, a trick of wind would send them tumbling sideways, turning them into ungainly bundles of feathers that skittered and scrambled across the sky. Then, in a sudden flare, they would spread their wings and resume their elegance.

Another voice screamed on the wind, trailing pain. It was the sound of a violin. I followed it to a tiny chapel on the beach. The sand had risen up its side and half buried it. Standing in the covered porch was Lisbon, playing his grief to the wind and rain.

He had been on the beach from dawn, trying to puzzle out an answer. 'What does it all mean?' he cried, putting aside the violin. 'If the girl in the coffin is not Sara, who is she?'

'Tell me about you and Sara,' I said. 'I think I could find the answer if you told me.'

He gazed out at the dark and swollen sea. 'We met in the wind chime hall, day after day. We loved each other.'

The Gift of Our Lives

The chimes hang in the windows, witnesses to the affair that is played out in the hall. Sometimes they are shaken passionately, sometimes they murmur sweetly, sometimes they are silent, and merely listen.

The two people in the room are making an ancient music of their own. When he lays a chain of kisses down the length of her arm to her fingers, he evokes a diminuendo of sighs. His fingers on her breasts stroke a cadence of small rising sounds from her. He puts his lips to the small of her back and the tempo shifts and she is undone in a scatter of random sounds. Her music swells and intensifies as he eases his mouth down one soft flank. They are locked together in a primal beat that plays the two of them, moving them in a rhythm as old as time. Afterwards, they talk.

'What do you love most about me?'

'Your voice. That is what I first knew about you. And the minute I heard it, I knew you were meant for me.'

'And if I couldn't sing?'

'Then I would ask you to return my love.'

'That I already do.'

I am a fool. I went back the next day. I couldn't stamp out all the hope in my heart. Just the smallest bit remained. So I went back. And I found them.

'What is that?'

'Just one of the chimes the wind has set off.'

'But there is no wind. Someone was at the door. Someone was watching us!'

'There is no one there. Come back to my arms.'

I saw them. It's her. It's her that he holds and kisses. She went to him. And now he loves Nina, not me.

'Does it matter to you who I am?'

'Of course, it does. You are Sara. The girl I love most in the world.'

'I mean, does it matter to you if I am a servant—or something else?'

'When we are married, it is I who shall be your servant. Your every wish my command. Tell me what you wish.'

'I have no wishes. I wished to find love, and that has come true.'

She has taken my name. And my love. And my reputation. They meet every night. And everyone thinks it is me. I get looks, sneers. I walked past the taverna today and they shouted things at me—such things! I cannot look at anyone. They all think that I am bad bad bad. And my heart is breaking. Nina swore to be my friend forever. And she took him.

Often, in the aftermath of their lovemaking, Lisbon is moved to music. He puts his violin to his chin and closes his eyes and fingers whisper music on the strings. The violin croons into the night, its voice trailing down empty corridors, wisping into abandoned rooms. The music finds a secret listener crouched in the dark. She listens silently to the voice of love attained, sweet love satisfied, and her cheeks are wet.

'Don't stop!'

'Now it's your turn. Sing for me.'

'Tomorrow.'

'Why tomorrow?'

'Tomorrow I shall sing a love song for you in front of the whole village. I am to sing tomorrow in the church. They will think that I am singing for them—but my song will be for you. Only you.'

Tomorrow I am to sing at a wedding. I know she means him to believe that it is her singing. But I will sing. Even if my heart breaks, I will sing. I have not forgotten my promise. Even if she has forgotten hers. She was my first and only friend. I will sing.

The voice rises clear and high and sweet from the choir stall. The song is Ruth's song. Though it is traditionally sung at weddings, it was first sung by one woman for another. Ruth, standing waist-deep in the corn, sang it for her, Naomi, who she was afraid to lose.

Wherever you go
I will go
Wherever you live
There will I live
Your people will be my people
And your God will be my God too.

Wherever you die
I will die
And there shall I be buried beside you
We will be together forever
And our love will be the gift of our lives.

The song soars. The voice is like a bird in the sky. It is like moonlight. It is like a river talking to God. It lights those listening back to the moment when love first suffused their world.

A mother of five remembers a night on the seashore and the dark shadow of a boat, secret and cool. A great-grandfather remembers the sunlight at the door of the church and how it turned his wife's hair to amber. Crazy Charlie remembers an afternoon in the summer and how her skin was warm from the sun and salt from the sea. The inspector remembers a face in a window across the road that he watched for years.

Lisbon listens and smiles. His gaze travels across the aisle. It casts a shadow on his happiness to discover that Damon, too, is listening and smiling.

The eagles were gone, the sky darkening. The wind had started to drag at the coconut trees, flailing their wide fronds about. The thin line of the horizon was disappearing into smoky darkness as the rain advanced across the sea.

Lisbon stared at me in disbelief. 'Not Sara? What do you mean the woman I loved was not Sara?'

'You never saw her sing.'

'What do you mean?' asked Lisbon, bewildered. 'Of course, she sang. I heard her. It was her voice I fell in love with.'

I had to shout above sea and wind to be heard. 'You fell in love with Sara's voice. But the woman who came to keep the rendezvous was not Sara—it was Nina.'

'Nina.' I saw his lips shape the name, but the wind snatched the sound away.

'It was Nina you had your affair with. Nina who came to you every night. And Nina who did not dare come to you the last night for fear that you would discover that she was not the singer.'

Lisbon stared blindly at the rolling grey walls of sea water. His lips were moving. I could see them shape 'Sara' again and again. He shook his head in denial.

I leaned close to him. 'Tell me. Would it have made a difference to your love if you had learnt she could not sing?'

'She asked me once, and I told her—yes.' He realised his folly. His face crumpled. 'She believed me. But—but it was not true!' He was frantic in his denial when it was too late. 'I never realised how much I loved her! She should have come to me. She should have told me. It would not have mattered.'

'Perhaps she chose not to come.' I advanced the second theory I had slowly been growing surer about. 'Or perhaps Damon stopped her. She was his fiancée.'

'Damon. Always him.' By a little trick of wind, the whispered words were suddenly thrust in my ear.

I watched him stare out at the roiling sea a long time. The rain was advancing in dark columns that leached the light from the sky.

I saw the new thought take root in Lisbon's mind. I saw his face change as it flowered into radiant hope. 'Then— does this mean she is alive? If it is Sara who is dead, is *she* alive? *My* Sara?' He still could not bring himself to call his love by another name. 'She is alive?'

I suddenly saw what I had led him to. Regret flooded me. 'Listen to me, I haven't finished …'

Lisbon was hasty in his eagerness. 'Don't you understand? The woman I love is still alive! I'll take her from him at any cost. I don't care who she really is. Nothing matters except that she lives! I must go to her.'

I grasped at his arm, but Lisbon's eagerness could bear no restraint. He brushed me aside and ran.

I shouted, 'She's dead! Nina is dead!' But the wind pounced on the words and shredded them. Hope gave Lisbon feet too swift for me to catch up. I followed Lisbon's headlong run down the seashore as best I could.

With foreboding I saw that Lisbon was heading for the path that led through the cemetery. For all that he dashed past him, Crazy Charlie still courteously inclined his umbrella. In the distance I saw a familiar figure in black.

Damon was standing by Nina's grave when Lisbon stopped beside him, almost too breathless to talk. 'Where is she?' he gasped. 'Tell me—*where is she?*'

Damon looked at him with hatred in his eyes. He bit out the word, 'Who?'

Lisbon barely had breath enough to say the word, 'Nina.'

Damon stepped back, his face darkening. Then he shouted, 'You dare to ask me where she is? *You* ask *me?*' Anger surged in him and he reached blindly for Lisbon. I arrived, out of breath, and shoved myself between the two of them. Damon stepped back, then turned on his heel and walked away.

Lisbon was about to follow him, when I put my hand on his arm and pointed. I had no breath to explain and did not think that I would find the words. Lisbon looked down at the tombstone. I watched the hope go out of him.

Nina Casimir
1921–1942
Beloved of her Grandmother and her Fiancé
We wait only till we are reunited with you

It was a blow to the heart. Lisbon dropped to his knees. I said, 'She died a few months after you left.'

Lisbon turned to me, eyes filled with desolation. 'Why do I find death wherever I look for love?' he asked.

I slowly got to my knees as well. I had seen what Lisbon was too grieved to notice. Beside Nina's grave gaped an empty one. The gravedigger's tools still leaned against the rough headstone. It said simply—'Sara'. I realised it was for the service I had so rudely disrupted.

We knelt together in the wet grass. A sudden dark thought possessed me. There were bones that lay unclaimed still in the church. And no name to them. What if the name was Nina Casimir?

I got to my feet. I picked up the pickaxe and stove a blow into the grave.

'What are you doing?' cried Lisbon.

'Sara is not dead,' I said. 'So, who was in the well? And who is in this grave?'

He stared at me, uncomprehending.

'You mixed them up in life. What if they were mixed up in death?' Sara and Nina. Nina and Sara. Friends until death do them part. 'The bones in the church are not Sara's. Could they be Nina's? Then, who is in this grave?'

I gave another blow of the pickaxe. The rain had soaked the mud and it yielded easily.

'Dig!' I said. 'Dig. The answer is in this grave.'

He hesitated. I saw a hardness come into his eyes. He nodded as he made up his mind. He grabbed a spade. Both of us attacked the grave.

A voice quavered behind us. 'I say,' said Crazy Charlie, 'you can't do that! The dead must be left in peace.' We ignored him and dug fiercely.

'I say—stop!' Only the scrape of spade and pickaxe answered him. He went hurrying out of the graveyard.

The sky slowly lowered until the dark stormclouds were just above our heads. I felt the first few raindrops splatter against my skin and stopped. We had been digging steadily for almost an hour. Lisbon was still feverishly wielding his spade. But the cold touch of the rain jarred me into an awareness of my aching back, my raw hands.

'I have to stop,' I said. There were blood blisters on both my hands. I was mindful of the treachery of my blood and dared not do further damage.

'I'm not stopping,' said Lisbon. 'I have to know.' He dug steadily on. It is surprising how much earth two men can move together. As the first few rumbles of thunder went prowling across the sky, Lisbon's spade scraped wood.

I said more insistently, '*Stop*, Lisbon. It's Damon.'

From my position inside the grave, my eyes were level with the grass. In the distance I could see Damon hurrying into the graveyard, with Crazy Charlie trailing behind him.

I turned to Lisbon and said urgently, 'Lisbon! He has a gun.' The rasp and scrape of the spade did not break for a moment. I hesitated, then grabbed my pickaxe and turned back to the grave. There was no time to lose. This was our only chance.

Damon came to the edge of the grave and looked down at us. Then he calmly raised the gun and cocked it. I shouted, 'Do something, Charlie!' even as I dug.

Charlie hesitated, then grabbed Damon's arm. The shot went wide and the gun fell into Sara's empty grave. I barely had time to brace myself before Damon's weight landed on me. As I grappled with him, I realised that the steady scrape of Lisbon's spade had been replaced with echoing blows as Lisbon tried to stave in the lid of the coffin.

Damon heaved me aside and grabbed Lisbon's arm. Lisbon was slick with mud and rain and he got no purchase. The two of them thrashed around. I managed to get my hands to the splintered coffin and wrenched at a spar of wood, wincing at the thought of cuts and hurts but not willing to stop. There was a rending sound and the wood gave way. I stared into the coffin.

Behind me Lisbon said with fierce triumph, 'I knew it! He killed her. He killed her and put her in the well and buried this!'

The coffin was empty. It gaped accusingly in the grave.

A ripple of quiet excitement edges outward from the graveyard. It shivers through the regular crowd at the taverna, stilling their chatter. It slips in whispers through the houses around the square. It even spills through the dining room at the nunnery, reducing everyone to silence. The ripple, now a wave, laps up at the steps of the white house on the hill.

Dona Alcina is in the family chapel, turning over the pearl beads of a rosary when the son she has made her own kneels beside her. He takes her knotted hands in his own. She turns her head. The inspector is standing there with two constables, looking ill at ease.

The taverna seethes with discussion of the find in the graveyard. It abruptly stops as Damon goes past in custody. He has the taverna's breathless attention but gives not the slightest sign of noticing.

Lorso is deep in an exhausted stupor when he hears the cell door open. He struggles to open his swollen eyes and cannot believe their evidence when he sees who is in the cell with him.

The Pride of the Casimirs

The bones wait. They have waited in still water for five years by the light of stars. Dry now, and laid in a coffin, they wait by candlelight.

The vestry door is hastily opened. Footsteps sound loud in the night. Who is it who visits these bones?

Aching knees clench around each step. Hands swollen and warped by arthritis hold the pews for support. On spikes and hooks of pain, the penitent advances down the aisle of the church. Dona Alcina shuffles to the coffin and stands beside it. The waiting bones are washed by lamp- and candlelight. She leans over and tenderly places her lips upon the ivory skull.

The wait is over, they have been claimed. These bones have a name now. Their name is Nina.

And so, we return to the question: where is Sara?

I had never been in such agony. My shoulder had locked; my back gave off sharp, shooting pains each time I moved. But worst of all were my hands. They burnt like they were on fire. But I was grateful. There was no blood. I sat with them soaked in a bowl of water and wished Tania would come so I could tell her what had happened.

Instead, a messenger came. It was a summons. It had come all the way from the white house on the hill. I rose painfully to my feet and went.

The room was dimly lit. Dona Alcina sat in a high-backed chair, staring straight ahead. The shadows claimed everything but her hands, which moved from bead to bead of a rosary. She raised a hand to dismiss the servant who led me into her presence. When she spoke, it was in English that was softened and bevelled by an edge of Portuguese.

'You have been asking too many questions. I thought it was time you knew the truth, so you can stop your asking.' The old lady leaned forward into the candlelight. Her eyes were marbled with cataracts. 'This was a happy house until that orphan girl came here. Nina was engaged to Damon. She loved him and was going to marry him.'

I said, 'She never loved him—'

Dona Alcina startled me by rapping on the ground with her cane. 'Stop interrupting! It was all decided. Nina was to marry Damon. They were to be happy together.' The hands picked at the rosary. 'And then that girl came into this house.'

Her milky gaze looked past me to the door where a young girl in faded clothes first stood under her gaze. 'I took her in because of Nina's pleas, and against my better judgement. The nuns had warned me already. But Nina insisted she was her friend. One year after that girl had brought her influence into this house, my granddaughter told Damon that she no longer wished to marry him. All that I had planned, all that I had hoped for, was laid waste!'

I said softly, 'Nina didn't love him. She loved Lisbon. Sara had nothing to do with that.'

The twisted hands knotted together. 'Oh yes, she did! I caught her passing notes from that musician to my granddaughter. In this very house!' Dona controlled her spasm of rage. 'I told her she was to take her wages and leave immediately. She was never to show her face in this village again. She went that night.'

I asked softly, 'And Nina?'

The hands fumbled for the rosary, began turning the beads again. The rage faded from the voice. Sorrow took its place. 'Nina went as well. That same night. I locked her in her room. I gave the key to Damon. But she got out.'

The voice wavered in the darkness, then steadied. 'We thought she had run away with that fiddler.'

I said, 'She was in love with him.'

'Love?' said Dona Alcina bitterly. 'Love? What is this love that will lead you to ruin a three-hundred-year-old name? To bring shame to your family? *Love*.'

Her hands trembled and she fumbled with her rosary. The familiar beads under her fingers stilled their tremor. 'To have the world know what had happened—no, it was intolerable. The shame! Damon thought of a way to cover all the gossip. We pretended that she was staying at an aunt's, while he went all the way to Portugal to search for her.'

Days and nights of searching. The railway station at Old Goa, the dockside in Vasco, the ferry at Panjim—Damon searches day and night, with nothing but a pocketful of questions. Subtle ones, obsequious ones, questions that disguised the actual query, questions that a knowing man would understand, opaque questions that the wrong people would not see through. Damon leaves his questions scattered far and wide and baits many a man with words and money. But, for all his efforts, he finds no answers.

His questions take him all the way to Portugal. To the home of the De Mirandas, to which they do not grant him entry. To concert halls across Europe where an orchestra is touring, featuring a young violinist, touted to be the best of his age.

They lead him to a confrontation with Lisbon after a performance. There are shouted exchanges, and the police are called. It is they who do the questioning, and are not happy with the answers they receive. Damon is deported back to India and told he cannot return.

'There was no word of her in Europe. No word of her here. When she could not be found after three months of searching, I suggested we bury her. Bury her so that there would be no scandal. We had the Casimir name to think of.'

'She was your granddaughter. Were you not worried about her?'

The Casimir pride flared from her angry reply. 'She was no longer my granddaughter! She had brought disgrace to the family name. She had gone against every wish of mine! She was already dead to me.'

'And so, you buried her.'

'Damon arranged everything. The story that she had fallen sick and died … the sealed coffin … I buried my granddaughter. I thought I had done with her.'

The empty coffin is lowered six feet on heavy ropes. But it is far from empty. It carries the weight of the Casimir pride, of Dona Alcina's hopes, of Damon's love. It carries a cargo of lies and anger and suppositions. All of them are taken and buried six feet deep. Earth is turned over and the matter left to dissolve into mould. Until now, when another set of pointed questions begins to dig up fragments and pieces.

The hands were moving on the rosary again. The beads jerked and moved on their fine gold links. 'I buried her. Now I must bury her again.'

I was puzzled. 'Why did Nina throw herself into the well? There was no need for her to. Lisbon was willing to marry her.'

Dona Alcina's words rang out sharply. 'That might be what he says now! I know men. He had already had her. What would he marry her for?' She controlled her bitterness with difficulty. 'I have lost my granddaughter. I have nothing now but Damon.'

'Why are you telling me all this?' I asked.

Dona Alcina came as close as a Casimir could to begging. 'Damon is not a murderer. He is an honourable man who did the best that he could. For his fiancée and for the family name. My heir is all that is left to me. If you would only leave us alone. There are no more questions for you to ask.'

That was not true. There was one question that yet remained unanswered. 'What happened to Sara?'

The words hissed from the shadows. 'I don't know and I don't care! This is where the story ends. Please leave us alone to mourn our dead.'

I was going to argue. But then I saw something was sparkling on her hands. Tears. Slow, difficult tears that cut deep trails in her pride as they fell. I turned and walked from the room.

Clues and Red Herrings

It was early in the morning when I went down to the police station. A small nagging rain was falling that covered each leaf with a fuzz of minute pearls.

At the door of the police station I found myself face to face with Damon Casimir. He brushed past me and walked free.

'Where is he going? You can't let him go like this!' I burst into the police station, disturbed and indignant.

The police station had suffered a change of fortune with the rain. The roof let rain through in a dozen places and there were patches of damp on the walls. I had to pick my way between a variety of vessels placed all over the floor. The rain dripping into them played a whole symphony of percussion in various keys.

The inspector had his desk in a relatively dry patch, and was mournfully regarding a drip that fell into a teacup placed in the middle of the polished expanse of teakwood.

'Why have you let Damon Casimir go?'

The inspector looked up from the drip. 'Dona Alcina came this morning. She explained everything.'

'Tell her to explain this.' I put the gun and the Goodbye Note on either side of the drip.

The inspector looked long and hard at them. 'Where did you get these?'

I said I had found them in the house. The inspector reached out a hand and unfolded the note.

Dearest,

   It can never be. Our worlds are too far apart to meet. I wish you well—always and forever.

   Felicidade seju sua sempre.

He sighed when he got to the end of it. 'This reads like a suicide note to me. Written by Nina Casimir. There you are. That makes everything clear. She killed herself. Mr Casimir had nothing to do with it.'

'And this?' I tapped the Casimir crest on the gun.

The inspector ran a rough finger over the crest. 'Nina jumped in a well. She died of drowning, not of a bullet. It can either be suicide or murder—it can't be both.'

'I found them in the house. It means Damon was in the house. Otherwise, how did the gun get there?'

The inspector carefully adjusted the cup so that the drip fell dead centre of the bowl. 'You're the clever writer fellow. You tell me.'

'Damon has something to do with all this. And with Sara's fate.'

'Ah,' said the inspector, 'but you yourself insist she's not dead.'

I sat silent. The inspector was right. It was a conundrum that I had no idea how to solve.

He got to his feet and began to move among the many makeshift rain-catchers that littered the floor. He paused to nudge each one with a foot so that the drip fell exactly in the middle. He had a passion for exactitude that led him to straighten papers in files and line up his pens in parallel.

I followed him, still arguing. 'I don't know what it's all about. But Damon knows. And you let him go.'

The inspector finished a careful adjustment and then turned to me. 'What do you want me to arrest him for? You can't arrest a man for burying an empty coffin.'

'He drove her to kill herself. He is a murderer!'

'That's different from actually killing her with his own hands. He can't hang for it.'

'But he has to be punished!'

'She was having an affair with another man. While engaged to him. Some people would call that a crime as well.'

'Not one that calls for a death sentence!'

The inspector abandoned the pots and pans and looked me straight in the eye. 'The case is closed. I have told Mr Miranda e Cabral that he is free to leave. I am sure he will wish to lock up the house. I hope you have finished that book of yours.'

I walked to the desk and reached for the gun. The inspector said, 'I'll keep that.'

I was quicker than him, grabbing it before he could. I said, 'Why? It's not incriminating evidence. There is no crime, remember? You let Damon go.'

'Maybe it belongs to Mr Casimir.'

'Maybe I'll show it to him myself and ask him.'

I firmly put the gun in my pocket and turned to go. The inspector called after me, 'Take him with you. I've no use for him anymore. As you say—Sara is not dead.'

At the far end of the hall was the jail cell. The inspector held the door open. Lorso stumbled out. His forehead was swollen. He held one arm awkwardly. Deep welts covered his legs. Heedless of Lorso's impediment, the inspector had done his best to make him talk. He scuttled behind me out of the station.

'Go away! Stop following me!' I walked as fast as I could. Behind me I could hear Lorso limping unevenly along. I glanced over my shoulder and he cringed away from my look. He looked like a dog whose master has whipped him. But still he followed me.

I stopped and told him repeatedly and fiercely to go away, but he trudged along in my wake. I took the path through the ruins without thinking. As I approached the place where he had last attacked me, my nerve failed me. I was alone in the ruins again with a man who had tried to attack me with a blade. A bump against my hip reminded me of the gun I was carrying. I pulled it from my pocket and turned around. 'Go away, Lorso!' I said.

The reaction was immediate. Lorso backed away, hands in disarray. His eyes were wide and fixed on the gun. I realised it was not me he was afraid of. He recognised the gun.

'You know this gun?' Lorso nodded. His hands shaped words.

'Someone threatened you with this? Who was it?'

It was the last answer I would have expected. Lorso signed, 'Nina.'

There are little fish that swim in the paddy fields in summer, slipping between the green stems. The paddy is high now and the fish are almost as long as a man's finger.

Lorso wriggles his toes in the velvet mud. He is crouched over, motionless, waiting for a fish to rise to his hook.

He sees Sara as a reflection that runs lightly on the surface of the water. She is crossing on sure feet on the raised dyke between the fields. Sun and sky and clouds frame her.

The fish scatter in silver sparks as he rises. He follows her, hook hanging forgotten from his hand. He has reached the edge of the fields when Sara stops. He reaches out a hand and she turns around. It is not Sara who faces him. The shawl slips from her shoulders and Lorso sees with dread that it is Nina he has mistaken for his friend.

'Hello, Lorso,' says Nina, smiling. 'I came specially to give you a message.' She raises her hand and she is holding a pistol, one that boasts an ornate 'C' on the butt. It is aimed steadily at him.

Lorso takes a quick step back. 'You have been bothering Sara,' Nina says. 'You can stop following her. I don't want you to bother her ever again.'

He has always been afraid of Nina. He has known her for far too long to think that she is joking. She is perfectly capable of putting a bullet in him.

'You be good now,' says Nina. She slips the gun into her pocket and is gone into the green fields.

Lorso's explosive gesture of frustration swings the forgotten hook loose. It sinks into the webbing between thumb and finger. He will have to remove it with pliers and will always carry the scar like a little white worm between his fingers. He dares not follow Sara anymore.

∞

'She scared you ... you stopped following Sara. You never saw her again until the night she disappeared,' I interpreted from Lorso's sign language.

He wiped the tears from his face with both hands. His hands were wet with grief as he signed. 'It's my fault she ran away ... I cut off her hair and frightened her ... I am sorry. I am so sorry.'

'Where did she go?'

His hands windmilled his puzzlement. 'I don't know ... I have searched for her all these years ... I don't know where she went. She was my friend.'

'Tell me the truth, Lorso. Did you do more than cut her hair? Did you hurt her?'

Lorso shook his head. His hands begin to move. 'I swear ... I swear by the angel ... I did nothing!'

He got to his feet and stood there, a sad, battered figure. Then he unexpectedly plunged into the ruins. I followed quickly and found him staring in disbelief at the remains of the shattered angel, spread in a great white burst on the ground. He raised his head to the sky and a howl of anguish came from his throat. He knelt by the head of the statue and began to beat his breast and weep. I looked at the broken man in front of me and lowered the gun. The blind eyes of the angel gazed at the sky.

I left, unable to witness his anguish. If Lorso had not harmed Sara, who had?

I arrived home to find Lisbon waiting on the porch. 'Where have you been?' he asked. I told him.

'And?' asked Lisbon eagerly.

'The inspector let Damon go. He thinks there is no evidence that Damon did anything.'

Lisbon looked at me in astonishment for a moment, then bitterness filled his voice. 'The Casimirs. They've reduced this entire village to being their servants. They are getting away with murder.'

'We don't know that,' I said.

'Who else could have done it? Do you have any suspects?'

I had to confess that I didn't.

'The empty coffin proves it,' said Lisbon. 'But no one will do anything. No one cares.' He turned to me. 'I am leaving. I am going to buy the first ticket I can to get out of here.'

'Why?' I said. 'You have to help me! We can prove that Damon did something.'

'Do you think they will accept your proof?' I thought of the Goodbye Note and the gun that the inspector had explained away and shook my head.

A thought occurred to me. 'Why did Damon attack you when he first saw you? Why did he ask you about Sara?'

'Because he's a murderer, afraid that I would ask questions. He was trying to pin it on me. Make out that I had made her disappear.'

'Why would he do that?' I asked, not fully satisfied with the reply.

Lisbon looked at me with a mixture of anger and scorn. 'Are you suspecting me? *Me*? You think I had something to do with Sara's disappearance? I didn't even know she existed!' He shook his head in bewilderment. 'I had no idea there were two of them!'

I was turning it over in my mind and was slow to respond. It moved him to anger and he grabbed my arm. 'What about *me*?' he shouted. 'What about all that I have been put through? The lies! And then ... coming back here thinking she was alive. Then dead. Then alive again. Then finding her grave.' I could feel his hand trembling on my arm with the strength of his emotion. 'I think I will go mad with it all! I can't bear to think about it anymore.' Lisbon put his hands to his head in a gesture of despair. I could think of nothing to say to him.

He said to me, 'I am going away. I can't bear it anymore.'

'I'm not leaving,' I said. 'I have to keep searching. I have to keep asking questions.'

'Why?'

'I made a promise to find Sara.'

He gave a bitter laugh. 'Don't you know you never will? They will never let you.' He gestured hopelessly and walked away.

Baptism by Water

I woke with a sense that something was wrong. It was a minute before I placed it. The rain had stopped entirely. I had lived so long with the cacophony of rain and wind and dripping roof that the silence felt strangely alive. When I looked out of the window I was amazed to see that the sun shone in a sky without a single cloud in it. Wherever sunshine dropped on the myriad shades of green they became incandescent.

My bags had been packed some time ago. The only thing that remained to be put away was all my writing. It had grown into quite a handsome pile that lay in the square of sunshine dropped on my desk. What was I to do with it? Ruefully I thought of my grand plans for a novel that would now never be. My ambitions of being a writer had been replaced with a simple determination. I had made a promise. I would keep it.

I made another resolve. I would leave the house, but not the village. I would find another place to stay. I would not leave until I'd kept the promise I made to Alice.

I put away the papers and set off down the hill, determined to ask around the village until I found a place to stay. I was delighted at the prospect of a walk without an umbrella and without wind and rain for companions.

Tentative birdsong had begun, as if the birds too could not quite believe that the sunshine was real. By the time I reached the ruins, there was a whole symphony of bird and insect sounds rising into the warm air. One deluded koel was singing as if summer itself had returned. I found myself smiling. I cheerfully acknowledged Crazy Charlie's greeting in the graveyard.

Gusts of music carried up the hill and into the graveyard. I thought how appropriate the cheerful horns, exuberant guitars and loud drums were to the day. 'San Joao,' Crazy Charlie explained. 'The festival of John the Baptist. The whole village will be at the square.'

The marketplace was a laughing, chattering riot of villagers. Everyone was dressed brightly, and most people wore flowers in their hair. It was, apparently, a tradition to be wreathed in flowers and the more creative villagers had wrought complex floral edifices. The contents of entire gardens could be identified on various heads.

More and more people were spilling into the square and the crowd was slowly shaping into long lines headed by various banners—'St Cajetan Union', 'Associacion de St Mark', 'Football Club of Chimbel'.

Children gathered around the red-and-tinsel band that played with gusto in the centre of the village square. The taverna regulars spied me on the edges of the crowd and hooted for me to come over. They enthusiastically adopted me. A glass was thrust into my hand. A tattered banner announced that they were the 'Infant Jesus Sports Club'.

I held the glass as far from my nose as I could. 'I have a problem,' I said to the man with the pig belly whose name, I learnt, was Castellino. 'I need a place to stay. The house I have rented is being closed up.'

'You can stay with us!' he said enthusiastically. It seemed they really were a club. They had a clubhouse that consisted of two rooms. One room had a carom board and a broken piano. The other was filled with a load of rubbish. 'We can clear it out,' Castellino assured me. Such was my determination, that I accepted their offer of a single room filled with rubbish.

The others joined in with equal enthusiasm.

'Come join our club. You can be a soldier for Infant Jesus!'

'Can you play carom? We play most evenings.'

It was Castellino who said, with a sly look in his eye, 'There is a condition.'

'What?' I asked, trying to furtively put the glass down somewhere.

'You must drink with us,' said Castellino. His condition was met with much noisy approval by the lot of them.

'Go on then,' said a man with a fierce squint. 'Drink up and you have a place to stay.' An absolute chorus broke out, urging me to drink up.

I held my breath resolutely as I brought the glass to my mouth. I had no idea that you could not swallow if you were holding your breath. I choked and gasped and the drink seared its way down my throat. Castellino refilled my glass. There was no escape. I had to drink the foul stuff.

A wave of light washed across the square, turning the band to catherine wheels of gold and red. The regulars assured me that the rain would come down soon. 'It is San Joao. It always rains on San Joao.'

'John the Baptist, you see. Water.'

The excitement reached its highest pitch as the priest arrived, resplendent in purple robes and preceded by several altar boys swinging censers. The band changed its tune from riotous to hymnal and the procession proceeded towards the riverside. I joined the happy crowd, urged along by my new friends. I was surprised at how many people nodded and waved to me.

The procession stopped at the riverside and awaited the arrival of St John. A flotilla of gaily decorated boats came down the river to the sound of drums and singing. A boat docked and disgorged the saint himself. St John was the local baker, thinly disguised by a rug wrapped around his waist and held up by string, and a bedsheet that served as a cloak. The villagers roared their welcome. The saint was escorted by a Roman soldier, three disciples in petticoats and what looked like an attempt to represent the Queen of Portugal.

The priest greeted the baptist, then turned to the crowd and thundered, 'It is time to be reborn into Jesus!'

The crowd began to line up at the bank of the river. All the Infants lined up for their baptism as well. With great difficulty I managed to wriggle out of their clutches and lurked among the crowd.

With roars of '*Viva San Joao!*' people began to leap into the water. Some merely keeled over and fell in. There was confusion and roiling water and I feared for my companions. But then, abruptly, they began to stand up. The water was only waist-deep. Someone threw the Infants a bottle. They continued their drinking waist-deep in the flow. More people were leaping in, flinging themselves with abandon into a baptism by water.

I found myself in the middle of the band and a large trombone was thrust into my arms with an injunction to keep an eye on it. The band trooped to the water and leapt into it in great arcs of gold and red. When they emerged, sopping wet, they took up their instruments and launched into vigorous dance tunes.

In no time, wet and drunken revellers were kicking up their legs. The women shrieked with laughter at their antics and some older matrons were bold enough to join them. Women moved through the throng, handing out round bread, sausages and fruit.

I looked up. The sky was a clear blue. We could have been in the middle of summer. Of all the days of the monsoon, today looked the least likely to rain. The taverna regulars rebuked my lack of faith. 'It *will* rain today. San Joao will make it.'

The morning extended into a long afternoon, so warm that the ground began to steam gently. Whenever the band tired, some old gentleman would leap up and seize a fiddle and begin cranking out sprightly tunes. The dancing grew more riotous and erratic under the influence of plentiful food and wine. St John himself flung aside his bedsheet and joined in.

All afternoon the boats went up and down the river, steering more and more erratically as the spirits of the boatmen rose. They had names like 'St Anthony's Social Club' and 'Virgin Mary Associacion'. From time to time a boatman tipped over and fell into the river. Attempts at rescue depleted the crew even further.

I have no idea how many glasses of that foul drink I had to down. Every time my glass was empty, somebody filled it and stood over me until I drank from it. Suddenly, the Infants discovered that I was not wet.

'You have to jump in the river! It's San Joao.'

'I am a Parsee. No rivers for us. No holy water. Only holy fire. Give me fire, I'll jump!' I declared.

Not that refusing did any good. They led me to the river and then I was so hot it seemed to be a good idea to jump in. The water shimmered invitingly. I took the plunge. There was thick mud at the bottom of the river and I floundered in it before I found my feet. All the club members cheered.

Standing in the river, muddy and muddle-headed, I had another glass thrust into my hand. I raised a toast. 'To my mother. I am doing everything you told me never to!' I found myself laughing. Everybody drank to it.

Then, to my surprise, I found myself in the middle of the dancing crowd, moving vigorously to a compelling rhythm. The music began to revolve around me. The crowd blurred at the edges. I staggered away, thinking to myself, 'I must be drunk.'

Everything was moving in a wheel of unbearable brightness of which I was the unsteady centre. I put my feet down carefully. But even the earth beneath my feet began to shift and move. I fell to the ground. I heard roars of, 'Viva San Joao!'

I was dimly aware of feeling raindrops on my face and thinking, 'It did rain after all.'

Then there was darkness.

Risen from the Dead

I am a bug in a box. A man in a room that sits tight around his shoulders. A snake, blinded and choked by its own shrinking skin. An ant buried in a vial of salt.

I am dreaming and I know that I do not like this dream. It closes around me in the darkness and I am afraid that soon I will not be able to breathe.

Somebody is knocking to be let in. Strange bursts of knocks. Scattered and random. Who is it who knocks? Why can I not open the door and let them in?

Someone else is in this room with me. Even in the dark I can sense the shape of a head on the pillow. Cold it is, and pale. A face that gleams white in the darkness. She sleeps on the pillow beside me and I do not know her name. I must open my eyes. I cannot scream because my mouth is full of something. I cannot move because my hands and feet are tied.

My eyelids are weighted. I lift them slowly, slowly. My head is throbbing. I tell myself—open your *eyes*! I open my eyes and it is …

Darkness. Deep night.

On the pillow beside me is a face that gleams white in the dark. Cold it is, and pale.

I realise I have crossed the boundary from dream to waking—and the reality that trails me is still the same.

I cannot scream. I cannot move. I am a bug in a box. A snake, blinded and choked by its own skin. An ant buried in a vial of salt. I am secured and locked in a coffin. And beside me, lies Nina.

Rain was pouring down as the priest said Mass. The clods of earth in the hands of the faithful were sodden and wet. They fell with deadened sounds upon the coffin. Damon stood bareheaded as mourners filed past, throwing their tithe of mud into the grave. The downpour made it impossible to tell if he was crying. Dona Alcina was veiled in black lace. Her back stayed ramrod straight, only her hands moved and twisted around her rosary.

The funeral was well attended. This was the biggest scandal the village had ever witnessed and no one wanted to miss out on any details. All the men were in their best suits. The women were alert in mourning black and expectation. Whole families had turned out, eager to see what would happen next. There were speculations about arrest warrants and police investigations.

The sexton struggled to hold the umbrella up against the wind. The pages of the Holy Book flipped and turned like the devil was in them, and the priest kept losing his place in the Mass for the Dead. Mercifully, he came to the end of the ceremony.

'May the soul of Nina Casimir rest in peace.'

Clearly and distinctly was heard the sound of knocking. It came from the coffin.

There was instant pandemonium. Fat matrons ran squelching through the mire. Gentlemen screamed as loudly as the ladies. Two old ladies fell to their knees in the mud and began confessing their sins. The priest dropped his Bible and pointed his crucifix at the coffin like a gun. A taverna regular was to date his giving up the Influence to that moment.

The knocking sounded again.

Spectacles were broken and umbrellas lost in the stampede as almost the entire population of the village ran for the gates of the cemetery as fast as they humanly could.

Damon stood there, frozen, staring at the coffin. There was no mistaking the knocking. It was getting louder and more frantic.

The inspector was the only one to keep his head. After all, he did not believe in ghosts. He grabbed a grave-digger's shovel and jumped into the grave. A bent nail had been used to fasten the latches on the coffin. He flung the lid open.

Light! An epiphany of light and air. And rain in the eyes, mouth, hair. I lay there gasping and wet and helpless. The smell of wet earth was in my nostrils.

My legs would not support me. The inspector held me up with one determined shoulder. He carried me out of the cemetery and eased me onto the nearest seat in the church. It happened to be the confessional. The priest fluttered in the background, clutching his Bible, not sure whether what had just happened was a miracle or an abomination.

'Some water please, Father.' The priest promptly sprinkled me generously with holy water from the font.

'I'm sure that's helpful,' said the inspector dryly, 'but I meant some water to drink.'

The priest scuttled off to fetch it. The sacristan had vanished with the stampeding crowd and would not return for three days.

I carefully felt my head. 'Is there blood?' I asked the inspector. 'Anywhere?'

The inspector scrutinised me. 'Not that I can see. I think you were drugged.'

I nodded and felt like my head had fallen off and rolled rattling down the aisle. 'Something in a drink I had. I thought I was dead.'

The inspector said, 'You should be—but you seem difficult to kill.'

Now that the inspector had said it, the thought finally shaped itself in my mind. It was a sledgehammer shattering half my notions to bits. 'Someone actually tried to kill me!' Even more bewildering was the realisation that it was not for the first time.

The inspector nodded. 'You'd have disappeared without a trace. We would never have thought of looking for you in a coffin buried six feet under.'

'A trick that has been tried before,' I said. 'Only, that time, the coffin was buried empty.' A thoughtful silence hung between us. 'Now that I've nearly died—do you believe that Damon is guilty?'

The inspector coughed. 'Yes. But I'm not quite sure of what.'

I eagerly said, 'Nina! He killed Nina. And Sara knew it. If we could find her, we could pin it on him. Nina didn't jump in the well. She was pushed.'

The inspector considered this point of view. 'Maybe.'

I said, 'Sara is the key. But I can't find Sara! God knows I've tried.'

'Keep trying,' said the inspector. 'If he tried to kill you—you're close.'

I grinned with gallows humour, though it made my

head throb. 'And when I'm dead—then I'll definitely have found her!'

The priest came hurrying back with a glass of water just as the inspector lit a cigarette. At the priest's outraged look, he realised what he had done. 'I'm sorry. Damn!'

The priest raised an eyebrow at the cuss word. The inspector looked guilty. 'Sorry. Sorry!'

The door to the vestry scraped open and discordant sounds echoed loud in the silence of the church. Damon had organised pallbearers and the coffin was being carried back into the church. Nina would not be laid to rest today.

The inspector and I watched the shaking, frightened crew cringing under their burden.

'Twice already, Nina has refused to be buried. Surely there is a reason.'

'Interesting,' said the inspector, 'but not evidence. Bring me evidence, and I will see she rests in peace the third time.'

'Is the case still closed?'

'Yes,' said the inspector. 'Unless you turn up some evidence.'

'Why me?' I asked indignantly.

'You started this, Mr Irani,' said the inspector. 'You're a stubborn fellow. I suspect you won't let go till you've seen it through.'

I was a bit surprised to discover he was right. Sitting there, head still heavy with the effect of an unknown drug, the fear of being a bug in a box still upon me, I knew I wouldn't stop till I got to the end of this story. 'You will write it,' Tania had said. And I will.

A Coin for the Ferryman

The drug was still upon me and the journey up to the house was part of a dream that faded at the edges. The ruins melted and flowed around me. The house was a jaw that unhinged and opened to swallow me whole. I fell across the bed and closed my eyes and dropped into the dream that was waiting for me.

I was standing on a broken wooden jetty on the bank of a river. The river was in full spate and the swollen black water raged down to the sea. At my back were strings of drying fish hung on black lines that flapped and undulated in the wind. Sara stood on the far shore. She was too far away for me to see her face, but she was calling to me. The wind that whipped the fish into flying strings of silver carried her words away. I slipped a hand into my pocket and felt a coin cold under my fingertips. I knew I had wished upon it, and now I was to give it to the boatman who would soon arrive.

Sara screamed across the breadth of the dark, uneasy water that separated us. Again and again, Sara called from the distance. But I could not understand the words she was mouthing. The wind snatched them away.

My eyes opened and, on the threshold of sleep and waking, I had a sudden moment of epiphany. Sara was calling the words from the Goodbye Note—'*Felicidade seja sua sempre.*'

I crossed the border from dreamtime into consciousness and was fully awake. Tania was sitting by my bedside. She made no noise, nor could I see her. But I sensed her presence as clearly as if she had called out my name. Her voice came out of the darkness, small and scared. 'I heard you were buried.'

In the darkness I could say things I would not dare hold up to the light of day. 'I thought I was dead.'

'Don't!'

'I wasn't afraid of being dead. But I thought I would never see you again ... then I was afraid.'

Tania's voice wisped out of the darkness, 'I am afraid all the time.'

The darkness wrapped us in intimacy. I took a deep breath. 'Tania—'

'Don't say it!' Her voice drew a quick line before the words I was about to spill. 'Not now.'

'Why not?'

'Now is not the right time.'

I smiled in the darkness. 'When will be the right time?'

'You will know.'

We sat quiet for a while in the dark, neither saying the words that pressed so hotly against our lips. A sudden sense of loss told me when she left.

Early the next morning I went down to the police station. The inspector was not surprised to see me. He pushed an envelope across the table. 'It arrived yesterday. From your mother.' It was marked '*Urgent*'. The letter inside was typed on our letterhead.

My dear son,

You must return immediately. I have news that is not common knowledge yet. The British are going to advance the schedule for the partition. It will be upon us before anyone is ready and we must prepare or we will lose much. You have to return to help me. Or everything that this family has built might be lost to us. Give up this foolish conceit of yours. You are an Irani. You come from a proud and honourable line of businessmen and you must claim what is yours if we are not to lose it all in this madness of partitioning this country.

An agent is on standby in Panjim to book your return journey the minute you get this letter.

'Well?' asked the inspector. 'Bad news?'

I pushed the letter across the table for him to read. He was thoughtful. 'The papers say there is chaos in India. Radcliffe has arrived to partition the country. There are demonstrations everywhere. Jinnah refuses to climb down from his demand for a separate country. No one knows how this will end. I suspect it will be a time of great disaster. And, for the right people, a time of great opportunity.'

'I'm not going,' I said flatly.

'Heirs to great fortunes are not free to do as they please,' he said.

'No,' I said. 'And when I return I will never again be. So let us not waste any more time.'

He gave me a grin and an approving nod. Then, sitting at his table, a steady drip marking time, we tried to puzzle it out.

'Someone tried to kill you. So, someone is covering up a crime.' Together we marshalled the facts, the inspector stroking his moustache thoughtfully.

He told me that Lorso had admitted to attacking Sara. He insisted he never killed her. Damon admitted nothing. I had seen Lorso with the hot madness on him. I had seen Damon stand cold with a gun in his hand. If Lorso could kill for love, could not Damon have killed for pride? He had been cuckolded. The woman promised to him was in love with another man. Did he do more than just bury a coffin to save the pride of the Casimirs?

'Damon,' I said firmly.

'Lorso,' said the inspector, laying his bet on another horse. 'He's attacked you before. He could have had an accomplice.'

'Damon,' I said stubbornly.

'What about your fancy boy?' said the inspector.

'Lisbon?' I asked. 'What motive could he have had?'

'The skeleton was in his well. He was the one who had the affair. Maybe he got her pregnant.'

'He says he locked up and left before it all happened.'

'He says,' said the inspector with irony.

'He didn't even know there were two girls,' I said.

'He says.' Lisbon stayed firmly on the inspector's list of suspects.

Time and time again we tried to order the events of that night. There were gaps in the sequence and I was sure that if I could lay the events out all neatly, I would know what had happened. 'They both disappeared the same night,' I mused. 'Dona Alcina threw Sara out of the house. Nina ran away to Lisbon.'

'But Mr Miranda e Cabral says she never reached there. Something happened to her before she could reach him.'

'Whatever happened, she ended up in the well of his house. Couldn't that have happened *after* he had left?' I persisted.

The inspector shrugged. 'No way of telling after all these years.'

'Where does the gun come into it all?'

'Perhaps it doesn't.'

'But what was it doing in the house, then? Did Nina carry it there?'

'A bit of an unusual thing to take on an elopement,' said the inspector dryly.

All we could think up were questions and not a single answer. We sat and thought in silence.

'Sara,' I said firmly. 'She is the key to all this. Surely she knows the truth.'

'If she is alive,' said the inspector.

'I know she is,' I insisted.

'And why is that?' asked the inspector, leaning forward keenly.

'Someone told me. A whisper in the wind,' I said, rather pleased with the subtlety of my reply.

'You sound like you've been talking to Crazy Charlie,' said the inspector, with an astuteness that astounded me.

'She is alive. Maybe she is in hiding because Damon threatened her and she is afraid of him. Her testimony will give us the truth. We must find her.'

The inspector shrugged eloquent shoulders. 'She's been gone five years. All the best with that.'

'I will find her. I must!' I said. I was determined to find out. If this bit of the story did not come to me, I would go out and fetch it.

'Do you know what a peeshaw is?' asked the inspector.

'Some dish or the other,' I hazarded, 'that has to be stewed a long time.'

'It's a stubborn donkey,' said the inspector. I grinned at him, quite happy with the appellation.

I left the police station and went back to the village to ask questions. I discovered that people were now willing, even eager, to talk to me. They regarded me with awe, even the sodden taverna customers reaching out occasionally to touch me with tentative fingers. I was Lazarus returned, and they the bystanders, not quite believing in the miracle. They asked me about being buried alive, of being locked in a coffin and shovelled six feet under. I traded my story time and time again for information.

Time and the Thirsty Man

I had several drinks in the taverna, I waylaid Lorso in a leafy lane, I even called upon Sister Ursula and was unusually polite. Through it all, I collected bits and pieces of information.

I wrote down all that I had learnt, piecing it together. Whispers and innuendoes and suppositions. Small nuggets of fact. Frayed hearsay handed from person to person. As I sifted out the fact from the chaff, I found myself scribbling in the margins, trying to draw up a sequence of events on the night that Sara disappeared. The scribblings grew until they sprawled over several sheets of paper. They grew until they became stories themselves. I found myself reaching for more and more paper.

This is how the stories told themselves.

There is a man who goes down to a well to draw water. There he meets Time playing with the rope that is used to lower the bucket. Time has tied the rope into many knots and chuckles when the man tries to undo them. The man is thirsty and the thought of the sweet water makes him angry with Time. Try as he might, he cannot get the knots free.

Time is bored, and so, he proposes a little arrangement. The man is to tell him stories. 'With each story you tell me, I will untie one knot. When the last knot is free, you will have rope enough to draw water from the well.'

The man begins with a dry throat.

The Devil in the Bottle

One day, the Devil went for a stroll through the village in search of someone to share a smoke and a chat with. This was how he had usually accomplished all his mischief. What he left undone, the cigarettes finished for him.

This time, to his surprise, the village was empty of all men. No baker shovelling pao in the bakery, no butcher trimming pigs' trotters on the chopping block, no candlestick-maker ladling and measuring hot wax. He could not find a soul. But what he did find was a smell. A most pee-culiar smell.

It is of old socks and perfume, mould and mangers, dried fish and sugar. Satan Baab finds himself drawn by the nose like he has inhaled a fishhook and is being reeled in. The reek leads him straight up the hill to where the cashew trees are in fruit.

The men of the village are gathered in the grove. The butcher is in charge of crushing the fruit. The baker, in charge of boiling it. The candlestick-maker pours and measures with precision. They are illicitly brewing feni. Satan Baab arrives and is glad to see they are doing so well without his help. But he cannot resist stirring up a little trouble.

'Surely,' he tells the baker, 'your job is the worst of all in the whole business.'

He sneaks up to the candlestick-maker and whispers in his ear. 'Your job is the most important. Without your precise measuring, the whole endeavour would be in vain.'

He swaggers up to the butcher and tells him, 'Your job is most crucial—everything depends on it.'

A spirit of mild dissension enters the process of feni-making. Each of the three eyes his partners at work and weighs and measures their contribution and is sure that he does more, himself, than his fair share. As the feni simmers, dissent boils in their hearts. As the liquor distils, it becomes a source of minor argument. By the time the feni is siphoned off and bottled, the argument has become a deadlock. Seeking to do further mischief, Satan Baab suggests that they have a drink before they continue. All three break off their heated argument and reach for glasses.

Satan Baab has reckoned without the Goan fondness for feni. One drink becomes two. And then three. By the fourth, all are casting sentimental glances at each other. At the fifth, they are embracing. At the sixth, they are swearing eternal friendship. And at the seventh, a befuddled baker comes upon the truth: 'We never would have quarrelled but for *him*.'

They return to their work in perfect harmony. The baker and the candlestick-maker nab Satan Baab. The butcher says, 'On the count of three, now, boys ... one ... two ...'

Satan Baab describes a short arc through the air and lands straight in the vat of feni. He surfaces spluttering and muttering all manner of curses.

Ever since then, the Devil is in the bottle.

One night, many decades later, and five years ago, the Devil in the bottle has kept two men sitting on a deserted bridge until late at night. They have nearly finished the bottle and the Devil's own mischief is at work on them. A girl comes hurrying out of the darkness, swathed in her shawl. The two men on the bridge know who she is well enough. The village has been buzzing with the gossip for weeks.

Prompted by the Devil, one of them rises to block the narrow path. 'Not so soon, Sara, my love. There is a toll to be paid on the bridge.' The girl shrinks back from him and his fetid breath.

The other man steps up behind her to block off her retreat. 'Why so shy now, Sara? Why don't you spend the night with us tonight instead of going up the hill?' They advance on her.

A voice stops them. 'Leave her alone.'

Damon is standing on the far end of the bridge. He advances on the two. The men back away hurriedly. The girl does not dare move.

Damon turns to the girl and says, with contempt in his voice, 'And you—go home.'

The girl fumbles her shawl closer around her head. And in that hasty gesture, Damon spies a ring upon her hand with an ornate curlicued initial upon it. No servant girl has ever worn that ring on her finger. He snatches the shawl away and Nina looks Damon calmly in the face.

'He was angry enough to commit murder,' says Missing-Tooth, crossing himself and quickly downing the feni that I had bought him. 'He grabbed her by the hand and dragged her home. That was the last time I ever saw her. Or anyone did.'

All the taverna regulars chipped in.

'I think she must have been pregnant.'

'He is too proud to have taken that easily.'

Time taps the first knot lightly and it untangles in a quick slither. He is eager for the second story.

The Fairy Gift

Nina Anastacia Esmeralda Casimir is born a Princess. And the Princess is allotted a Fairy Godmother, like all babies so favoured are.

The Fairy Godmother has marked the Princess's birthday on her calendar and spends much time every year planning a gift. Like Fairy Godmothers are supposed to, she sends her fabulous and useful things.

One year, the gift is Courage in Adversity held in the mouth of a fish made of silver of cunning workmanship. Another year, it is Loyalty to Friends closed up in a jewelled egg. Another year it is Strength of Will in a basket made of adamant and crystals. Another birthday it is Compassion for the Less Fortunate, all done up in peacock feathers.

But on her ninth birthday she sends the Princess Simplicity and Humbleness in a rush basket. The Princess hates the present on sight. 'What is this?' she demands. 'Why! We keep the onions in the kitchen in a basket like this!' The Princess stamps her feet and is furious.

'My,' says the Fairy Godmother when she hears about the tantrum, 'what a temper she has! I take my gift back. Let me give her another gift in its place: May whatever she says in anger always come true.'

And so, when Damon surprises the Princess in her nightly wanderings and drags her home, she is far from repentant. Dona Alcina speaks to her of her good name and upbringing, hoping to shame her. Instead, Nina storms at both Dona Alcina and Damon, telling them that she loves Lisbon. That if she knows one thing in life, it is that she is meant to be with him.

Listening to it all is the kitchen girl who has crept up the stairs and hidden in the shadows.

Burning in anger, Nina makes a promise, 'Tonight I shall be with him—or I shall be dead. I swear it.'

Damon cringes to hear her say the words. He has never ever yet heard her make a promise she did not carry out.

To prevent her hasty words from proving true, the Princess is locked in her room and the key hung carefully on a chain around Damon's neck.

The rope is an old one and has hung swaying over the well for many years. The second knot creaks and mutters as it is closer to undone.

The Thief of Dreams

I met a man once, who was a professional thief like no other in the world. He stole dreams right from the pillow on which people dreamed them. I believe there is indeed a market for such things and he made a very good living off it. He refused to divulge the actual method, but he told me how, once, he had come close to being caught. It was the night that he went to steal the dreams of a haughty Princess, blessed by destiny.

Strangely, asleep on her silken pillow, the Princess is dreaming of how she longs to be free of her destiny. Of the man chosen for her. Of the house that she is bound to. Of the ordered life that awaits her.

The thief puts out a quick hand and slips her dream into his satchel and is off. But as he tiptoes out of the house he pauses in the kitchen. In her hard bed, on her lumpy pillow, the Kitchen Girl is dreaming a dream of such singular beauty that he cannot resist it. It is a dream of love, innocent and pure and true. He has never stolen twice from the same house but that night he breaks his rule. He puts out a careful hand and closes it around the glowing dream.

Unfortunately, indigestion wakes the cook at the exact same moment that he finishes his thievery. She cries out in alarm. Other servants awake. A small dog attaches itself to the thief's leg. In his hurry to get away, he drops his bag and the dreams fly out getting hopelessly mixed up. Thus it is that the Princess finds herself dreaming the Kitchen Girl's dream of a man who has come across the sea and is in love with music. She dreams of notes under a door, and an assignation.

And the Kitchen Girl dreams of opening the door and running free of Pride and Honour and her Destiny. She dreams of leaving behind the perfect life that has been ordered for her from the moment that she was born. In the dream it closes around her in silver fetters so tightly bound that she cries out in terror.

Sara's heart is large and, having dreamt Nina's dream, she understands her deep longing to be free. She watches Dona Alcina and Damon turn the key in the lock. When Damon and Dona Alcina are gone, she creeps to the door and bends to whisper through the cracks.

Nina writes a note and passes it underneath the door. Sara climbs out of the kitchen window and sets off for the house on the hill where Lisbon waits.

'I saw her go running through the graveyard. I called to her to stop but she would not.' Crazy Charlie remembers that evening still. 'She had something in her hand. A note.'

The third knot is thirsty for water and rasps dryly as it falls open at a touch.

The Singing Tree

There once was a tree that grew in a garden of sorrow. It was watered by bitter tears and washed by dark rain. For in the house lived a woman whose love had died. He lay buried in the garden under the tangled roots of the tree. She had planted a sapling on his grave and now it shadowed the green mound. It was on his heart, bones, eyes that the tree fed. It was of her tears that it drank. And it grew straight and tall.

At the time where day and night cross, she would steal out into the garden and whisper her sorrow to the tree. She had no one else she could tell it to. Her love was gone and she was left there to mourn it. For many twilights the tree listened to her voice speaking her pain. When the wind moved through its leaves the whispers that fell from it were laments, soft dirges, mourning songs.

One evening the woman did not come. The tree stood alone in the wild garden for years after that, wafting its funereal lamentations upon empty air. Then it was cut down by a passing stranger.

The tree yielded fine wood, soaked in sorrow and seasoned with pain. Many things were made from the tree.

And from the heart of it was fashioned an instrument—an elegant narrow-necked violin.

But this was no ordinary violin. No sooner would bow be put to string than the saddest sounds would well from its throat. Even the sprightliest tunes became imbued with dolour. The player would find himself filled with a deep yearning, a sense that something had been lost and buried in the earth.

It earned a name and people said it in whispers— *Saudade*. Sorrow. Yearning.

It is a saudade tune that Lisbon chooses as he waits for Nina to come to him. They have planned to run away together. She will go with him to Portugal. She will leave her destiny behind.

He touches his bow to the violin strings and the music that wells from it is yearning. It has been made from a tree that was watered with tears. It calls urgently into the night, calls to the woman that he is waiting for.

A young woman has come to the house. She pauses on the doorstep. The music that carries from the inside fills her with despair and sorrow like she has not known before. She thinks her heart will break. It seems an eternity of mourning has passed before she raises her hand to knock.

The knock cuts the music off. Lisbon flings open the door thinking it will be Nina. But instead it is Sara. His eyes are eager for his love and so he scarcely sees her face, will not later remember what she looked like. She holds out a note.

Felicidade seja sua sempre, the note says. Our worlds are too far apart to meet. It cannot be. It cannot be.

Wild with despair, Lisbon writes another note begging his love to trust him. To come to him! Come to him!

He takes up his violin to fill the despairing time and sends music into the night to call her name with yearning. Call to her to return to him.

Sara runs back through the darkness. Crazy Charlie sees her in the graveyard running swiftly between the graves.

'It was late. The moon was rising. I had been at the grave much longer than I usually was. I saw Sara on her way back. She used to stop to say hello to me. But that night she ran back through the graveyard and was gone.'

'Where was she going?'

'Back to the house. Where else did she have to go?'

The fourth knot is stubborn and opens only after much prying and untying.

The Messenger

There was a Princess in India who paused by a lake. The lake held the reflection of a sky full of clouds. 'Show me the face of my beloved,' she asked the clouds, and the clouds cast his image across the sky and the water held it. 'Take a message to him,' she commanded the wind, and it listened to her whispers.

Cloud and wind went in search of the man she loved. Across the land they roamed, one remembering his face, one whispering her words over and over to itself so it would not forget.

But the man she loved had been betrothed to another, and cloud and wind arrived only as the seventh turn around the sacred fire was done.

The Princess waited eagerly for their return. Every day she would scan the sky for clouds. Every night she'd open the casement and wait for the whisper of the wind.

One day wind and cloud returned together. The skies were overcast. The trees whipped from side to side. 'Tell me!' cried the Princess. 'What did my beloved say?' The reply of cloud and wind fell upon her face in rain. Such was their sorrow that the rain poured out of the sky for days, and so seasons were born.

Wind and rain are far away. It is now Sara who is the messenger who comes running to the house on the hill. But when she tries to slip the paper under the door, a cane catches her a burning welt across her hand. Dona Alcina stands there, spitting in fury. 'The nuns warned me about you! I should have listened to them.'

Anger gives the old woman's arm strength, and she raises her cane and brings it down across Sara's shoulders repeatedly. The servants come running. Dona tells them to seize Sara and throw her out of the house. Lock the door and bar it. She is never ever to come back.

'Where will I go in the middle of the night?' begs Sara. 'To die,' says the old lady.

The servants shut the door upon the weeping girl.

Lorso will not look at me as he talks. He turns his head away, but his hands move. It was late at night when he saw Nina go past. He was in the ruins.

'Are you sure you saw Nina first, and not Sara?'

He nods his head vigorously. He tried to hide from her. He was afraid of her after the incident with the gun. But she saw him and came up to him. She gave him a message to give Sara.

'Come to me. It is a matter of life and death. Remember your promise and come to me.' Lorso's hands hold the memory of that night still. 'Nina said to tell her that. To find her and tell her that, urgently. Then she ran to the house.' His finger points to the house where I now live.

Lorso crouched in the ruins, wondering what to do. Then he saw her. Sara. 'She came to the ruins alone. She was weeping. She had been thrown out of the house and did not know where to go.

'I told her Nina had been there. I gave her the message. She turned to go and I grabbed her hand. I told her that she could come with me. I would take her. We would be together always. I asked her to marry me.'

The fifth knot is tied in the fashion called 'Love's Purse'. It opens with a sigh.

The Sickle Moon

The Sickle Moon will not be pleased. She sighs and frets and bites her fingers and nothing at all can engage her. All night she has been discontent, fretted by she does not know what. 'Tell me a story,' she demands of her love, the North Star. But he has no stories for her. Constant in his love, troubled by her unease, the North Star takes her to the casement to gaze down upon the rivers below. She leans out of the window to look at her face in the paddy fields. Her reflection sails serene in dark fields of young rice, shivered by the passing of a lone heron.

The paddy fields hold a mirror to another image. A girl running lightly on the embankment.

'Surely,' says the Moon, her interest caught, 'this is an assignation.' She leans out of her casement to watch the girl pass, slight as a silver ghost through fields and dark trees and ancient ruins.

The girl pauses in the shadows of a broken church. A man is waiting there, by the feet of a stone angel. But his is not the assignation that the girl hurries to. She speaks to the man, rapidly, urgently, entrusting him with a message. Then she is gone—her feet hurrying to the white house on the hill.

The paddy fields frame the Moon and the reflection of another girl. One so like the first that they have been confused for each other often enough. This one does not hurry. Her feet are slow and aimless. She has nowhere to go.

The girl is weeping. She stops in the shadows of a broken church at the feet of a marble angel.

Someone comes out of the darkness to her with a message. It is a man who has lost his voice and searched for it all his life.

His hands are eloquent in the moonlight. They plead his love and devotion. They shape a destiny together and ask a question. The Moon hangs breathless in the sky, wondering what the answer will be. But the girl is adamant. Her friend has left a message calling her. She must go to her friend and redeem the promise she has made in blood.

The Moon sees the girl turn to go. She sees the eloquence slip from the hands of the lover, and anger clench them. She sees the sickle flash and rise.

The Moon gasps in horror and draws back from the window. When she dares to look again the girl is gone. The lover stands there holding a hank of hair.

'Where did she go?' asks the Moon. 'What has become of her?'

But that is another story.

Time strokes the sixth knot and it eases open in his palm and lies there quiescent.

But the man at the well does not have the story that will untie the seventh and last knot. The rope is an inch away from water, thirsty and whimpering, but he cannot lower it any further.

Time leans forward and whispers. He has long, yellow teeth. 'There was a man once who drew a sword and cut through the knot that confounded him. But that takes inspiration and vision. It also takes a sword.'

Only one person had given me an answer when I asked time and again: 'Where is Sara?'

Sister Ursula had looked at me and said, 'Gone. Gone back to the gypsies.' I asked her how she knew. 'Her shoes,' said Sister Ursula. 'The night after she disappeared, I found her shoes lying in the middle of the road. I knew she had flung them off and gone back to being what she was before we found her. Do what you might, you cannot change them. It's in their blood.'

Sara slips now on quick, bare feet through the ending I have constructed and runs free. I cannot not find her. For that I need the seventh story. Seven is the mystic number, the one that seeks—and finds.

I would have despaired, but I thought of Tania. Of how her heart had led her unerringly to the true story every time. I put aside all the bits of paper and sat back. What would Tania have said?

She would have believed Sara. That she wasn't a bad girl. That she told the truth. That she kept her promises. I thought of Alice. Her faith had kept watch in the ruins for five years. Surely, such strength of belief deserved a convert.

Sara was not bad. Sara did not tell lies. Therefore, no matter what transpired, she would have returned to her sister in the ruins. Something had prevented her from returning to her sister. The answer was simple enough when I looked at it that way. Nina's murderer had prevented her from coming back. The ending lay with him.

I fetched the gun. The truth was, I didn't even know if that gun worked. And with only one bullet, there was no way to check.

I put the gun in my pocket and set off to hunt down a murderer with words.

The Unworthy Slave

The church was scented with camphor and mould.
Though it was afternoon, the day was so dark that
branches of candles had been lit on the altar. The
pews were shadowy trenches, empty of the faithful. Only
Damon knelt in the first row, gazing down at the coffin
that lay before the altar. After all these days, the bones
were still unburied.

The coffin was banked with white lilies that had come
all the way from Bombay. Their sweet cloying scent was
heavy in the air. Damon had spent every waking moment
in the church since the bones were named. He would be
waiting at the door when the sacristan arrived at dawn,
and he kept vigil until the priest asked him to leave late
at night.

My footsteps echoed in the empty church. I slipped
into the pew beside Damon and made the sign of the
cross I had learnt from Tania. My whisper was loud in the
silence. 'Praying for Nina? They say that if someone has
died an unnatural death, their soul does not rest in peace.
It wanders in torment until it is avenged.'

Damon gave no indication that he had heard me. I
leaned closer and whispered, 'The dead will have their
vengeance.'

His head lifted. He looked at me and simply said, 'I pray that is so.'

I saw with shock that he had withered. His face was haggard, his eyes ringed by dark circles. He looked like a man who walked in the shadow of death.

'I pray with all my heart that it is so,' he whispered.

This man who knelt before Nina's coffin was broken. There was no menace in him. The thought that came to my mind was that Damon was dying. The heart went out of what I had planned to say. Suddenly bereft of words, what I really wanted to know tumbled out without warning. 'Tell me about Nina.'

I had a sense that he had been waiting for this. Waiting at the edge of living to confess. His eyes stayed upon the bones. They were unseeing. He was looking past them to the moment when he first saw Nina. 'She came down the staircase of the main hall,' he began.

She descends on light feet. Her hair is a cascade to her waist. She is dressed in white, and until then, Damon has not known that such clean, such pure white, actually exists. Seeing a princess, he is suddenly aware of how he is soiled. He is aware with burning shame of his muddy feet on the tiles, the dust that covers him, his uncombed hair and the torn edge of his shirt.

The girl approaches. She takes his hand and leans forward to whisper, 'Since we are now cousins, I can kiss you welcome.' Her hair touches his face in silken strands and her breath smells of fruit as she places her lips on his cheek. He is branded with flames, burnt forever.

Dona Alcina beckons the boy closer and taps him critically with her cane. 'Stand straight, boy, don't stoop.

You are a Casimir now.' The cane taps him across the shoulders, on the knees, on the head—and Dona Alcina is satisfied that he is sound of body.

'Do you understand what that means? It means that all this will one day be yours.' Her gesture takes in the house—the gilded rafters, the gleaming porcelain, the painstakingly polished silver, the large 'C' that twines and weaves through every object so pridefully displayed. 'All of this.'

Damon's mind is still shrunken by the circumstances that have been his all these years. He cannot possibly imagine what it means to have a future like this. But he knows that if he were by some impossible, miraculous chance to have only one thing, then he knows what he would give his tomorrows for.

Dona Alcina waits for his reply. She notices where his gaze is straying. Her hand descends on his shoulder and she smiles for the first time. She whispers, 'Do not be shy. One day, you will marry her, and she, too, will be yours.'

And ever since, Damon has waited for that day.

The Story of the Slave and the Princess

Once upon a time, a Princess who lived in a castle was presented with a new Slave. The Princess clapped her hands with delight. She had been lonely for some time now, and the Slave had been promised to be hers, and only hers. She commanded him to play with her and he did. What games they played together! Hide-and-seek up in the attic, races through the long corridors of the palace, guessing games, strange games the Princess invented with five shells and three beads. They hid, crouching, breathless from stifled giggling, in the storeroom, hands full of stolen apricots.

Her servants could never find the Princess, she was always missing. And when they could not find her they did not bother looking for the Slave either. He was sure to be with her. He was bound to her by hours minutes seconds. Never could he leave her.

Her smallest wish was his command. 'Be *bad* for me. *Steal* for me!'

They would plan for hours what he would steal. Then he would climb trees in the afternoon, when everyone was sleeping, and rain mangoes down on the laughing Princess. At other times, it was cashew fruit, or guavas. And one shining morning, it was Crazy Charlie's false teeth. How they laughed to hear him spraying spit and spattered syllables, inarticulate in his rage, and incomprehensible without his teeth.

'I want you to *lie* for me. Tell a terrible lie.'

And so, the next day, heart trembling, he went to the priest to tell him that Dona Alcina was very, very sick. She was dying. The priest left his ablutions and ran all the way to the old house, terrified that a patron as good as Dona Alcina was leaving the world so precipitately. Why, she had only just made a promise to contribute towards repairing the roof of the church! He found his patroness eating finely cut sandwiches off china that had been imported from Venice.

The Princess was quick to the Slave's rescue. 'He said it because I told him to. I thought you were dying, Grandma. I dreamt it! Such a terrible dream.' Her sobs were quick and hard and heart-rending. And Grandma melted, and retribution was stayed, and both of them were given a special cake with custard poured on it lavishly.

The truth is that the Slave had loved the Princess from the time he first set eyes on her. And even if she had not been a Princess he would have done every single thing she ever commanded.

But the Princess was his just for one enchanted summer. Then, the Slave was told that he must be off to a special school so that the slave husk of him could be polished and rubbed off. He was eager to shed his skin as well, and glad to be off.

In boarding school, the Slave learns the subtle differences that separate the boys. The pure-bred Portuguese sneer at the half-breeds. The half-breeds sneer at the full-Indians. Those who go to Portugal for the holidays are a rung above those who merely have relatives there. A father in the government is worth twice one in private service.

There is an intricate tree upon which they all hang, crucified or redeemed by their lineage. With a three-hundred-year-old name, a Casimir would indeed be in the top branches, if he were not so obviously an adopted charity boy. The charity boys come at the bottom of the pile.

Damon learns to hold his spoon and fork correctly and sneer at the charity boys along with the rest. The Casimir name becomes all-important. It is his salvation, his one key to opening doors to higher things. He becomes prouder of that name than even Dona Alcina is. He learns the names of every ancestor, the stories of achievement and glory, and is glad that he is the Chosen One. He will never let the name down.

Holiday time, all the way home in the carriage he thinks, 'This time ... this time, I will see her, and I will not be a Slave'. But each time, when he sees her, he is undone. He knows that his feet are still dusty, and in his heart he is still a Slave.

But now the Princess's whims have turned in other directions. One hot summer day, they are scavenging for guavas in the graveyard when she turns to him with a new command. 'Kiss me.' He dares not. His heart trembles within him.

The Princess taunts him, 'Scaredy cat!'

And so, the Slave lays his lips against the Princess's. 'Ugh!' she says. 'I don't like it. You smell of fish.'

He turns away from her. He finds himself running as fast as he can. He wants to hide. Hide away someplace where no one will see that he has been cut in two and is bleeding.

The Princess finds him in the attic. His face still bears the marks of the burning tears that he has shed. He is curled underneath a table with three legs.

'Come out of there!' she commands. Even wounded and bleeding, he obeys her. She kneels before him, looking curiously at his face. She touches the marks the tears have left on his face. And the Princess says that she is sorry.

But the Princess has discovered that she can make him bleed—and ever after that, she cannot resist pricking him.

The Slave strives tirelessly to prove his utter devotion to her. Fervently, on Sundays, he whispers the lines from the Mass that have become his own private incantation. 'Only say that I am worthy—and I shall be healed.'

But with time, there is no healing. The unkind cuts grow deeper. His Princess is tiring of her Slave.

In the hushed silence of the church, Damon cried, 'Holy! Holy!' upon the name of his love. Always and always, it would be Nina. I looked at him and realised that I had come to catch a murderer, but found a lover instead.

Damon's head dropped into his hands. But I knew that the words were not yet done. Damon was making his last confession. He was giving of the bread of his own living. I was receiving the sacrament of another's truth.

'She was meant to marry me. The date had been set. We were to be married at Christmas. And then I stopped Sara on a bridge and discovered it was Nina. She was going to him.'

Damon's voice is raw with pain. 'I knew about them. I watched them, you know,' he says. 'I watched them through the window.'

So many evenings watching the Princess. Watching her climb the hill to another kingdom. Watching her through the window, unable to turn away. Watching through eyes seared almost blind with tears. So many nights awake, knowing he will never be worthy. Never. She will never say the word. He will never be healed.

He is not the only one watching. Dona Alcina has been hearing rumours. When Damon brings Nina back home, her grandmother is waiting. Nina will not be allowed to tarnish the pride of the Casimirs. The only way to keep it bright and shining is to lock it away.

The key is placed in the Slave's hand. It has an ornate initial upon the haft. The initial of the name that has been given to the slave. The Pride of the Casimirs is now in his keeping. He holds the key.

Late at night he hears the shouting. The servant girl has been found passing notes to the Princess from under the door. She is cast out of the house and goes weeping into the night.

When silence returns to the house, he goes and stands at the door and hears something that he has never heard before. The tears of a Princess. He falls to his knees and whispers to her to stop weeping. The Princess whispers back. She too is on her knees. A Princess on her knees to a slave. She begs him to let her go.

He unlocks the door, knowing that he will never be worthy. He lets her go.

'I let her go,' Damon says. 'I had the key. I opened the door and let her go. I held her happiness above mine. I set her free—and she went to *him*.' He spat out the last word.

'I told no one. When Dona Alcina insisted I search for her, I pretended to.' He hesitates, then says, 'I went to Portugal. I went to see her one last time. To know that she was happy. I stood in a concert hall and heard that man play. There was no sign of Nina. I accosted him after the concert, shouted questions at him that he would not answer. It must have sounded like a brawl in the offing. The police were called. They escorted me to a plane the next day, telling me I would not be welcomed back to the country.'

Damon raises his eyes to the coffin. 'I came back and buried an empty coffin. And every night I prayed that Nina was happy. That she was with him. But I didn't know for sure. Such torment, not to know!'

I remembered the task I had set myself. 'What did you do to Sara? Where is she?'

'Sara? The little orphan girl? I felt sorry for her.'

He turns his gaze back to the coffin. The sacristan is moving in the darkness behind us. We can hear doors being shut, the distant jangle of keys.

Without much conviction, I try to goad a reply from him. 'You know what happened to her. You are the reason she never returned.'

'Sara? I know nothing of what happened to her. I have often wondered. I would have never sent her away. She was my last link with Nina. She loved her, too.'

He falls silent. I can hear the footsteps of the sacristan coming down the aisle. I am running out of time. 'Finish the story!' I say urgently.

'And then that man came back. I learned that he had returned alone. That he had never been married.' He hisses the words at me. '*He had never been married!* Where was she? What had he done with my Nina? I tried to choke the truth out of him. I would have killed him if you hadn't intervened.'

He turns back to the coffin and there is so much sorrow in his eyes. 'Then, to find the bones. To find her like this. In his well. Alone all these years.'

I look back at the coffin. At the bones lying there, gilded by candlelight. I know what it is to lie in a coffin. To be a snake, blinded and choked. An ant in a vial of salt.

Remembrance hardens my heart and brings back my conviction. This man has tried to bury me alive.

The sacristan coughs in the darkness. It is time to leave.

I get to my feet. 'Nice story,' I say. 'I can tell, because I am a storyteller myself.'

'You think I lie?' cries Damon, turning to look at me for the first time.

'Yes,' I say. 'You never let Nina free to join Lisbon. You killed her rather than let her go to him. You tried to kill me. You are not a lover. You are a murderer.'

Damon is quick on his feet and starts towards me. 'Don't you dare say that!' he hisses and grabs me by the throat. I raise the gun and hold it to his head. We both freeze in place.

The alarmed sacristan wrings his hands. 'Remember where you are! Please! This is a sacred place. You cannot quarrel here! Put down the gun.'

'Liar!' I whisper into Damon's ear. We stand, as close as lovers.

'You will never know how much I loved her,' he whispers back. There are tears running down his face. 'I would be happy to be bones in that coffin today if it meant that she was spared.'

'*Help*!' cries the sacristan. 'Father! Help! *Murder*!'

At the cry of 'murder', Damon's hands loosen. He steps back and I fall into a pew, wheezing and gasping.

Damon turns and walks away down the aisle. The anxious face of the sacristan looms over me.

'Are you all right? Are you hurt?'

I shrug off his concern and rise shakily to my feet. I have my seventh story—and the last knot still remains unpicked.

The Long Goodbye

It was the third time I was packing to leave that house. Twice, it had refused to let me go. Or, say rather, that the story had refused to let me go. It sought to be ended. And I was a poor writer who could not find my way to that resolution, all doubts resolved, all questions answered, all threads knotted.

The last thing I gathered together was the large pile of typed manuscript that sat on my worktable. I sat down and read it all from end to end. It was almost a novel. But for that stubborn ending!

Though I may not be certain of finding the ending or Sara, I am certain, however, that it is Damon who is behind it all. When his fingers closed on my throat last night, all my doubts vanished. I have no doubt he has loved Nina deeply. But is it not the thwarted lover who might choose to make a quietus for that love with his own bare hands? I can think of no stratagem to shake the truth from him.

With a start, I realise I have been reading at the table for a long time. The children have been let free for lunch, and the tumult of their cries reaches me. When the bell rings half an hour later, the house returns to silence. It is a saudade silence, deep with the unsounded notes of separation and departure.

I walked through all the rooms again. I rummaged through Miss Miranda's collection of records and put one on the turntable. It was to the strains of Beethoven's *Opus 109* that I drifted through the house. As the music swelled into the Third Movement, I came upon Tania sitting in the wind chime room in a shower of chime-song.

The clouds were moving over the valley. From our place in the window apse, I could mark the progress of the rain by the moving tide in the trees below us. The rain stalked up the valley and soon we were cocooned in a haze of grey. The house was an ark and we were adrift in an uncharted sea of our own.

It was our last day together, and we both knew it. By an unspoken understanding, neither of us mentioned Sara. Instead, we simply talked. A girl and a boy, shyly learning about each other on the last day that they could be together.

I made her laugh with stories of my childhood as a Parsee prince. She told me about the orphans in Mater Dolorosa and all the small ways in which they took their petty revenge on the nuns. I sang her nonsense songs, quoted from poets that I love, described my library. She told me about the games she had played with her friends and the stories they told each other.

The light slowly began to ebb from the day. We had wandered through the house for all the afternoon. But now, with the dusk, the knowledge came upon us that our idyll was ending. With that, our paradise returned to being an old, mouldering house, rank with smells and riddled with leaks. Dolour came upon us, and the knowledge that it would soon be time for me to go.

I wondered how to say the words that I had carefully prepared as I walked through the house in the day. I had a sudden inspiration. We were in the music room. I placed a record on the turntable and held out a hand. 'Will you dance with me?'

Tania looked at my outstretched hand. She held out hers, but it did not touch mine, her fingers hovering an inch above my hand. Mischief danced in her eyes. I couldn't help laughing. I accepted the unstated condition. My vow could not be broken.

The music began. Tania's bare feet rose on tiptoe and she stepped into the dance. We danced without touching, inches from each other. We separated to dodge the drips from the roof, returned to a handspan distance, inched dangerously closer. Tania judged each turn carefully, dancing out of reach at exactly the right time. Her feet were quick upon the warped boards.

Stiffly posed ancestors watched us spin in the eddy of music, reflected as we were in the photo frames that lined the walls. The falling darkness blurred our images, and then, erased them.

I did not pause to light the lamps, and so darkness fell upon us like an unstoppable enchantment, and we kept dancing. I blundered like a blind moth; she danced joyously like one drawn to the light. She dipped towards me and curved away at the last minute, evading my outstretched hands, my desire.

As the darkness deepened, I strained to place Tania. I listened for her breath, for the sound of her feet upon the floorboards, but I heard nothing. She may as well not have been there.

Then came the inevitable moment when I was tempted to break my promise. I had been straining every sense against the dark. Now I reached out in triumph. Instinct made Tania step back quickly—and my outstretched hand snatched at the air not even a thread away from her. Just at that moment, the record stuck. The phrase repeated itself to the point of what seemed like idiocy. Tania began to laugh. The moment was broken, vow left intact.

The dance had left me winded and disappointed, and I did not feel inclined to laugh. But the sound of her delighted giggles, tumbling through the darkness, made me smile, reluctantly. I went to replace the record and light a fresh candle.

I took a long time at the gramophone, gathering up courage to say all that I knew must be said today. I turned back to Tania. 'Before I say anything, you have to promise me that you won't run away. That's all you do. Run away.'

She gave me a dimpled smile, but refused to give me a promise.

'I am taking a room in the village. I'm not going anywhere. Please come to me there. Promise you will.'

But Tania refused to make any vows in return. 'I can't.'

'Why not? You must. You must meet me again. There is something I must tell you.'

'I won't listen.'

'You told me I would know when the time was right. The time is now.'

She backed away from me, shaking her head in denial. 'No. Not yet.'

I reached out, spurning all the promises I had made. She saw the resolution in my face and turned and fled from me. I started after her. This was no game. I was chasing her now in earnest. She fled, down the length of all those rooms. I blundered in the dark, knocked over sudden chairs and furniture, but did not desist in my pursuit.

I cornered her in the hall filled with dusty animals. I leaned against the lion, holding my side and struggling to get my breath back. 'There is something I have to say to you. Listen to me, Tania!'

Tania shook her head. 'No! Not now. Not yet.'

'Listen to me!'

'No!'

The clatter of someone knocking on the door fell like a death knell through the house. Distracted, I turned my head. When I turned back, only the empty glass eyes of the animals gazed back at me. All I saw reflected in their stares was myself, standing there, empty hand outstretched.

Lisbon was wet through, and stood dripping on the doorstep. 'I've come to lock up,' he said.

Worlds Too Far Apart

We locked the chapel first. The drunken caretaker had repaired the hole in the roof, but anything of the slightest value was already gone. Still, Lisbon insisted on locking it again. He produced a large chain that he threaded through hasps and hinges and secured with a large padlock. We went back through the house in silence. My feet dragged, reluctant, through that walk.

None of the rooms felt strange any longer. There were memories in each of them. In this one, Tania and I had wound up the gramophone and listened to it playing for hours. Here, to the tune of the wind chimes, she had wept for Alice, so sadly deserted. To me they were a kingdom rich with remembrance, that I was being forced to abdicate.

Lisbon made awkward conversation. 'There is a car waiting for me in the village. I am going to Vasco and catching a train to Bombay.'

My slow feet came to a pause in the music room. Shadows from the lamp I carried danced across the photographs of Miss Miranda's career. 'I have a favour to ask,' I said. Lisbon turned courteously to me.

I gestured to the disc kept carefully on the Chinese table. 'Do you want the recording? I was wondering if I could have it. You play beautifully.'

Lisbon smiled. 'Of course. Please keep it.' I picked up the disc.

Lisbon said, 'I haven't thanked you for all you've done. I don't know whether we will meet again.' He held out his hand. 'Felicidade seja sua sempre.'

I looked at the hand held out to me. Sara's voice came calling to me across the black water. With brittle care I put the record back down on the Chinese table.

Then I said to Lisbon, 'Sit down.'

'I have to leave. A car is—'

'Sit down! You're not going anywhere for a while.' The gun was cold and heavy, but my hand was steady.

Lisbon looked from the gun to me. 'Have you gone crazy?'

'There's still a bullet in it. Sit down. There's a stool behind you.'

Lisbon stepped back until he banged into the stool and sat down. I sat on the winged armchair beside the little table. The gun felt awkward in my hand. I had no idea if I could actually pull the trigger if I needed to. To my own surprise I found that I was calm. My mind was busy feeling out this ending, trying to fit it into the rest of the story.

'I came here to write a novel. And all I've done since I arrived is try to find Sara.' Lisbon was watching me carefully, his eyes dipping away to the gun from time to time.

'I tried to write my own ending. I wrote many alternative endings of what happened to Sara and Nina, but none of them fit. I didn't have a chance of getting them right. You know why?' I wondered why I had never thought of all this before. 'I got the characters wrong. I had Damon cast as the villain and you as the true lover. But I was wrong, wasn't I?'

I looked at him sitting there on the piano stool, listening intently. 'Why did you kill Nina?'

'Kill Nina?' Lisbon held out a conciliating hand. 'Calm down. You've lost all touch with reality. You've got so wrapped up in solving this missing Sara business that you don't know what is fact and what is fiction anymore.'

He started to rise, but I raised the gun. 'Sit down! I've come too far not to know how it ended. That's the problem with a really good story. You must know how it ended.' Lisbon sat down again. He made an attempt to speak.

'Shhh!' I gestured for him to be silent. I was concentrating fiercely. 'Listen. I'm going to tell you a story. It starts like all good stories should, with "Once upon a time".'

Shadows danced around the hall. The lamp washed us in gold. Both of us were bound within the circle of light until the story was told.

'Once upon a time there were two friends called Sara and Nina. One was a Princess, and one a servant. A handsome man—romantic, a musician, oh, so irresistible—came into their lives. Both of them lost their hearts to him. But one of them gave him more than just her heart. She came to him in this house and became his lover. It was the perfect romance. Until the day she came to him and told him she was pregnant. Suddenly, it wasn't so wonderful. He hadn't planned on this. He'd just wanted a quick holiday affair to while away the time.'

The words were quick to Lisbon's lips. 'I loved her!'

I silenced him irritably. 'Don't interrupt. I'll lose the thread of the story. Where was I? Ah yes—and I'm making this bit up, but I think I'm right—I think he told her that he'd take her away with him. They'd both go to Portugal and live happily ever after. But he never planned to do anything of the sort. She, poor thing, believed him.

'But the dragon who guarded the palace she lived in, locked her up, and she could not go to her lover. The Princess remembered her true friend, the servant girl, and sent her with a message to her lover, telling him to come to her. Rescue her. And he sent the maid back with a note. A Goodbye Note.' I knew the note by heart. Why had it never occurred to me that the writing was not Sara's? I had learnt her careful hand so well as it led me through the pages of her story.

'Our worlds are too far apart to meet. It can never be. Felicidade seja sua sempre. What does it mean, by the way?'

'May you never be far from happiness,' said Lisbon.

The words were an admission. So lost was I in my story, that I didn't really notice. I nodded. 'A bit ironic in the light of the events that followed, don't you think?'

'You could say that,' said Lisbon.

'I had the note all wrong. The lover wrote it to her. Not the other way around. The Princess thought there must be some mistake. How could her constant lover, who had sworn to be true eternally—change? She was determined to go to him and plead with him. She begged her fiancé to let her go. And he made the biggest sacrifice that true love can make, and let her go. *He* was the true lover all along.' I thought of Damon praying night after night at the coffin of his Princess.

Lisbon did not say anything. He was listening carefully to every word. The pause stretched and he couldn't help asking, 'And then?'

'And then she came here, running through the dark night. I think she found the lover gone. Back to his world which was so distant from hers. Pregnant and desperate, her heart broken, she threw herself in the well.'

The flame of the lamp waxed and Lisbon's face flared out of the darkness. He was smiling. He shook his head, laughing. 'You didn't know Nina. She didn't come here to kill herself. She came to kill me.'

The note is flung in his face, and Nina stands there, furious. 'What do you think I am? Some helpless servant girl you can dump when you want? I am a Casimir.'

Pride smoulders in her anger. It holds her hand steady as she points a gun. A gun with an elegant handle, carved with an elaborate 'C'.

Lisbon gestured to the gun in my hand. 'She had that gun in her hand. And she did her best to put a bullet in me.'

Fling yourself sideways. Floorboards burning your face. Spinning desperately, the cock of the gun almost louder than the shot itself. Scrambling, twisting, turning over in time to see her pull the trigger again.

'Did you think I'd let you get away with it?'

Stink of cordite in your nostrils. Click. The gun is cocked again. Time has slowed. Your hand takes an age to reach out. To close around an ankle. Tug. She falls to the ground and fractures time so that it speeds up again and you are grappling on the floor, as your life counts down.

The gun fires again. You have no idea if the bullet has hit you. You grab the gun. She sinks her teeth into your wrist. You snap her hand sideways. She drops the gun. Your hand is still reaching for it when she pulls a chair down on your head. It slams across your temple. Sound explodes out of your ears. In dead silence you swing your hand into her face. She ducks. Another soundless explosion at the side of your head. Your sight dims and flickers.

'We fought all over the place. The bitch bit and kicked and scratched. She never gave up. One moment I'd be hitting her. The next moment she'd be on me screaming and slamming a chair into my face.'

Pain. Exploding from your jaw. Searing up your arm. You gather your fist and slam pain back into her face. She rolls with the blow. Grabs the doorstop from the floor. Stabs fresh agony into your hand.

Lisbon shook his head in reluctant admiration. 'She was a devil, that one. I picked the wrong girl. Actually, I did think she was a servant girl who wouldn't say a word. Sara the angel. And I got Nina the devil. Oh, she meant to kill me.'

He sat there smiling to himself. It was the smile of a survivor. 'We both lost the gun early on in the fight. But then she got the damned candlestand.'

It is a trident of metal, topped with sharp spikes to impale candles. It slams into the floor inches from your face. You scramble to your feet. Run. She is running after you, screaming. You realise that you are screaming as well.

She is gaining on you. You turn to look over your shoulder and she is Nemesis, hair flying, eyes of glass. And in that moment, you skid. Your feet go out from under you. You go down screaming and feel her weight fall heavy across your legs.

You open your eyes and she is sitting across you, candlestand raised in both hands, tines pointed to your heart. She whispers, 'Die! Die, you bastard!'

'I really thought I was going to die. She had me on the floor and raised that vicious thing to shove it into my chest.'

Your brain has frozen. A sudden flash of what you had shared with this woman sears your mind. You heave your groin in a grotesque parody of climax. Unseat the girl. Grab her hair. Slam her head against the floor. Again and again. You are locked against her from breast to groin. The rhythm picks up and you are melded into an act that is love and death together. Slam her down again and again and again, until she stops moving.

'We had ended up in the kitchen. I picked her up and carried her to the well. I could barely walk. I balanced her on the rim. Then I let her go.'

Silence. Her arms flying open as she spins down the dark throat of the well. The distant sound of water opening and closing around her. Soft guttural lappings ... sibilant sucking sounds ... silence.

There was silence in the room. Somewhere, a solitary heron called. I sat frozen in place, staring at Lisbon. Lisbon shrugged off the gaze angrily.

'You don't understand. I have in my hands—greatness. I am the youngest violinist since Maestro Andre to be invited to play for the German Philharmonic. Do you know what an honour that is? It is recognition that I am the best of my time.' He flexed his long fingers, held his hands out to the light. 'I am an artiste. We need our inspirations. But we can't marry all of them. You are a writer. You will understand.'

He leaned forward. 'I have been given The Gift. In each generation one person has had The Gift. But none have had the chance to hone it and polish it like I have. How I have worked! Played till my fingers were bleeding. Used my talent and mind until I was emptied. Europe will remember my name not just in this century but in those to come. You must understand. I couldn't have some little villager from Goa hanging around my neck.'

I said softly, 'Finish the story.'

Lisbon sighed. 'I thought it was over. Then the other one turned up.'

'Sara?' I leaned forward, intent and absorbed. Here was the ending at last.

Lisbon leaned over and, in one swift movement, he slammed his hand down on my wrist. Taken by surprise I let go my grip on the gun. Lisbon grabbed the gun as it fell. It was absurdly simple.

Hands suddenly bereft, I began to rise to my feet and found that Lisbon could hold the gun steady as well. 'My turn to tell you to sit down. Sit down!'

I sat down. Lisbon leaned close to the lamp. He spun open the chamber and checked that there was indeed a bullet in it. Then he pointed the gun at me and said, 'You really are irritatingly persistent. I shoved a statue onto you and it didn't kill you. I shoved you in a coffin and you rose like some bloody Lazarus from the dead.'

We stared at each other. A small moth clinked against the glass of the lamp. It was the only sound in the room until Lisbon sighed again. 'This is really upsetting all my plans. What should we do now, I wonder?'

I had no hesitation. 'Finish the story.' If I was going to die, I had to know how it ended.

There was moment of silence in the room. Lisbon threw his head back and laughed out loud. 'You writers are crazy people.' Then he shrugged and said, 'Might as well get it over with.' And so he continued to the ending I had sought for so long.

'I was lying there exhausted, wondering if Nina had broken any bones of mine, when I heard a knock on the door. I was so tired I just wanted to go on lying there on the ground, but the knocking wouldn't go away. Finally, I got up, found the gun and went to the door. The other one was standing outside, asking for her friend. The servant girl.'

I leaned forward. At last. Sara.

'I would have fobbed her off with some story, except at that moment I heard screaming. Screaming like all the devils had broken out of hell together! She heard it too. I slammed the door in Sara's face and ran back to the kitchen. It wasn't Nina screaming. It was the pulley.'

Screaming! Screaming like a woman in agony. The air bubbles with the banshee wailing. You stare at the moving pulley, mind struggling to absorb that this means it isn't over yet.

'It was moving. The bitch was trying to climb up the rope. She wasn't dead.'

I was riveted. I scarcely breathed, scared that Lisbon would halt his narration.

'She hung in the well, grinning up at me. I pointed the gun at her. I never got to use the bloody thing. The other girl came flying through the well window and grabbed my hand.'

The girl is a knot of desperation that clings to your hand. You slam her against the wall, claw at her hands, but she does not let go. She is a dead weight, a vice around your arm, the gun pressed against her flesh. And through it all, the screaming screaming screaming of that inhuman voice.

He looked at me. 'They were quite a pair, those two. I never planned to kill anyone. Those two just forced my hand. What was I supposed to do? Lie down and die?'

I said nothing. I was afraid to speak. Afraid that my words would somehow change the story and make it worse.

'We fought for the gun all over this kitchen floor. And all the time we were doing that, Nina was climbing up the rope, inch by inch. I can tell you, I thought I'd had it. If one of those witches didn't get me, the other would. Then I managed to pull the trigger. Once. Twice.'

I flinched.

The girl shudders twice. But her hands are around the gun and she won't let it go. Even as she falls, she is wrenching it from your hand, flinging it as far as she can. Her weight slows, hangs in the balance, then tilts and falls heavily to the floor. Your hands are free.

'I heard Nina screaming her name, "Sara! Don't let him go, Sara!". I ran back to the well and there she was, five feet away from the top, still hanging on and struggling to get her breath. The only thing that would stop her was a bullet in the head. But when I turned around, I just couldn't find the gun.

'I didn't know where Sara had flung it. I saw a knife on the kitchen table and grabbed it. But Nina was hanging just out of reach. Then it struck me. So simple. Cut the rope.'

I moved involuntarily. The long hands that made music clenched around the gun. Then Lisbon continued to unload the albatross he had carried around his neck for so long.

'I began to saw at the rope, and she began to climb up it, and that cursed pulley just shrieked through the entire thing.'

The knife slipping and turning in your hand, slick with Sara's blood and your sweat. The bite of it travelling up your arm as you saw away at the rope.

The rope thrums and shivers. She is climbing up it again. A hand appears over the edge. You raise your hand and slash at it. She jerks back and, with that, the last fraying thread parts.

Lisbon shook his head. 'It was close. But I won. I cut the rope. She fell back into the well. I watched her go all the way.'

The hollow echo of the girl falling into the water. Water agitated and roiling as she rises and sinks and rises and sinks again.

You count. Once … Twice … Turn your head. There is a blank space where the other girl was lying. And a streak of dark blood that leads into the shadows.

He looked at me. 'It never seemed to end. I just had time to notice Sara wasn't there, and there she was, coming at me with a grinding stone.'

The shadows are filled with intent. A sudden movement and a stabbing pain. Hot fire slammed against your temple. Darkness pours in from the shattered side of your head.

Lisbon fingered the scar over his eyebrow. 'Remember Sara? Of course I do. She gave me this to remember her by.

'I must have blacked out for a second or two. When I came around I couldn't see anything. I thought I had been blinded, but it was the blood in my eyes. I lay there dazed. I could hear the friends screaming to each other.'

The well magnifies the voices so that they call to each other across vast distances.

'Nina!'

'Sara!'

'Nina, hold on! You have to!'

'I can't. I can't any longer.'

'I'm going for help.'

'First make me a promise. Promise me you'll see him punished. Promise me he'll be punished!'

'I promise.'

Blood. The cloying blanket across your sight is blood. You wipe your eyes with a shaking hand. Slowly, something comes into focus but your mind cannot decipher the sinuous coil that lies beside you. Then you understand.

'"Promise" was the last thing she said. I came up behind her and picked up what was left of the well rope and put it around her neck.

'Then I stood by the well and watched until Nina went down for the third time.'

Her fingers are splayed against the wall. They have found purchase in a tiny crevice. But the water sucks at her. Her clothes are sodden and heavy, her fingers tear free and she falls into the maw of dark water.

Ripples run quick from where she has vanished. There is the sound of the water … laps and sucks … clicks and mutters. All swallowed by the well until only dense silence remains.

The night comes back for the first time with its sound of crickets and rustling wind. You lean your head on the edge of the well. It is cold and damp. You realise that you are crying.

A moth blundered against the lamp. Its wings threw shutters of light and dark across the room. There was silence. It was broken only by the moth's frantic spasms against the glass. I fought to hold back tears. My hands were clenched. 'You killed Sara? You killed them both?'

Lisbon said angrily, 'Do you think I meant to do any of it? I'm a musician, not a killer. I didn't mean to kill anyone.

It happened. They pushed me to it. Everything that night just happened. God. How I have suffered!'

I whispered the forlorn words, 'And then?'

Lisbon was impatient now to be done with the tale. 'I didn't dare go near that damn well. I found another place and hid Sara. Cleaned up the mess. Went back to searching for the gun. I just couldn't find the damn thing. Then it struck me. I didn't need to. It was so simple. Lock up the house and go. No one would ever know. No one did. Until you came along.'

We both sat looking at each other.

'You tried to kill me,' I said. 'To stop me asking questions.'

'Yes,' says Lisbon. 'You were just so damn persistent. Questions, questions, questions! No one gave a damn about Sara for five years. No one does still—except you.'

Here it was at last. I had come upon the end of my story. I could think of nothing more to say or ask. It was done. *Finis*.

'And now?'

Lisbon shrugged. 'You wanted to know how this story ends? The same way as last time. You wanted to find Sara? Well, you will. And I'll just lock up and walk away again. And this time nothing will bring me back. Nothing.' He gestured with the gun. 'Get up.'

I did not know where Lisbon was taking me. I walked as I was bid, through all the length of rooms, knowing only that I was being led to Sara.

Lisbon could not seem to stop talking now that he had started. He talked of music. 'I have to go back. I am the principal solo violinist for Liszt's *Consolation*. Yehudi Menuhin and I were both considered. They chose me.'

His voice was loud in the deserted rooms. 'It is not an easy piece at all. I don't mean technically. Anybody can fiddle on the strings. The difficult part is putting soul into it, and truth. Real truth in your interpretation.'

Lisbon began to hum, completely at ease in the situation. He had the concentration of a great musician. He was completely focused, now that he knew what he had to do. Then he stopped. His head snapped around. 'What was that?'

The merest hint of presence. Movement at the farthest edge of perception. Scarcely movement. As if the darkness itself rippled.

He peered into corners with the lamp, but there was nothing there. 'All these damn shadows. I'll be glad to see the last of this rotting house.'

He prodded me to move on, but I had scarcely taken a few steps when Lisbon stopped dead again. 'What was that?'

There it was again. The sense of a presence that followed us, a presence that hovered just out of our reach. But unlike Lisbon, I knew what it was. It was no ghost. It was Tania following us, her bare feet soundless on the ground.

'Perhaps the dead leave something of themselves behind,' I said.

Lisbon laughed. 'A ghost? I don't think so. If they did, those two witches would have haunted me to my grave by now.'

But from then on, Lisbon was uneasy. We traversed the next room in silence, Lisbon watching out of the corners of his eyes for movement. We were in the hall of stuffed animals and their glass eyes followed us as we crossed the room.

Lisbon looked around wildly. 'There was something there!' he cried.

I said, 'I saw nothing.'

'Is anybody there?' called Lisbon into the dark. Then he laughed at himself. Firmly, he said, 'There is nobody in this house but you and me.'

'And Sara,' I said. 'She is still here.'

'Be quiet! She is dead. And has stayed dead all these years.'

We hurried through the last room towards the wind chime hall. I saw Tania slip ahead of us. I wished Tania would leave us. There was still one bullet left in the gun. I feared for her, and I could not imagine what she could do to help.

As we came to the door of the wind chime hall, I spied what Lisbon did not see. Bare feet that hid behind the door.

Lisbon pointed the gun at me and gestured for me to step through the door first. As we came through the door, Tania panicked and ran down the length of the hall, shawl trailing after her.

I spun around, hoping to catch Lisbon off guard. Lisbon was staring after Tania. 'Did you see that?' he whispered. 'Did you see her?'

I said, 'I saw nothing. What is it you think you're seeing?'

'Her.'

He was sweating. His face was white and the scar on his forehead stood out like a slash. Lisbon wavered, then raised his gun.

Tania had fetched up at the door of the chapel and stood there, frozen, not daring to move. The gun shook and then steadied.

I had no weapon but words. I stepped quickly between the gun and Tania's figure and spoke. 'There's nothing there. What are you imagining? There is nothing there at all. Don't shoot!'

Lisbon whispered urgently to me, 'Turn around.'

My words stuttered and stopped. I turned.

'Can you see her? She's standing right there with a shawl over her head. Just like I saw her that night when she came to the house.'

I turned back slowly and said, 'I think you're overwrought. There's nobody there.'

Tania made a small movement. Terror washed through Lisbon. His hands were trembling. He could scarcely shape words. He stood there, rigid with fear. Then his finger began to tighten on the trigger.

I grabbed for his hand and struggled to wrest the gun from him. I was praying that it would not go off. There would be so much blood.

Abruptly, Lisbon let go of the gun and flung himself free, scrambling backwards, away from the shrouded figure that stood at the chapel door. 'Oh God! Can't you see her? She's standing *right there!*'

'Where is Sara, Lisbon? What did you do with her?'

Lisbon said, 'Can't you see her? She's there! Where I left her!'

Fear had reduced him to a series of shudders. His jittery finger pointed at the chapel.

'Open the chapel!' I said. Lisbon shook his head vehemently. He began to back away. I held out an urgent hand. 'Give me the key.'

Tania began to turn around. Lisbon's nerve broke. He dropped the keys. They scattered across the floor in jangling discord. I got to my knees and grabbed them up as fast as I could.

Lisbon backed away and blundered into the darkness.

I picked up the keys and ran to the door of the chapel. I fumbled the padlock open as fast as I could. The metal chain twisted and slithered and wrapped itself around my frantic hands. Finally, I freed them.

I shoved open the doors to the chapel. I stepped into it and raised my lamp. Tania followed me.

It was a bare room wrapped in shadows. But it had a shifting quality. When first I spied it through a crack, it was mysterious. When, led by the noise, I had come upon it, bathed in moonlight, it was scary. Seen through disenchanted eyes in the light of day, it was ordinary. Now, by lamplight, it had resumed its secretive and enigmatic air. Dark, rustling shapes huddled everywhere. The lamp picked out a few faint gleams of glass and metal. 'She's in here, somewhere,' I said, raising the lamp.

I began to search in a frenzy. Suddenly, I paused. My lamp had lit up a crucifix that was hanging on the wall. It was the one the robbers hit me with. The crucifix pointed like a giant arrow. Below it was the box bench that I had sat on. I knelt by the bench. My fingers hooked underneath the lid. The top of the bench opened like the lid of a chest. Inside was the ending I had sought so long.

The candlelight turned the bones that lay within to tarnished gold. They were a scatter of riches in the coffin. At last, the ending of the story. At last—Sara.

Tania dropped to her knees and crossed herself. I raised my lamp to see the woman I had searched for so long and so hard.

Sara was lying curled on her side, one hand slightly outflung. Something in the casket caught the light and glinted. The glint was nestled in the bones of that hand. Puzzled, I brought the lamp closer. It was a coin, shiny and new. A coin given to make a wish in a well. A coin given to make a wish for love.

Seven stories. Seven stories I had gathered and not found what I searched for. I had forgotten there is always one more story. The one that lies in the silences that weave all the others together. That hides between the words. That whispers in the breaths we take as we tell it, and is carried off by the wind.

The silence when I named her Constania, which I took for acquiescence.

The silence when I made a promise never to lay a hand on her.

The third silence when I urged her to make a wish in the well.

I realised that I had known it all along. This story had been given to me, and I had always known how it would end. I had heard the silences, but not understood what they wove till this moment.

I slowly raised my eyes to where the girl knelt beside the coffin. She was looking steadily at me. So many names. Constania … Tania … Saraswati …

'Sara.'

We looked at each other one long long moment. Then I put out my hand to finally touch her. I didn't break my gaze as my hand reached out. Slowly. So slowly.

A gust of wind caught the candle flame. It wavered— and there was nothing there for me to hold.

Lisbon crashes through the undergrowth, running wild with fear. His terror rides him like a bat, clinging to his hair, chittering in his ear. He cannot fling it off. In his mad, headlong rush, he is blind to the gaping maw in the stone flags. It is an old well, overgrown with plants, bearded with grass and almost invisible. He screams until he hits water. The hollow echo rises to the quiet evening.

A little girl appears at the mouth of the well. Around her hangs the miasma of neglect. She is about nine years old and is wearing a patched and ragged uniform. She stares curiously down at the man who rises and sinks and rises and sinks again. Ripples run quick from the space of his vanishing. Then she looks up and her face radiates joy. Her vigil is over. The one she loves has returned to her. 'Sara!'

The two sisters run to each other and cling together.

A voice calls through the darkness, 'Sara! Saaa—rah!' It is rough with panic and despair. '*Sara!*'

I came crashing through the trees into the ruins and stopped.

Were two sisters standing there, arms around each other, or was it only a trick of moonlight on the wall?

The time had finally come. I said the words that would make Sara's last unspoken wish come true. 'I love you truly. I will always remember.'

The words dissolved into the breeze. A swirl of leaves brushed past my vision, and I saw there was nothing—nothing there at all.

A Song of Ruth

The song rose in sweet voices on the evening air. It is a song sung by one woman for love of another. Ruth, standing waist-deep in the corn, sang it for her who had become everything in the world to her. Sara sung it once as a gift to a friend. The only friend she had truly had. She sang it as her heart was breaking.

Wherever you go
I will go
Wherever you live
There will I live
Your people will be my people
And your God will be my God too.

Wherever you die
I will die
And there shall I be buried beside you
We will be together forever
And our love will be the gift of our lives

The graveyard was filled with people. The entire village had turned out for the last rites. Speculation about where Lisbon had fled was rife. I had kept my silence. He deserved to lie where he was, alone in deep water, waiting.

The inspector swore that, wherever Lisbon was, he would find him. As the seasons turned and summer dried the well, eventually, he would.

Two coffins were lowered into the ground so that they lay side by side. Sara and Nina. Nina and Sara. Friends until death do them part. But even that churl, Death, had been unable to part them.

This time, Nina did not refuse burial.

When the bell had tolled for the last time, when the last hymn had been sung, when the footsteps of the last mourner had faded, I stood at the graves, listening. I was not alone. A figure in black stood by my shoulder, equal in his grief. I knew Damon would return day after day to the graves. I knew he would remember.

I felt a touch on my elbow. It was Crazy Charlie. I said, 'I did everything you told me to, Charlie. I listened. I broke my heart. I found my story.'

Charlie peered into my face. He drew back and hastily made the sign of the cross. 'Write it,' whispered Crazy Charlie.

I waited till the grave-diggers had filled in the grave. I waited till light was seeping from the sky. I waited until the wind was whispering through the long grass. Then I put a sheet of paper upon the grave and weighed it down with a stone. I knew the wind would eventually blow it away.

Constania.
Tania.
Saraswati.
Sara.

And what's in a name? Lisbon's love stole her name from another. I foolishly gave my love a name that was not hers. But does it matter what name you call your love by? By any name, would it not be as sweet?

Surely, any lover will tell you that his love has a dozen different names. That which he calls her in the light of morning; the name he calls her in the deep of night; the name he whispers into her nape when she is asleep; the name he teases her to laughter with after her tears. The true lover coins a dozen names from morning to evening with each new shift of love.

In the names we give our lovers, we grope to identify them, to feel out the real shape of them. Adrift in an unfamiliar new world, we lay our stake to this shape we have stumbled upon, that feature that we are learning to adore. But all such effort is doomed to failure. Love is the one thing that cannot be named. That lies beyond all the words we may seek to call it, all the categories we may try to confine it to.

What does it matter what name I gave to her? Take away her name. Only then do you come to the true heart of the matter. What have you really loved?

I have loved your bare feet seeing so surely in the dark. I have loved your eyes, laughing at me as we played hide-and-seek, filled with tears at the thought of your sister alone and waiting. I have loved your hesitations, your fears, your sadnesses. So much sadness, and I, too blind to see.

Forgive me, Sara. Forgive my pettiness and my pretensions. All my noble beliefs and my fancy words. My stumbling and my blindness and my stupidity. There is only one thing that redeems me. I kept all my promises.

I have been so proud of my words. I strip them all away now. I say to you the only thing that matters. I am whispering into the wind. Hear me.

I love you.

I will always remember.

Whisper in the Wind

The wind is blowing from the land outward to the sea. It is heavy with the smell of smoke from the cotton factories, the stench of open sewage, the sour, rankling smell of the fishermen's colony. It carries the sounds of people working, lovers quarrelling, devotees singing, teachers lecturing. Heavy with a hundred scents, loaded with sound, it arrives at last at a garden on a hill at the edge of the sea, and pauses to tease a wind chime. Someone has made the wind chime, knotted it out of odds and ends together with little bits of wire and string, so that it sings in its own unique scale.

The chimes hang in a window, in a tower, in a Parsee palace. The window overlooks a gulmohar tree, a jacaranda that is filled with crows, and a glorious laburnum in full bloom.

The broken music of the chimes drips from the window into the room.

I sit at a desk, looking at the book that lies upon the table in front of me. It is a handsome book, bound in dark blue leather, with gilt lettering on the cover. It is a limited edition sponsored by a mother's pride.

Whisper in the Wind
Written by
J. Irani

I open to the first page and read.

I met a madman today who told me that all the stories in the world are whispered in the wind. 'Listen!' he said— and the wind will blow a story into your head.

There are many stories in this house. I can hear the wind stirring them.

Which one is my story—the one that I alone can tell?
Listen.

Acknowledgements

Many thanks to all my fierce warrior friends who have fought so long and hard to hold on to the idea of a gentle and gracious Goa—Claude and Norma Alvares, Dean D'Cruz, Reboni Saha, Patrician Pinto, Oscar Rebello, Sabina Martins, Miguel Braganza, Prajal Sakardhande, Vizilia D'Sa and so many more. Deo Borem Koro.

Where would writers be without readers willing to give feedback on work that is still in progress? Many, many thanks to Madhuri Kale, Amrita Narayanan, Arindam Basu, Nithya Dorairaj, Vidya Madabushi and Lubna Khan. Thanks also to those in the Goa Writers Group who read this book a long time ago and urged me to finish it.

And where would we be without the editors who pour over the words again and again? Thank you Deepthi Talwar. For the really haunting cover—thank you Nandini Varma.